JUSTICE BY ANOTHER NAME

To Rob,
just another tale
of southern charm –
greed, corruption, sex
and murder
ciao [signature]

Justice by Another Name

by E. C. Hanes

Distributed by John F. Blair, Publisher
1406 Plaza Drive
Winston-Salem, North Carolina 27103
blairpub.com

COVER ART BY JOEL SHELTON

Library of Congress Cataloging-in-Publication Data

Names: Hanes, E. C., 1945- author.
Title: Justice by another name : a novel / by E. C. Hanes.
Description: Winston-Salem, North Carolina : RaneCoat Press, [2017]
Identifiers: LCCN 2016037058| ISBN 9780895876850 (hardcover : alk.
paper) |
    ISBN 9780895876867 (ebook)
Subjects: | GSAFD: Mystery fiction. | Suspense fiction.
Classification: LCC PS3608.A71428 J87 2017 | DDC 813/.6—dc23 LC
record available at https://lccn.loc.gov/2016037058

10 9 8 7 6 5 4 3 2 1

To Gordon and Copey Hanes,
who showed me the way

PROLOGUE

They glistened wet and radiant as in their first hour from the womb. It was hard to tell which boy was brown and which was white since each wore a plastron of chalky Carolina clay.

A violent storm had dumped over six inches of rain on eastern North Carolina in less than two hours, leaving the August air heavy with the watery smell of rotting bog mud and broken pine limbs. Worse was the ammoniac stench of hog waste from the catch lagoon on Wallace May's farm.

Paulie Reavis and Hank Grier slid, whooping like a war party of Lumbee Indians, down the greasy clay bank next to Mitchell Creek. They laughed and shouted, slapping high-fives as they watched the loamy brown waters leap and swirl between the crumbling banks. Huge tree trunks that had once sprung from those banks, now sank beneath the onrushing tide and its pounding froth. The boys' usual haunts had been transformed into new, wonderfully dangerous places.

Hank and Paulie tore along the shoreline until they came to the mouth of a rough-hewn gully opening into Mitchell Creek. At its junction with the creek, the root-filled gully was fifteen to twenty yards wide, but at its origins, some fifty yards to the east, it was only a matter of feet from rim to rim. A cascade of tainted water, funneled from the farm's soybean and peanut fields, poured over the narrow rim of the drainage cut and flowed in a frothy stream to an eventual merging with the angry Mitchell.

"You 'member the pictures of those gigantic falls in geography class?" Paulie said.

"You mean the one that flowed over that humongous stone cliff?" Hank replied.

"No. The ones that cut that huge canyon . . . uhm . . ." Paulie paused, trying to think of the name.

Hank brightened. "You mean the Grand Canyon?"

"That's it," Paulie answered.

"Well then, this is our Grand Canyon. This is—'The Grand North Carolina Canyon,'" Hank replied.

"Too long," Paulie said, shaking his head. "This is Mitchell Canyon."

Hank thought about this then nodded. "Too bad we ain't got a flag to stick in the ground. Explorers always stuck a flag in the ground when they named somethin'." They looked around for something to use.

"We can use one of the tomato stakes we brought for swords," Paulie said.

"They're not real tall, but I guess one of 'em can work for now."

Hank pulled a red shop rag taken from his daddy's garage out of his pocket and tied it to the end of one of the tomato stakes. Paulie smiled and raised the stake over his head.

"No," Hank said. "We can't stick the flag here. It won't look right. We got to go to the top of the canyon." They clambered up the slippery bank, carefully walking to the narrow point of land that protruded between the canyon and Mitchell Creek. Standing there, high over the surging creek and holding their banner aloft, they looked down on the foaming, debris-filled water flowing all around them and felt a surge of pride. They were mighty explorers indeed.

"We claim this canyon for Hogg County, North Carolina,"

Paulie said, thrusting the tomato stake deep into the wet, leafy ground high above the gully. The two friends stood gazing at their discovery, as proud as if they'd found the source of the Nile.

"Look at that!" Hank said, pointing to the edge of the creek.

At the junction of the creek's turbulent water and the water from the canyon, just at the edge of the backwash near the bank, they saw a whirlpool of heroic proportions. Only a few feet across, it was still bigger than any whirlpool either of the boys had seen. They stood mesmerized, watching as pieces of flotsam circled the eye of the whirlpool, then disappeared.

"Man, is that neat!" Paulie yelled. "Watch this!"

He grabbed a piece of pine bark and threw it into the water above the whirlpool. Within seconds the twelve-inch piece of bark, now a raft loaded with westward-bound pioneers, arrived at the spinning water, circled a few times and vanished. Hank and Paul raced along the canyon rim and began pitching pieces of bark and small sticks into the rushing water. As these made their way down the canyon toward the Mitchell, they too were transformed from mundane bits of vegetation into the war canoes of pursuing hostiles or the keelboats of river pirates.

Mud clods they hurled from the top of Mitchell Canyon exploded in the water below like cannonballs fired from the ramparts of a wilderness fort. The boys were Meriwether Lewis and William Clark forging through the virginal wilderness of the American West; they were Daniel Boone and Davy Crockett driving back the savage Indians of the Appalachians; they were happy. Of course neither boy was supposed to be anywhere near the stream during flood conditions, but what were the admonitions of anxious parents to two fearless explorers and Indian fighters?

—✦ ✦ ✦—

"Paulie, I'm going to the clinic for a few hours," Lana Reavis had said at breakfast. "Dr. Jeffers needs me to clean up some paperwork, and then I'll be home. Don't you be runnin' off more than a few blocks, okay?"

He squinched up his mouth and mumbled, "Unhunh . . . I won't," knowing that the minute his mom was around the corner he would be on his bike and headed toward Hank's house two miles out of town.

Nancy Grier had told her son Hank, as he came sliding around the corner of their house, almost the same thing.

"Ain't it neat, Momma? You ever seen so much water?"

"Isn't it neat, Henry. I know you're excited and I know you want to go and mess in those woods, but not today. The stream will be out of its banks in an hour or so, and I don't want you near it. You understand?"

Hank mumbled, "Yes'm, I understand," knowing that he would soon join Paulie in those splendidly dangerous woods.

—✦ ✦ ✦—

Hank dragged a twelve-foot pine log down the bank and halfway up the drainage cut to the far side. The creek had risen two feet since the boys first got there and continued moving up the canyon. The runoff from Wallace May's fields was slowing, so if they wanted a dam it had to be now.

"Stick your end of the log into the bank behind that root on your side. I'll try and wedge mine behind this rock over here," Paulie said.

The boys bent to their tasks. Dirt flew from their cupped hands, and small rocks yanked from the sticky clay rolled down the canyon walls as Paulie and Hank worked to anchor the pine log.

Neither boy heard the dull roar made by Wallace's collapsing containment wall surrounding the hog waste lagoon two hundred yards away. They didn't hear the five million gallons of putrid black hog feces and urine coursing their way across Wallace May's fields toward Mitchell Creek, the Roanoke River, and eventually, Albemarle Sound and the Atlantic Ocean.

As the nauseating wave burst over the rim of the gully, the boys looked up just as their world was engulfed in unspeakable filth. The smell of ammonia burned their nostrils. Hydrogen sulfide stung their eyes and skin. Their gasps were choked with sludge. Pinned by the torrent, they were swept away in the rush of animal waste made mobile by the recent downpour. The boys were exploded out into the raging brown waters of Mitchell Creek, now black with its own turbid waste. The tide of filth swept down the Mitchell, tarring the creek from bank to bank.

Hank tried to understand where he was, where he was going, but the force of the water disoriented him. His shirt was torn from his body and his arms were jerked back with such force that both shoulders were dislocated. He retched, spinning out of control beneath the surging water. His chest heaved from the ingested offal. Reflex took over and he gulped for air just as the pounding water threw him clear. Half out of the torrent, his face slammed into the root ball of a sweet gum tree dislodged by the flood but still anchored to the creek bank. His arms felt like they'd been torn from their sockets. His throat and eyes burned.

"Help, Paulie, help . . . !" he gagged calling to his friend, then vomited again into the tangle of the sweet gum. As it swept down the creek, the tip of a root tore at his face cutting a deep red swath across the smooth umber of his cheek. He couldn't reach the cut to soothe it, only cry out in a weak and gurgling squeak. Then something, some object carried in the torrent, smashed against his head and forced him further into the root ball. Hank tried to maintain consciousness, but unsuccessful, soon drifted into a coma.

Paulie Reavis had vanished, sucked into the swirling hell of Mitchell Creek.

1.

Will Moser pulled his brown patrol car into one of the ambulance-only parking spaces outside the hospital emergency room. No danger of both spaces being filled that day since he'd just seen the older of the county's two emergency vehicles balanced on top of the hydraulic rack in Dodson's garage. From the look of the garage floor, the tired 1970 ambulance was suffering from its own emergency. Piles of metal engine parts and rubber hoses littered the oil-covered concrete pad beneath the lift.

The Hogg County Regional Hospital emergency room, while newer and better equipped than the EMS vehicles, was only a bricks-and-mortar prayer for holding death at bay. But it was still better than a ninety-mile-an-hour dash to Raleigh's Rex Hospital.

Will closed his eyes and rolled his head from side to side to ease the tension building up in his neck, then reached over and picked up his white Stetson on the seat. The morning weather forecast had called for temperatures in the nineties, but that didn't take into account the multiplier effect of an asphalt parking lot. The soft black tar pushed the ninety-plus degree heat

7

to almost a hundred. Will always said Vietnam was the hottest place he'd ever been. Today Hogg County cooked under the wet-hot Asian sun of his memory.

Vietnam returned to Will Moser often. It might come with a noise, a smell, the heat of an oppressive summer day, or a body mutilated by bullets from the pistol of some drunk or drugged lunatic. Today it was the heat. He pushed open the car door and carefully stepped out, looking up at the early afternoon sun. Pushing his Ray-Bans higher on the bridge of his nose, Will started for the emergency room doors. His limp, the result of a piece of shrapnel still in his lower back and a couple of steel pins holding his hip in place, felt more noticeable than usual.

By the time he'd gone twenty feet, a perspiration patch the size of a softball had blossomed between his shoulder blades. Two orderlies were standing on the sidewalk between the hospital and the patient parking area. One was clearly agitated, his arms waving, his voice rising and falling. The other leaned against the railing and smoked a cigarette, his expression both annoyed and bored. Will nodded as he got near the emergency room doors. The two men acknowledged with a nod and a pair of weak grins.

—✦ ✦ ✦—

The cool of the emergency room engulfed Will the minute he walked through the door. The chief admitting nurse, Florence Reily, was on duty.

"Afternoon, Flo, Bob Velez in?" he asked, removing his Stetson.

She smiled, "Hey, Will. I haven't seen him since lunch, but I know he's here since you can hear that man from a mile away. I'll page him for you."

Dr. Robert Velez was the senior physician at Hogg County Regional, one of the first doctors the hospital board had recruited following its last growth spurt.

Almost before he could turn around, Will saw Bob Velez hurrying down the long corridor leading to the waiting room.

He was moving like a man on his way to a fire, a habit that came from being one of six doctors in a hospital that needed ten.

"Will, thanks for coming." Bob looked around the reception room and then down the hall leading to the small clinic. "Uhm . . . let's go to my office."

Will followed the doctor down the cracked, faded linoleum corridor, past the X-ray room, and through the clinic's double doors. Dr. Velez walked around his cluttered desk and sat in the seldom-used chair behind the pile of papers. Will looked around the room, then flipped his hat onto the loveseat against the far wall and settled into the leather chair facing Bob's desk.

Neither man said anything for a few seconds. It was going to be an uncomfortable conversation. Bob took a deep breath, then said, "We did the autopsy on Paulie this morning."

Will nodded.

"I've seen a lot of shit, Will, a lot of shit, but that boy today. . ." He shook his head. "That boy died the most horrible death I can imagine. I mean the decay that . . ." He stopped, then blinked, sitting perfectly still, his eyes riveted on Will's.

Tears ran down Will's cheeks, his face pale and anguished. His raised hand asked for silence and he shook his head, trying to regain his composure.

After a moment, he cleared his throat, "I can't believe it. It wasn't even a year ago that I saw his father beneath that bull-dozer, and now the son, stolen away, drowned in that filth . . ." Will's lips moved but no words came. He shook with grief . . . and anger.

He knew Bob Velez was looking at him, so he kept his head down while he fought for control.

"I'm sorry, Will. I didn't think . . ." Bob twisted slightly in his chair.

Will shook his head. "That's all right. You . . . it's okay. I been thinking about Paulie nonstop since yesterday." He looked up. "You know, that boy wanted nothing in this world more than a pat on the back, a hug, and a few words of encouragement. Paul was the same way. I guess we all were. Taking Paulie out to fish or camp was kinda re-living the times me and his daddy had when we were young. I liked to think I was helping Paul and Lana out sometimes. You know, Paul always so busy with his business. I figured I was giving them some time for themselves."

Will ran his fingers over his mouth. "That's not entirely true. I may have needed our times together more than Paulie did. Seeing the excitement on that little boy's face gave a cynic like me new life. I reckon that's a kid's gift to the world, clean views of old scenes. Plus, you know, somehow it was like Paulie was . . ." He cleared his throat. "You know, like we were . . . related. Close, like me and Paul were close as boys." He smiled and gave a little shake of his head.

"Paul was a lot like my father about his business. It wasn't the only thing, but it was the number one thing. I obviously understood it better with Paul than with Father. I was too young to understand Father. No child can really understand a parent. Not supposed to, though. What I knew was that he loved his business first and me and Mother next. I mean it wasn't like we never did stuff together. He taught me all I know about bird dogs and quail, and a good deal about calling mallards into hardwood river bottoms. Still, it was the fishing and hunting trips that Paul and I thought up that stick in my mind the most. I guess my time with Paulie was a do-over of sorts."

Bob Velez listened without comment, this being the best medicine for Will, but when Will stopped speaking, Bob said, "Will, you ought to have kids. You'd be a great dad."

Will smiled. "I hope I will someday, but thank God Shelby and I didn't have any."

Bob tilted his head to the side. "Shelby?"

"Shelby Moser, the Raleigh deb of the century and my ex."

"Damn, Will. I never knew you'd been married. I . . . never mind. None of my business anyway."

Will smiled, "Oh well. I'll do better next time."

Bob nodded and smiled, "Marie and I have been lucky."

—✦ ✦ ✦—

Will took a deep breath, "Tell me about Henry Grier."

Dr. Velez paused a moment to make sure he kept his response short and without unnecessary graphics. "I talked to the doctor in charge at Duke and he said the boy was doing as well as could be expected. Not out of the woods yet, but he should get there." Will waited for additional information but when nothing else was offered, he simply nodded.

The phone rang and Bob picked up. "Dr. Velez. Yes. Okay. All right, I'll be there in five minutes." Will started to get up. "Hold on a minute, Will. Since you're here, how's Lana doing?"

Will settled back in his chair. "I'm not sure. She's all over the place. I don't know what she's thinking most of the time, but I do know she's got a lot of work to do to get back to flat ground, or maybe even survive. She doesn't know who to grieve for sometimes. She knows her son just died, but then she'll flash back to Paul's death and be talking about him.

"She's always thought there was more to Paul's death than just an accident. No matter how many times I tell her that we didn't find any evidence of foul play, she still insists that Paul knew heavy equipment better than anybody in eastern North Carolina and getting crushed by a dozer with a slipped clutch didn't make sense. She blames everybody.

"One day it's Oris Martin, the next it's somebody else. I've tried to talk to her about tossing around unfounded accusations but haven't gotten very far. Now she's got it in her head that because Paulie was killed by a Martin Farms–inspected lagoon, they're responsible. She doesn't listen to me, or her mom. She needs help, Doc. You can see it in her eyes, a desperation I've not seen before, even after Paul's death. Losing a husband is hard, but losing a child doesn't have words for it, so I'm worried. I think she needs somebody trained in post-traumatic stuff. A lot of the guys from 'Nam needed help for years. But right now all I want to do is get her through the next few days."

Bob Velez nodded and reached for a book on the shelf behind him.

"I know a guy in Raleigh, at Rex, who has a lot of experience in trauma. He works at Dix Hospital part-time. I'll call him and see what he says. In the meantime, I'll drop by and see about a few sedatives. She needs rest."

Will nodded and got to his feet. He took a step to the couch to pick up his hat but instead turned back and looked at the doctor.

"You're not telling me the truth about Henry Grier, are you? I'm going out to the Griers' when I leave here and would like to know the truth."

Bob nodded. "All right. His brain waves are near normal-looking and he's coherent, but they're still afraid of scarring in his bronchial tubes and lungs. He's in a partial body cast for the dislocated shoulders. That boy was mighty lucky considering how long he was probably underwater."

Will stared at Bob, his eyes narrowing, "Scarring?"

"A hog lagoon is a nasty place, Will. The main ingredients of pig shit quickly become ammonia and hydrogen sulfide. Hydrogen sulfide is extremely volatile and forms sulfuric acid. Ammonia is a base, and its effect on the human body, in combination with the hydrogen sulfide, is to dissolve fatty acids and burn tissues. The internal tissues are particularly vulnerable, especially in the throat, mouth, and lungs . . . basically, we're dealing with sulfuric acid and ammonia.

"But, he's hanging in there. I don't think he would have made it if he hadn't gotten hung up in those tree branches. Still, the amount of fecal bacteria in one of those hog lagoons is so intense that he could still come down with diseases we don't even have names for. Plus there's still his brain function. Like I said, he was underwater for a long time."

Bob Velez stood up and walked around the desk as Will finally retrieved his hat, slowly sliding the brim through his fingers. It was clear Will had something else on his mind, so Bob waited.

"Bob, I was over at the Griers' yesterday. Odell and Nancy told me they've had a few ... uh ... unpleasant calls, plus somebody threw a dead raccoon into their yard night before last. Some asshole in a pickup racing by yelling stuff out the window. You know the kind. Anyway, I would appreciate it if you could drop by the Griers' and see if Nancy needs something for her nerves. She's driving between here and Durham every day, a long hard trip."

Velez nodded, "I was afraid this kind of crap would start. Those folks have gone through enough these past few days. I hope you don't let some asshole redneck do anything to endanger that family. I'll definitely get her something for her nerves—and needs be, I'll park my car outside their house."

Will nodded and stepped past the doctor. "No need for that, Doc, I've got deputies checking by on a regular basis."

Bob Velez stood directly in front of Will, not more than a foot away, and said, "I've lived in this town for a pretty long time now, and see it as a comfortable and caring place, but there are still those people ... those dangerous, pig-eyed, ignorant people who scare the shit out of me." He moved into the hall and started walking toward the emergency room. After a dozen steps, he turned around.

"You know, there are times, deputy, when I don't feel like taking care of a damn one of them."

2.

The black Ford pickup was moving so fast when it turned off the hardtop and into the feed mill parking lot that it kicked up a twenty-foot rooster-tail of brown peat dust and yellow corn fines. It slid to a stop in front of a small brick building, disgorging, as the dust settled, a heavy-set, fifty-five-year-old man wearing a pair of khakis and a red-and-white plaid short-sleeved shirt. As the roiling cloud of dust following the truck began to settle, he smiled and waved to the small cluster of men standing by the grain elevators and dump trucks parked at the rear of the two-acre lot. Putting his right hand over his mouth and nose, he trotted toward the cement steps.

The single-story red-brick building housed a dozen offices and a small conference room with crank-out metal windows. An eight-foot red-and-white-striped metal awning covered the front door. To its right a small brass plaque identified this modest agricultural facility as the original headquarters of the now-burgeoning porcine empire known as Martin Farms, Inc. Martin Farms had close to 300,000 pigs squealing and defecating in hog sheds all over Hogg County and six other eastern North Carolina counties.

Even though Martin Feed Mills was only a tiny part of his corporation, Oris spent almost as much time in these unassuming offices as he did in the ostentatious suites of his corporate headquarters. More comfortable in the dust and noise of the feed mill, he came here when he needed to make a tough decision, one that might involve a little nut cuttin'. He could smell the mill, taste the dust in the air, and be around men he trusted. Men who knew him, were loyal, and more importantly, men who needed him.

Martin Farms, Inc. took pork from the hoof to the meat counter. It bred pigs in giant farrowing sheds—up to three thousand sows per complex—shipping the piglets to independent farmers to raise in large feeding facilities, which, of course, used feed and medicine bought from Martin Feed Mills. Later, Oris's trucks returned to the farms and picked up the newly fattened pigs, taking them to a slaughterhouse either owned or affiliated with Martin Farms, Inc. From there the sliced, diced, and neatly wrapped pork went to wholesalers or to large retail operators.

It wasn't an original idea. Holly Farms Poultry had done the same thing years before in the chicken industry, thus saving hundreds of small mountain farms from certain destitution. Oris Martin simply moved the concept from poultry to pork, and while finding the logistics of breeding pigs more difficult than those for breeding chickens or turkeys, he also found it considerably more rewarding.

Being the originator, and by any measure the largest practitioner of vertical hog processing, Oris had come to be known in the state as "The King of Hog County." The name angered many of the citizens of the real Hogg County since they felt the ironical play on their county's name was disrespectful of its origins.

Hogg County had been named for General Josiah Moir Hogg of Revolutionary War fame. Josiah had immigrated to America from Scotland in 1756 having endured the crushing power of the British monarchy for his entire life; thus, to breathe the air of freedom and independence was to him especially precious. He carved a working plantation out of the Carolina wilderness and had no intention of losing it to his former antagonists. Highlands

Plantation covered over a thousand acres south of Mussel Ford along the Roanoke River.

The family was large and prosperous, with numerous sons and daughters, many of whom became leaders in the North Carolina colony. Josiah became a trusted member of General Washington's fledgling American army, and had, along with his older brother, volunteered for military duty immediately after the start of hostilities. He served with honor for almost six years, until his death at the battle of Guilford Courthouse. General Nathanael Greene, for whom Greensboro was named, said at Josiah's funeral, "Our new nation has lost a courageous leader and one of its most dedicated citizens. North Carolina has lost a devoted son."

The vast land holdings of the once-prosperous Hogg family had, over the years, been divided among generations of children, grandchildren, and great-grandchildren. In fact, there weren't many current residents of the county who couldn't trace a family connection to one of the dozens of Hogg progeny.

It was understandable, then, that a great many of the citizens of Hogg County, being justly proud of their origins, didn't appreciate a slur making light of their famous ancestor.

Actually the animal husbandry faculty at N.C. State had come up with Oris's new title. Based on his very generous financial contribution to the university, his alma mater, and the creation of the Oris Martin Distinguished Professorship, the administration had awarded him an honorary degree. During the presentation, the chancellor had, to the enthusiastic applause of the faculty, anointed Oris "The King of Hog County." So by chance or by fate the ascendency of pork in the agri-business sector of North Carolina's economy made Hogg County the fiefdom of its largest practitioner. Naturally, Oris took the "king" part of his new title a bit too seriously, but then humility was never one of his defining traits.

The pork industry's growth was greatly accelerated when the big tobacco growers in the East, based on current mores, were forced to find other sources of income. Tobacco, for decades the mainstay of eastern North Carolina agriculture, was under attack, and it didn't take a genius to see that the tobacco companies were now the road-kill-of-choice for the legal vultures circling the American economy.

—✦ ✦ ✦—

Oris walked into the conference room and took off his sunglasses.

"Boys," he said.

Rufus Austin, Charlie Summers, and Eugene "Popper" Winslow sat at the conference table drinking coffee. Rufus and Charlie could have been brothers. Both were approximately the same age, fifty-five, and both stood over six feet. Rufus was stockier, Charlie, grayer and more weathered. Both men gripped their coffee cups in large, fleshy hands made hard with years of outdoor labor.

Popper was different. A small man, some would say "wiry," with thin, graying hair. A large bald spot spread from the back of his head toward the front. Charlie and Rufus' open-faced friendliness was missing in Eugene. His face was drawn and hard, his eyes close together and watery. His left eye seemed always to be looking in a different direction than the right, so when you looked at him you never knew exactly which eye to focus on. They weren't stupid eyes, shallow or vague, rather they were warning signs.

Oris was the only one to go to college, but that caused no friction here. He had always been the smartest, and Rufus and Charlie had always deferred to his judgment, even when they were young. Eugene required something more for his complicity. Nothing tangible, rather a favored position: first among equals. But then he delivered more.

As boys, they all had had some type of .22 caliber rifle, and all were pretty good shots by the time they were ten. Eugene was way beyond good; he was scary. In the summer they went to the river to take pot shots at the turtles clustering on top of the logs and rocks on steamy days. The others would occasionally hit the shells of the sunbathing turtles, but Eugene would only shoot at the turtles in the water, the ones with just their heads showing. From the top of the bank to the water line was fifty to sixty feet. From there it was up to the turtle how far away it got.

For his long shots, fifty yards plus, Eugene lay in the grass to rest his gun on a rock or a piece of wood. For any less challenging shot he simply stood and shot off-hand. The results were nearly always the same: eighty percent hits and twenty percent near misses. Eugene only used hollow-point shells because he "loved to see the heads pop off." It was hardly surprising that he was nicknamed "Popper."

Oris walked to the metal file cabinet that held a dozen or so coffee mugs and plastic jars of sugar and fake creamer. He picked out a red-and-white Martin Farms mug with a picture of a pig wearing a Santa Claus hat and a big ribbon around its neck. It was one of the thousands he'd sent out to all of his contractors one Christmas. Oris smiled as he poured himself a cup of black, caffeine-rich New Orleans coffee.

"You know what I love about coming to this office?" The other men shook their heads. "I love being able to get real coffee instead of that fancy designer shit they drink at headquarters."

He sat down, blew on the coffee, and looked around the room, "I appreciate you boys coming in here on such short notice."

As if any of the three would say no.

"I been thinking a lot about the Reavises . . . first Paul, and now his boy . . . it's a real shame . . . a real shame. I know how Emma and I would feel if that'd been one of our young'uns. Lana Reavis has got to be real broke up. By the way, anybody seen her or talked to Ray or Robert?"

Ray and Robert Reavis owned and ran Riverside Farm Supply Company. Paul Reavis had been their nephew and young Paulie their great-nephew. While Ray and Robert had never been that close to Paul, though he was their brother's son, his death, and now his son's death, was a tragedy for all Reavises . . . at least that was the face they'd instructed their respective families to wear in public.

Rufus looked at Oris. "Evidently none of us have, but I understand that Ray is trying to help Lana. Apparently she's about at the end of her rope. Doctor Velez had to give her a bunch of sedatives. Lana's mom has been staying at the house, plus Will Moser's been there quite a bit."

Oris had gotten up and was staring out the window. He watched a man wearing a pair of blue coveralls push an augur from one of the feed bins into the back of a five-ton dumper and start loading it with cracked corn. Without indicating that he had even heard Rufus, Oris walked over to the outside door of the conference room, opened it, and yelled across the yard, "Othello, yo Othello, put your damn mask on!" He slammed the door and walked back over to his chair.

"This is the kinda thing that causes sides to be taken," Oris said. "The Reavises are good people, and even though Paul's side of the family hasn't had much to do with Riverside, at least recently, out of pride, Ray and Robert may have to find a villain. Me, I think they oughta be pissed at that nigger boy who got young Paulie out there in the first place. He still alive?"

Rufus and Charlie shrugged. Popper twisted his head around, "You give a shit?"

Oris sipped and went on. "Anyway, y'all know what happens when a momma decides that somebody has hurt her family. Lana has already had more on her than most folks, but with her boy dying so soon after her husband, she might just go off the deep end. You boys keep your eyes and ears open."

Popper was leaning back in his chair, staring out the window at the departing work crew. His left eyelid fluttered a few times and his mouth turned down in a ropey frown.

Oris finished his coffee. "I'm gonna talk to John Keaton. I need to make sure he's got Wallace under control. We don't need some halfwit screwing things up."

Wallace May was what many in Hogg County called a slow

pitch. He was a nice young man with limited capabilities, who only through the intervention of his uncle, John Keaton, had been able to get a feeding contract with Martin Farms. John Keaton had sold his nephew, on time, a hundred acres along Mitchell Creek with enough land to build eight feeding sheds and a two-acre waste lagoon, plus enough land adjacent to the sheds so Wallace could spray out the sewage from his lagoon. The state allowed hog-feeding operations only on farms with enough adjacent fields to allow the farmer to pump his sewage onto active crop land, thus using as fertilizer the millions of gallons of waste as well as controlling them.

Wallace had struggled, but with the assistance of his uncle, a partner of Oris Martin in numerous business ventures, he was doing all right. At least he had been until his waste lagoon ruptured and killed Paulie Reavis.

—◆ ◆ ◆—

Popper stood up and walked over to the window. Without turning around he said, "Hey, Oris. Sheriff's just drove up."

Oris shifted his weight in the chair. "I thought Ernie was in Rocky Mount today."

"It ain't Ernie. It's Will Moser."

Oris's mouth turned down and he made a kind of harrumph. "Well, well, boys, if it ain't Mr. Fancy Pants himself. Wonder what brings a Moser out to common-folks country." Popper leaned against the window sill with his back to the yard, then crossed his legs and arms. After a minute there was a knock at the door. No one said or did anything. Another knock. Popper looked over at Oris who smiled, licked his lips, then motioned his head toward the door. Eugene leaned forward, took a couple of steps, and slowly pushed the metal door out into the sun and dusty heat.

Will Moser stepped into the cool of the conference room. He was a head taller than Popper and bigger by thirty pounds. He pushed his Stetson back on his head and, without looking at him, said as he walked into the room, "Eugene."

Nobody said anything or got up. Will took off his dark glasses and put them in his shirt pocket, then nodded and smiled at the two men sitting across the table. "Charlie, Rufus." He paused then turned his gaze to Oris, who sat frowning at the head of the table.

"Oris."

Oris set his mug down and slowly stood up. Putting his hands on his hips and stretching, he walked over to the window and looked out at the now almost vacant mill lot. Without turning around he said, "So, Will, what brings the law out to see working folk in the heat of the day?"

Will removed his hat and without taking the seat that hadn't been offered, replied, "Well, you know me, Oris. I like to mingle with the little people every now and then. You can certainly understand mingling with the little people, being the king and all."

Oris turned around and smiled, "Well, then, on behalf of the little people, we're honored to have you."

Greetings over, Will continued. "I'm doing some investigating into the events surrounding the death of young Paulie Reavis. The folks from DEHNR are coming out our way and I'd like to have a head start on getting some information together. Thought you might be kind enough to tell me how I can get a copy of the inspection reports done on Wallace's lagoon by your folks at Martin Farms?"

Oris stared at Will, not saying or doing anything even after Will finished. After a few beats, just long enough for Oris to establish his control of the conversation, he said, "I can do that. I'll need some kind of order or something. You understand, Deputy, these are private and confidential matters."

"Fine. I'll have a request brought out today."

"I'm not going to be here very long today," Oris cautioned.

"Then one of these gentlemen can bring it to you," Will said, looking around.

"They're not going to be here either."

"Then find somebody who is. I'll need the information at my office by tomorrow afternoon. Let's say, four o'clock. And Oris, any king worth his salt should have loads of loyal subjects hanging around whom he can order up for delivery jobs." Oris didn't say anything, just kept a stony face.

With a suitable eat-shit smile still on his lips, Will put his Stetson back on and retrieved his dark glasses. He nodded at the two men across the table, said "Boys," then turned and walked out of the conference room, making sure to leave the door open into the hot, dusty yard.

Popper pulled it shut and went back to his post by the window. Oris slowly moved his gaze from one man to the next, then said, "I'll tell you what, I'd rather be a nigger with a broke back than a snotty-fuckin' Moser in Hogg County. He ain't no different from his holier-than-thou daddy, 'cept he ain't runnin' Moser Hardwoods like his old man. Still, that don't keep him from strutting around like his shit don't stink."

Popper said, "You gonna give him the report?"

"Sure, it ain't no big deal. They all say the same thing. Every lagoon built on a Martin Farms contract facility is top of the line. Something happens, it's the farmer's fault 'cause when it was built it met all of the state standards. If they think not, then prove it." He said to no one in particular, "I'll have somebody bring a report to him sometime after five tomorrow."

Rufus got up and motioned to Charlie. "I reckon we'll be getting home, Oris. You coming to the Reavis boy's funeral?"

"Yeah, I'll be there somewhere. I don't imagine Lana much wants me there, both her men killed at or near a Martin Farms facility, but not goin' would look suspicious to folks. I reckon I can't fault her."

After Rufus and Charlie left, Oris looked at Popper. "You need to be there too, Eugene."

Popper nodded.

"And keep an eye on Wallace. You know goddamn well that Will is gonna be all over him and his place. And tell Weldon to keep an eye out. I don't want Wallace talking too much. You understand?"

Popper frowned. "What do you think, Oris? You think I'm as stupid as Wallace? You think I want him running his mouth?"

"I didn't say anything about being stupid, Popper. I'm just remindin' us both to be careful. And don't tell Weldon more than you got to, just enough so you can have some idea about what deputy hot-shit is doing and who he's talking to. Okay?"

"I'll take care of it, Oris. I always do." Popper opened the door and shuffled down the stairs toward his oversized black Ford dualie.

—✦ ✦ ✦—

Oris stood for a while on the steps, gazing out over the empty, dust-settled yard. The afternoon sun had dipped behind the grain bins and the pigeons were starting to settle for the night in the rafters of the two-story, wooden processing plant. A quail, calling together its scattered family, whistled in the creek bottom behind the mill, and evening stole into the yard on the back of a warm southwest breeze.

The smells of an approaching late summer storm blew through the wooden buildings and deserted alleys of Martin Feed Mills. Then a pair of big tomcats strolled around the corner of the equipment shed and headed into the feed building for a night of rat hunting.

Oris looked around the yard. It had been a long road. From the time his daddy had bought out the Reavis interest in the mill until now had been twenty-five years. Twenty-five years of busting his ass every day. He couldn't remember a time when he could rest, when he could just coast. Not until now. Not until he finally had the muscle to get his way not only in Hogg County but across the whole damn state. Martin Farms, Inc. was a power . . . bigger even than Moser Hardwoods, and he wasn't about to let some third-generation wannabe sheriff screw it up.

Oris watched the two tomcats saunter into the feed building.

"Good huntin', boys. Kill a rat for me."

3.

Will drove between two iron gates and under a sign that said in foot-high letters, "No Trespassing. Violators will be Prosecuted." He got it. The danger of contamination and disease spreading through a feeding or farrowing facility was enormous. Any number of hog diseases and even some human diseases could wipe out several thousand pigs in a matter of days. Like an early winter cold spreading through a kindergarten class. Will was surprised to find the gates open until he remembered that Martin Farms had already hauled away Wallace's pigs following the rupture of his waste lagoon.

After passing through the gates, Will turned left down a long alley of bent and broken pine trees lining the dirt road leading to the feeding sheds. The storm that dumped so much rain on Hogg County had in its fury also done considerable damage to the timber in the county. It had taken Wallace a whole day to clear the road following the storm. As a matter of safety as well as security, the sheds were located far from the public highway; however, it was never difficult to sense a hog facility was in the neighborhood—its foul odor permeated the air for miles around.

At the end of the tree line, Will drove between two enormous piles of pine logs and slash, emerging into a large soybean field. The hog sheds were another quarter-mile across the field against a stand of hardwoods. As he got nearer he heard the clanging sound of heavy equipment.

Will parked next to the trailer serving as the feedlot office. In the heavy heat, the rank odor of the now-empty lagoon was already seeping into his car. Will climbed the three steps onto the porch and knocked on the trailer door. When no one answered, he walked to the far end of the wooden porch and looked around the corner. Wallace, sitting atop a D8 bulldozer, was pushing dirt into what had been the break in the lagoon wall. Will covered his nose with his left hand. The stench, even with the majority of the sewage vacated, was overpowering.

He waved his hat in the air to get Wallace's attention, who, when he finally saw Will, turned off the dozer.

"Hey, Wallace. You got a minute?" Wallace waved and got off the bulldozer, walking toward Will without raising his eyes from the ground.

"How you doing, Will?" Wallace said.

"Fine, Wallace, hope you are." Wallace made no reply. The deputy turned and slowly walked with Wallace back to the front of the trailer.

"Sorry about your troubles, Wallace. I hear the state boys were down here yesterday."

Still no reply.

"Wallace, were they here?"

Wallace looked up. "Yeah, they was here. Uncle John come out and they was a bit of a ruckus. I didn't git what they was so riled up about, but I reckon it's okay now. Anyhow they done gone." He looked over at the entrance to the farm. "Uncle John is coming back today. You reckon he'll still be mad, Will?"

"I don't imagine so. He's just looking out for your best interest. He's real proud of you, Wallace. He said so." Wallace smiled at this and started to say something when he saw John Keaton's Cadillac turn the corner by the pile of downed pines and head to the office. Will watched as the Cadillac sped into the feedlot yard and slid to a stop in front of the trailer.

John Keaton, a man in his mid-sixties, slung the door open even before the car's engine was off. From the look in his eyes Will saw he wasn't pleased.

"Goddamnit! Do you people have nothing better to do than harass us every damn day of the week?"

Will stood on the first step of the trailer porch. "Not sure who 'you people' is, John."

"You bureaucrats . . . state, federal, local. It don't make a shit. I spent a couple of hours yesterday with two stone-brained bureaucrats from DEHNR. We've told everything we know. Now how about leaving us the hell alone?"

Will took his sunglasses off. "John, I just need to find out if you've got the original paperwork done by Martin Farms when the lagoon was first put in. I need it for our files. The sheriff's department has to have a complete accident report on file for any occurrence that involves an injury or death. No need to get so worked up."

Keaton nodded and walked over to open the office door.

"Wallace, get me the big file from the cabinet marked Martin Farms."

Wallace walked over to the steel cabinets that stood against the wall behind the only desk in the trailer. He pulled several files from the top drawer and walked over to where John Keaton was sitting and handed him the stack of legal-length hanging files.

"I ain't sure which one you mean, Uncle John, so I got 'em all." Will stood by the window looking down on the partially repaired lagoon. John Keaton picked a file and began thumbing through it.

"Okay, Deputy, I think I got what you need. Wallace, make a copy of this for Deputy Moser." Will turned around as Wallace stood by the copy machine feeding papers into the auto loader.

"I'm sorry about your troubles, John. It wasn't anybody's

fault. Just a terrible accident."

"Yes, I know, Deputy. Now that you've got your paper, let's be done with all the prying around and questions. Wallace needs to get his lagoon fixed, inspected, and back into operation as soon as possible." Wallace finished making the copies and turned the copier off.

"Here they are, Uncle John."

"Thank you, Wallace. Why don't you wait for me outside while Deputy Moser and I talk." Wallace nodded and went out onto the porch. When he was gone, John Keaton looked from the door back at the deputy.

"Will, that boy is sick to death about young Reavis dying on his place. You know damn well he didn't have nothing to do with it. It's about time everybody left him alone."

Will didn't speak until he had the file. He thumbed through the dozen or so papers and looked up.

"John, nobody is harassing Wallace, but a death is a serious thing, accidental or not. We are required to be thorough."

"Right, thorough but not a pain in the ass. Anyway, I thought you already had what you needed. Oris said you was out at his place asking for the same kind of stuff."

Will looked at the older man and smiled. "Lot of talking going on, looks like. But hey, I'm not going to argue with you, John. I'll review this material and if I have any more questions, I'll call you. Okay?"

"Fine. Now are we through?"

"Almost," Will said still looking in the file. "Maybe just a couple of things. Like, who was the inspector from Martin Farms that did the final inspection? This only states that the company completed the inspection in May of last year. It isn't signed or at least I don't see who did the final inspection. The other thing . . ." Will walked over to the window looking down on the empty lagoon, "is that I noticed while Wallace was pushing the dirt back up, how little clay is in the soil. I thought the base of all lagoons had to be compacted clay. The soil out here seems to be real fine loamy soil." John stared at the deputy for a few seconds then looked back at the pile of papers in the file and muttered something under his breath. Within a few minutes he looked up and handed Will a paper marked "final approval."

"I'm guessing the fellow who signed this is the final inspector. If you want to be sure, you probably need to call Martin Farms back. As far as the clay content of the soil is concerned, I have no idea what the requirements are. As a matter of fact, I don't imagine you do either. Why don't we let the people who know what the hell they're talking about figure that out. I imagine that Martin Farms, having built about a thousand of these damn things, knows what constitutes a safe facility. But I don't imagine they figure on the amount of rain in one hour that we had the other day. Now unless you got a question that I have a clue how to answer, I got things to do."

Will took the paper and put it with the others. "Thank you, John. If I have anything else I'll let you know, and John, please give my best to Oris and the three stooges." John Keaton didn't crack even a tiny smile.

"I'm sure you want me to tell Oris that," John said, then stretched his neck from side to side. "You ain't impressing anybody with your Perry Mason impersonation, Will, but if I was you I wouldn't screw with Oris Martin or his friends if you know what's good for you."

"I'll be sure to remember that, Mr. Keaton, and I'll be sure to tell the sheriff you send your warmest threats to him as well."

Wallace paced back and forth in front of the trailer door. He was worried. Any expression of anger made Wallace nervous. While no one would ever say that he was retarded, he was definitely slow. But slow or not, he was a sincere, likeable young man who tried hard and always had a pleasant word for everyone he met. In Mussel Ford, he would have won a popularity contest way ahead of John Keaton or Oris Martin.

Will walked out of the trailer and patted Wallace on the back. "Good luck to you, Wallace. I'll talk to you later."

—✦ ✦ ✦—

From behind the desk inside the trailer, John motioned to Wallace to come in and sit down. He'd been on the phone for almost thirty minutes and was by now almost yelling. "I know, Robert, I can read the papers as well as you, and you may be surprised to know that the people in Raleigh aren't the only ones who read the *News and Observer*." He banged his fist down on the desk.

"Robert, I don't give a good goddamn what the pressures are. You're paid to keep those jerks in line, and I for one don't think that the drowning of that young boy should have a damn thing to do with new regulations on hog feeders. Yes . . . I know that . . . all right . . . all right . . . but listen to me, nothing can stand up to six inches of water in an hour, nothing.

"Wallace was in the direct path of that storm. If it had run over my lagoons, the same thing would have happened. All right. . . . I'll probably see Oris tomorrow . . . all right . . . yes . . . good-bye." He hung up and slowly stood. Wallace stayed in his seat but kept his eyes glued on his uncle as he walked over to the windows.

"I'm glad you did what I told you to do about the berm. We don't need any pictures of that hole showing up on the front page of the *News and Observer*."

"I borrowed Mr. Eugene's 'dozer like you said, Uncle John." Wallace's hands opened and closed. He glanced at his uncle, then reached into his pocket and took out a small piece of stone, rubbing it between his fingers.

"Okay, Wallace, now listen. If anyone else calls, don't say a thing. You call me and let me take care of it, okay?"

"Okay, I will, Uncle John. When is the funeral? I want to be sure I'm there on time."

John Keaton turned from the window. The boy really didn't get it. He started to say something caustic, but then looked into Wallace's eyes and understood, cynicism aside, how deeply

Wallace felt about the death of young Paul Reavis.

"Wallace, I know you want to go to Paulie's funeral, but it would be better if you didn't come. Lurella and I will go for you. You just have to understand that some of the folks there may be feeling a little angry about the accident, and they may be mad at you. I know that you wouldn't have had that dam bust in a thousand years, but it did, and some folks just won't understand. Let things cool down a little and then I'll go with you to see Lana Reavis. Okay?"

Wallace looked hurt and confused. "Uncle John, I'd give anything to bring that boy back alive. I would. I don't want his momma to think that I don't care. Maybe I could wait outside. Maybe I could just wave at them and . . ."

John put his hand on Wallace's shoulder and whispered, "Wallace, calm down, son. Lurella and I will tell Lana Reavis how sorry you are. We'll tell her that we asked you not to come to the funeral because of the hard feelings that might be around. She'll understand. Just give it a while, then I'll take you to see her." He patted Wallace on the back.

Ever since Wallace's father had died, John Keaton had tried to help his sister raise the boy. It hadn't been easy but when he finally arranged with Oris to let Wallace be a contract feeder, it looked like he had found the perfect job for his nephew. He sold him enough land to build on and made sure to check in often enough to keep everything on track. His accountant kept the books so all Wallace had to do was keep watch over the pigs during their feeding.

"What you got there?" John asked, looking at the stone Wallace was rubbing.

Wallace looked down at the chipped piece of flint and quickly put it back in his pocket.

"Oh, nothin', just an ole arrowhead I got. It's a kovis point, real old."

"You mean a Clovis point," John said, making sure to pronounce the *l*. "Clovis is one of the oldest kinds of arrowheads. Named after Clovis, New Mexico. Where'd you get it?"

"Found it."

"Well, that's a lucky find. Clovis points are rare. It's probably worth a lot of money to some collector."

With that John turned toward the trailer door, "Wallace, I've got to go. You finish up with the 'dozer, then return it. I'll call you tomorrow. Don't worry, son, everything will be all right."

Slamming the door behind him, John Keaton stepped off the small stoop beside the trailer, got into his Cadillac, and drove through the soybean field and down the pine alley toward Mussel Ford.

Wallace stood by the desk and watched through the window as his uncle drove down the alley of broken trees and toward the gate. After a few minutes, he opened the door onto the porch and walked out into the warm afternoon air. Turning toward the fields behind the sheds, he took the arrowhead out of his pocket and began rubbing the shallow grooves along its side. He marveled at its shape and tried to imagine what the person who made it had been like. He looked at the wood line of Mitchell Creek and wondered where along its banks those Clovis people had lived. And thought about the young boy who had found it and given it to him.

"I'm sorry, Mrs. Reavis," he whispered, "I really liked your boy. I always thought he was real polite. I promise I'll come over and tell you so. Uncle John said I could come."

He paused for a brief wipe of his eyes and then added, "I'm sorry about your husband, too. I never come by to tell you, but I'm sorry about him, too."

4.

There were three cars at Lana's when Will got there, Grace Albright's blue Cutlass parked to the right of the porch, a brown Malibu around back next to the big, blue hydrangea, and Ray Reavis's red Cadillac clogging the middle of the driveway in front of the house.

Will didn't have much use for Ray Reavis, or his brother Robert. But then greed and dishonesty are hard to admire. After promising their dying brother, Carl, that they would look after his son, they proceeded to make working at Riverside so miserable that after seven years Paul had had enough and asked to be bought out.

The truth was that Ray always intended for Ray Jr. to take over Riverside, while Robert, seeking support for his two morally challenged daughters, needed a friend at the head of the family business. Siding with Ray's succession plan seemed the best bet.

Will parked behind the house and, while balancing a squash casserole and pan of turkey tetrazzini on his arm, entered through the kitchen door. Doris Cleveland and Roberta Pressman were sitting at the kitchen table writing down the names of everybody who brought food by the house. Will put his two covered dishes on the table.

"Afternoon, ladies," he said, then walked over to the dining-room door where he heard Ray's high-pitched drawl floating in from the living room.

"Lana, sweetheart, I've got to go now. Don't you worry about coming to the viewing unless you're totally up to it. Blanche and I will be there, as well as Robert and Eunice. Lana, you hear me? Hon?"

Grace Albright, Lana's mother, was standing next to Ray and before he could say anything more, she took his arm and led him to the front door.

"Ray, thank you for coming. Lana really appreciates it and don't worry, she'll be at Foster's sometime after seven. She's a little tired now but she'll be okay before long. I'm gonna see if she won't rest for a while. We'll see you tonight."

The screen door slammed shut as Grace gently pushed Ray onto the porch and toward the front steps.

Looking around the kitchen door, Will whispered, "Grace, hey Grace. Y'all by yourselves?"

"Come on in, Will. I heard you when you drove around back. I thought I'd never get Ray out of here." She rolled her eyes. "He hasn't done a damn thing for Lana since Paul died and now he wants to play the grieving uncle?"

Will looked into the living room. Lana was sitting in a large Lawson chair staring out the window. Grace took his arm and walked him back to the kitchen.

"Lana's not real talkative this afternoon, but she had a good visit with Dr. Newell a little while ago. That is the sweetest woman. She's come by several times in the last day or so. Lana's mighty lucky to work with such fine folks." She moved closer to Will's ear and lowered her voice.

"You know, Will, Dr. Newell told Lana that she should come

back to the office as soon as she wanted, next week even. I didn't want to say anything, but I think that's way too early. Don't you?"

Will thought for a moment and then said, "I don't know, Grace. Maybe, but then again it might be just the thing. Sitting around the house with all the pictures and memories could be worse than getting back to the office. Vicky is a good friend in addition to being a good boss. Lana might be better off with Vicky and work than sitting alone, thinking about what she's lost. I don't know, but let's not talk it down just yet."

Grace nodded. "Okay, if you think so."

Lana called from the living room, "Will!"

Will pushed open the dining-room door and looked into the living room, "Yeah, Lana, I'm here. What you need?"

"I need to talk to you."

Grace tapped Will on the arm and nodded, then motioned to Doris and Roberta to follow her. Will walked into the living room and sat down in the wing chair opposite Lana.

She blinked a few times then focused on Will. "I didn't feel like talking to that sanctimonious bastard, so I just played deaf and dumb. I haven't seen Ray or his phony wife Blanche in months, but now they've decided that 'We're here whenever you need us.' So, where the hell were those two when Paul needed them? Where were they when I needed them?" She tightened her jaw.

Will explored her face for a sign of how far she'd come in her grief, looking for a tear or catch in her breath. Nothing but her clenched jaw and steady stare returned to him, though her face occasionally tightened as if reacting to some sharp pain, then relaxed and went cold. What only days before had been smile-crinkled blue eyes were now red hollows, the smile a distant memory. Her russet blond hair, always glowing with a healthy sheen, hung dull and lifeless. The pair of tortoise shell combs usually perching on either side of her head lay on a small table beside her chair. Grief had slapped Lana's face a stinging blow, bringing age to what had been a clear, ageless beauty.

"Lana, hon, your mom and Roberta are gone. What can . . . "

"Just wait," she said in a strange, wounded voice, her eyes narrowing and her finger suddenly jutting out and to the side. Not in his face, but a warning nonetheless.

Will, his eyes wide, slid back into the recesses of the chair.

"God must hate me," she said. "And I can't figure out why. I've always tried to be a good person. I mean, I am human, we're all human. You, you haven't always followed the straight and narrow, I surely know that, but God doesn't seem to hate you. God hasn't taken away your whole family. Why me? Why my family?"

Suddenly her composure completely dissolved and she fell into a heap on the floor, beating the carpet with her fists and crying amid engulfing hopelessness. Will dropped to his knees and tried to put his arms around her, but she pushed him away. When she started to beat herself, to hit the sides of her head with her fists, Will grabbed her, pinning her arms to her side. He held her tightly against his chest until her screaming had stopped, then loosened his grip as she sagged against him and merely shook with sobs.

"Lana, shhh. Please. I'm here. I won't leave you." He didn't know what else to say. Nothing he could think of was profound enough or wise enough to satisfy a soul believing itself damned in the sight of God. He simply held her until Grace returned, looked into the living room and then left again. Her emotions spent, Lana lay against him like a favorite childhood bear, its stuffing largely gone. She was of above-average height, so her head rested on his shoulder and her arms circled his neck. He loosened his grip and slowly separated from her, keeping his eyes locked on hers.

"Lana, hon, let me get you something. A coke, tea, milk." He cocked his head to the side and downward so he could look into her downcast eyes. "How 'bout a bourbon? Maybe even a double," Will added.

She straightened up and sat back on her heels. Her face, though streaked and red, appeared for the moment calmer and more open.

"Thank you. A double would be splendid."

Will helped her back into her chair, then headed for the kitchen and the glasses. As he went through the dining-room door into the kitchen, he glanced over his shoulder and realized that Lana was behind him, following him. She sat down at the kitchen table while Will went over to the cabinet. He took down a half-full bottle of Maker's Mark and poured two or three ounces in each of two glasses.

"How's Hank doing? I haven't even called about him," Lana said.

"He's doing okay." Will replied. "He's still in Durham, but . . . he's okay."

"Will, you're hedging. Is he okay really?"

"They think so but he's got a way to go yet."

Lana said, "Please tell Nancy and Odell that I asked. If they are up to it I'd also like for them to come to the funeral, and by the house afterward. Would you please tell them?"

"I'll call but I think Nancy is in Durham with Hank, and I don't imagine Odell is too keen on coming by himself."

Lana cocked her head to the side. "Why not?"

"'Cause I think he feels uncomfortable with the feelings around here."

"What do you mean?"

"He thinks people are blaming him or at least Hank for Paulie's death."

"That's absurd. Those boys were thick as thieves and fed off each other. If it's anybody's fault it's mine."

"It's not your fault any more than it's Nancy's. They're boys and boys follow the same paths their fathers and grandfathers did."

"Well, it sure as hell isn't Odell's fault!" Lana said.

"Yeah, I know that, but not everybody agrees with you. The other night somebody threw a dead raccoon into the Griers' yard and yelled something like 'This ain't gonna be the only dead coon around here!'"

Lana shook her head and her lip started to quiver. "I just

can't imagine what kind of person would do something like that. I . . . I don't know."

Will put the glasses on the table, sat down beside her, then poured another healthy shot into each glass. Lana picked hers up and started to drink, but Will gently put his hand on her arm and touched his glass to hers.

"To Paul Reavis Senior and Junior, Man and boy . . ."

But Lana shook her head and put her fingers against his lips. Tears were pouring down her cheeks as some of the whiskey in her glass spilled onto the table. When she found her composure, she raised her glass toward Will and without a word, downed her whiskey in a single gulp. Will poured another. Her eyes eventually wandered from the glass to the notebook Doris and Roberta had left on the table. She flipped open the cover and started to read.

"Arlo Byerly brought a whole fryer, how sweet. And Ruth being dead for only four months. I wonder who fixed the chicken?"

Will smiled. "I saw Arlo the other day and he asked about your pigeons. You know he had the best time helping me and Paul and Paulie catch those guys." Will looked over at Lana and then into his glass. "Those were some good times, Lana, fun memories."

She nodded, but didn't acknowledge his comment; rather she kept on reading from the visitor book. "And Muriel Westmoreland . . . I'll bet that she was up all night fixin' that pecan pie. She can barely walk. Mr. and Mrs. Dunbar Kaster . . . how very proper. Smoked salmon, of course."

She looked at Will for what seemed a long time, as if she was trying to decide whether to tell him something. Finally she said, "I called Mr. Kaster this morning. I asked him about representing me in a wrongful death suit against Martin Farms, John Keaton, and Wallace May."

Will slowly shook his head and pursed his lips. "What does Martin Farms have to do with Paulie's accident, Lana?"

"I checked up on them. I talked to one of my cousins. He's

got a hog-feeding operation and does business with Martin Farms just like Wallace. The contracts between feeders and Martin Farms gives Martin Farms almost total control over all aspects of feedlot construction. While the farmer or contractor may own the land, Martin Farms controls the whole process of construction and even operation procedures after construction. If the lagoon wall was bad, they must have known it, and if they didn't, then they were negligent."

Will narrowed his eyes, "Look, Lana, I know you still got feelings about Martin Farms and Popper Winslow after Paul's accident, but this is different. You know as well as I that Wallace isn't smart enough to plan or actively be involved in something dishonest. He only got a contract with Martin Farms because his Uncle John is such a good friend of Oris's. Trust me, Wallace is all to pieces over this thing.

"I was out there this morning. John won't let him come to the funeral and Wallace doesn't understand why. Really, I'm on top of this. In fact, I've been out to Martin Feed Mills as well as Wallace's. If I find even a hint of negligent behavior, believe me, I'll take action. But as far as naming John Keaton in a suit, he doesn't even own the land. He sold it to Wallace."

Lana's eyes never blinked. "Yeah, I'm sure there're all kind of legal things that protect everybody, but we both know this thing smells worse than that busted lagoon. There's gotta be some justice left in the world. My little boy is gone. He's gone and . . ." She stopped. "I want them to feel the pain that they've caused."

"Them? Who, Lana, Oris Martin? You think he was supposed to inspect Wallace May's lagoon? Popper Winslow? John Keaton? Look, I know how you feel, I . . ."

"No, you don't. You're not his mother."

"Of course, but I did love that little boy. You know that. But latching on to a conspiracy theory isn't going to help."

Lana never took her eyes off Will. They bore into him, silent and glaring with the fury of unquenchable grief.

Uncomfortable with the silence, Will went on.

"We're going to be as thorough about this as we were with Paul's accident. In fact, I've been to Wallace May's twice since Wednesday morning. Plus I've been to Martin Feed Mills and told Oris that I want to see the inspection records for Wallace's operation. The state inspectors were at Wallace's just the other day; let's let them decide who, if anyone, is at fault."

Lana narrowed her eyes and twisted her mouth, finally speaking. "You think you were thorough with Paul's accident? You did everything you could? You questioned all the Martin Farms people who were out there that day? You talked to all the truck drivers and construction workers who were on the site from start to finish? You talked to neighbors? How long did you question Eugene Winslow and Weldon Goins, those bigoted pricks? Who were the delivery people that day?

"Could it be, Will, that who you mainly talked to was Ernie Tasker? The same man who talked you into coming back to this one-horse town to run for sheriff when he retired. Will Moser, the fair-haired boy of Hogg County law enforcement. Tell me, Deputy, how much time do you think Oris, Mr. King of Hog County U.S.A., allowed Ernie to spend looking into Paul's death? Probably more than he'll spend looking into Paulie's."

Anger stretched and wrinkled her face. The calm of moments before was now consumed by a hopeless realization of her son's death. Fear, hate, and grief had anesthetized her soul and loss had turned it cold.

Will looked at her, then took a sip from his glass. It wouldn't matter what he said, so he said nothing.

After a few minutes, Lana raised her eyes from her glass, "Maybe that's unfair. Maybe you did look hard, but you missed something 'cause I'll never believe Paul did something so stupid, and I'll never believe Wallace's lagoon met state standards."

Will took another sip and waited for her to do the same. "If I thought there was any reason to suspect foul play in Paul's death," he said, "nothing, and I mean nothing, would keep me away. I know Paul wasn't careless. I know that Popper and Oris aren't always on the up-and-up. But we just didn't find anything suspicious, Lana, you gotta believe that."

Lana watched him without moving. "I don't gotta believe anything. What I do believe, Will, is that something's out there. Something is out there that you missed. I'll bet if we went out to Popper's we'd find something. I think I could feel it even if I didn't see it. Come up with some excuse, Will. There's something out there."

Will shook his head. "What do you think we'd find . . . pictures, a confession, a smoking gun lying on the ground? Lana, I got no reason to go back to a place where an accident happened over a year ago."

"Not a year yet!" she said.

"Okay, eleven months and a few days. But listen to yourself. Go out to Pine Bluff and look around. Conduct some kind of séance." Will leaned back in his chair and sighed. "Hey, if it'll make you happy, I'll ask around some more. I'll go look. Just don't you even think about going out there."

Lana shook her head, then rocked back and closed her eyes. "Don't worry about trying to make me happy, Will. Nothing can make me happy—not asking around, not re-opening the investigation, nothing. I've got nothing left. No husband, no child, no . . . life . . . nothing." She took another drink then looked across the table holding Will firmly in her gaze. The blue in her eyes seemed fired almost purple. Her neck was taut and her jaw set forward.

"I want justice, Will."

Will cocked his head. "Maybe what you really want is revenge."

Lana didn't say anything, but slowly turned her eyes from Will to the world outside the kitchen window. She narrowed her gaze as if looking for a ship far out on a violent sea. Then, more to herself than to Will, she said, "Maybe so. But then what's revenge but justice by another name."

Will didn't reply. Anything he said would sound like a cliché, and Lana was way beyond clichés. Vengeance would be her sustenance now.

"Anyway," Lana said, "Mr. Dunbar Kaster said that my chances of winning a wrongful death suit for Paulie were about one in a million. He said the storm would be blamed, and Martin Farms would show that they'd fulfilled all their responsibilities, including having Wallace follow their directions to the letter. How did he put it?" she asked, affecting the manner and voice of Dunbar Kaster, "A matter of force majeure, my dear, an act of God. Your lovely son was the unfortunate victim of an act of God." Lana leaned back in the chair and slowly shook her head. "You want to know something funny?"

Will nodded.

"I thought he said force manure. I remember sitting there and thinking, what the hell is he talking about! Force manure. That some kind of pig joke?"

Will smiled but didn't laugh. He needed to watch her. She had a puzzled look, like something had just occurred to her, something she'd need to ponder. She looked around for the pen and made a note in the back of the notebook.

"Anyway, as far as going after Wallace May, Dunbar said that being retarded has a way of working for you if you're in front of a jury. He also said the same thing you did about John Keaton: he doesn't own the land. As far as suing Oris Martin and Martin Farms . . . well, what can I say, he doesn't want the case. I guess I'm just going to have to find someone else. Maybe I can get one of those high-priced ambulance chasers from Raleigh or Charlotte. They got more hungry lawyers in Raleigh than Oris has pigs in Hogg County."

Will got up. "Even if you could find an attorney from somewhere else, he'd need local counsel. Without local counsel, any lawyer coming into Mussel Ford would get eaten alive by a Hogg County judge and jury, and a local attorney who took a case against John Keaton or Oris Martin wouldn't work around here much longer. It's not fair, Lana, but it *is* reality."

She gazed into her glass as if she wasn't listening, then looked up. "Maybe . . . Maybe you're right. But I'm not going to desert my family. I'm not gonna quit on them."

They heard Grace pull around to the back of the house, and Lana shivered.

"You need to go home, Will. You need some rest and so do I. But if you don't mind, I would appreciate you taking me and Momma to Foster's tonight. I don't want to stay long, but I won't have Ray and his cow-eyed family playing like it was their son that drowned. And Will, no open casket. I've got a hundred pictures of Paulie in my heart; I don't need one of him in that casket. Call Mosby and tell him no viewing."

5.

The Hogg County sheriff's office was quiet. Most of the deputies were out, and the dispatcher was sitting with her headphone cocked back and her feet up. She was reading the latest gossip in *The Enquirer*. Will walked into the waiting area and buzzed through security.

"Hey, Sue. What's new from the Venusians? Any new reports of rectal exams? Egg or sperm thefts?"

Sue Honeycutt looked up with a smirk. "No, Major, but word has it the Venusians have run through all available rectums. They're looking for new meat. I'd watch out if I was you."

Will smiled and walked back to his office, putting his fingers into the opening between the second and third button on his shirt, trying to get some air next to his heavily perspiring body. He hated vinyl seats. Every time he got out of his patrol car the back of his shirt was soaked from top to bottom, and the seat was slick with moisture. The front of his shirt was so splotched with sweat that it looked like one of the new oak leaf camouflage patterns worn by the deer hunters in Hogg County.

He sat down in a big swivel chair. His chair was cherry, and like the desk, made from wood milled by Moser Hardwoods, Inc. Together they represented the only two possessions of his late father that Will had in his office. The same was true of his house. One or two paintings and a dining-room table were all he had taken from his childhood home. His mother had offered rooms full, but Will had rejected her offer, saying he didn't want to strip her house of its carefully planned décor. The truth was that he wanted his home to reflect his life, one that didn't revolve around lumber cut from the forests of eastern North Carolina and milled at Moser Hardwood.

He was a cop, an officer of the law, maybe even a pig, as the hippies would once have called him. In fact, a particularly apropos title for the chief deputy of Hogg County.

Will's choice of a career had always been a point of contention in the family but with his father's early death, the pressure on Will to assume his mantle had subsided. But was never forgotten.

—✦ ✦ ✦—

On the wall opposite his desk, hanging in no particular order, were a half-dozen eight-by-ten photos of him with his parents, army buddies, teammates, and of course Lana, Paul, and Paulie. Next to these were two plaques from the Boy Scouts, one from the Hogg County United Way, and one from his MP unit. Finally there were his diplomas from Vanderbilt and Infantry Officer Candidate School, his Army commission, and his Purple Heart and Silver Star certificates.

Will put both hands on his face and slowly pushed them against his cheeks and eyes and then over his forehead and scalp. It had been a long day, with an evening at the funeral home still to come.

He exhaled, and with his eyes closed, stretched his neck from side to side. Opening his eyes, he focused on unfinished paperwork that covered his desk. He picked up the top folder, but before he had read the first memo his radio came alive.

"This is Deputy Canipe. I have a 10-39 for Major Moser." Will activated his shoulder mike.

"This is Moser."

"Major, we have an 11-80 on NC 521."

"Roger that. 10-6 to ops 5."

Both men changed their frequencies to a channel that couldn't be monitored.

"Will, we got a bad wreck out here."

"Where are you, Tommy?"

"I'm on 521 just south of Tomkins Road."

"Where exactly?"

"There's a high bank on the north side of the road, the O'Neil place, they're doing some timbering."

"Okay, I know where you are."

"Looks like some logs come off the bank and crashed down on the road hitting a pickup in the process. It looks bad, Will. It's Odell Grier's truck and Odell was driving." Will's heart almost stopped.

"What's the status, Tommy? Is he alive?"

"Yeah, he's alive but he's mighty beat up. The EMS boys just got here and they're trying to get him out now. He's conscious but there sure is a lot of blood."

"Can you tell what the hell happened?"

"Not really. They got a skid loader on top of the hill and a bunch of pretty big hardwood logs . . . red oak, mainly. Looks like something came loose and a damn big log rolled over the edge of the hill and down onto the road. Odell was just unlucky enough to come by when he did."

"Who's doing the logging, Tommy?"

"I don't know, but the skidder belongs to Eugene Winslow, plus he's got a mid-sized dozer up there as well."

Will leaned back in his chair and stared at the far wall. His eyes focused on a picture of himself in Vietnam. He was wearing a flak jacket, holding an M-16, and standing beside a beat-up

APC. He had just come off a road sweep with the First Cavalry and had lost two armored vehicles to booby traps set by the VC. Roadside demolition was easy to set out and hard to find.

"Tom, I want you to take pictures of the log pile and the surrounding area. If you don't have a camera, call Robert, I know he carries one. Listen, before anything else you need to cordon off the area. Tape off all road entrances and anywhere else that looks like an access to the area. I don't want anybody coming in or out until we have a chance to inspect everything."

"Okay, Will, but . . ."

"Do what I'm telling you, Deputy, and don't say anything to anybody until we've talked. You got that?"

"Roger that, Will."

"Look for tracks, any sign of an explosion, equipment that's been tampered with. Look at everything, Tommy. I'm going to the hospital now. I'll meet you there."

"Okay, I'll . . ." but Will had already clicked off.

—✦ ✦ ✦—

Below the Vietnam picture was another photo. It was of Paulie's ninth birthday . . . a group shot in front of the Raleigh Coliseum. There, in a line, were Paul and Lana, Paulie, two of Paulie's friends, and finally Will, smiling at the end of the line. They'd gone to the state fair instead of having a regular party.

Paulie was holding a huge stuffed animal. It was a four-foot version of the Tasmanian Devil and was almost bigger than Paulie. Hank Grier stood to Paulie's right wearing an Alabama teeshirt and holding a three-foot plush snake. He was looking at Paulie and holding the snake as if to bite Paulie's devil. Both boys were laughing. Will drummed a wooden pencil on the desk.

Either Odell has had some really shitty luck or something was going on. This can't be just bad luck. Bad luck was the hog lagoon busting. This is too neat. Logging operations are dangerous places but with nobody there, if indeed nobody was there, it should have been fairly safe.

He shook his head then mumbled as he got up. "Wait and see, Will. Don't jump to any conclusions. Let's just see."

—✦ ✦ ✦—

Bob Velez came out of the emergency room and removed his mask. Will was standing next to the door leading into the waiting room and motioned with his head for Dr. Velez to follow him.

"I have to take care of something first, Will. I'll be in my office in five minutes."

Will nodded and headed down the hall. He kept his seat when Bob came into the office.

Dr. Velez sat a minute, then said, "Okay, Odell has a broken leg, a couple of broken ribs, a slight concussion, possibly a spinal fracture, but without question the damnedest supply of good luck I've ever seen."

Will breathed out in relief. "That takes a load off. I have to call Nancy and tell her, and I was hoping I'd have relatively good news. I mean good compared to really bad."

"I know what you mean, Deputy. And yes, it is relatively good news. He'll have to be in the hospital for a few days for observation and a few more tests but he's a lucky man. Deputy Canipe tells me the truck is a pile of junk."

Will nodded and smiled. "Thanks, Bob. I'll look in on him later tonight, if that's all right. I'm taking Lana to Foster's for Paulie's visitation, but I'll come by afterward to check on Odell. I'd like to ask him a few questions."

"Let's take it a step at a time, Will. If he's feeling up to it, then okay but maybe tomorrow would be better."

Will nodded and stood up. "Thank you, Bob."

—✦ ✦ ✦—

Deputy Canipe was in the waiting room when Will came out. Will nodded toward the front door. When they got outside Will walked to the side of Officer Canipe's car.

"So, what'd you find?"

The deputy shook his head, "Nothing really, Will, but then I don't exactly know what I'm looking for. What I did do was take one hell of a lot of pictures. I even took close-ups of all the tire tracks in the area. What do you think, Will? You think somebody tried to kill Odell?"

"I don't know. Too early to tell anything. I always figure that accidents may not be accidents, at least until it's obvious that they are. How long after Odell got hit did you get there?"

"About twenty minutes, I guess."

"Who called you?"

"I got a call from dispatch. They said someone called the accident in and that they'd already called EMS."

"You know who called it in?"

"I don't know 'im but it was a guy lives over in Gates County. He was on his way home from somewhere over near Oxford. The guy is a mechanic or electrician. I'm sure dispatch has his name."

"Did he see the accident?"

"I don't think so. I think he come by after Odell was already off the road."

"We need to talk to him." Will looked at his watch. "You cordon off the area?"

"Yes, Will."

"Good. See if you can find out who was working the logs and when they left. See if anybody saw anything, and be sure to get the name of everyone who worked today. I have to go to Paulie's visitation tonight, so you need to stay on this thing. I've got to get Paulie and Lana taken care of." His voice began to crack and he had to stop talking.

"Will, you don't need to worry. Robert Joyce took most of the pictures and he's got a lot more experience at investigations of this kind than I do." Deputy Canipe tried to put a good face on events. "Odell sounds like he'll be okay. You just focus on taking care of Lana." Will nodded his head and started toward his car.

"Will, I'm real sorry about Paulie. I . . ."

Will held up his hand.

"Anyway, I'm sure this will probably turn out to be just a freak accident,"

Tommy said, though Will knew better.

6.

The usual mid-afternoon August breeze was late. It was well past six o'clock before the broad leaves of the tulip poplar in front of Lana's house began to flutter and sigh.

Will wrapped his arm around the nine-foot white column at the top of the porch steps and leaned out to take in the cool air. He closed his eyes and breathed in the fresh eddies swirling around the house. There was no smell of rain, just the calm sense of the earth exhaling after a hot muggy day.

He looked down the street, and then over at Ernie Tasker, sitting on the top step to his left. It had become unbearably hot in the house and after an hour of greeting and sympathizing with the crowd of mourners who'd come by after the funeral, Will and Ernie needed some air. Their conversation, such as it was, with all the porch people behind them, stopped as the blue pickup neared the mailbox in front of the house.

Ernie turned his eyes from the street and up toward Will.

"Will, this is the third time in the last thirty minutes that that boy has come by."

"Yeah, I know," Will mumbled, keeping his eyes fixed on the man driving the blue truck. Wallace glanced nervously over at the crowd on the porch. His features were fuzzy and confused, like he'd been crying. Will smiled and nodded as Wallace slowed down. He'd seen him at the cemetery . . . standing behind a holly hedge at the north end of the property.

When Wallace saw Will smile, he quickly looked away and accelerated north on the hot asphalt of Roanoke Street.

"John Keaton should go out and tell him to park his goddamn truck and come on in. I mean give the guy a break," Ernie said.

"Forget it, Sheriff." Will said. "There ain't no need to start a hassle. You know damn well that that boy'd freak if he put foot on this porch. "

The porch crowd started to move around. Some were looking for the best place to catch the breeze, others for a good spot from which to make their getaway when the time was right.

The house, even with the funeral over for an hour, still pulsed and bulged with mourners. Ray and Robert Reavis, along with wives, children, and grandchildren, continued to dominate the inside rooms. They all wore sad, bedraggled smiles, playing the role of grieving family members.

Popper Winslow and Charlie Summers stood by the window in the dining room eating ham biscuits and speaking in hushed tones. Oris and Emma Martin had come and gone, staying long enough to be seen, but not long enough to be obvious. Will had engaged Oris in a superficial exchange of niceties, and as usual got the feeling that Oris was too preoccupied and uninterested to talk further. John and Lurella Keaton sat on the living-room sofa talking to the Crumplers while Bob Velez and his wife took turns standing in the hall outside Lana's bedroom. She was, with the help of Dr. Velez's sedatives, sleeping calmly.

It seemed like the whole town had turned out for Paulie's funeral. His death, like his father's, was a major event in the life of

Mussel Ford, and folks wanted the Reavis family, Lana especially, to know how much father and son had meant to the community. Fortunately, not everyone from the service came to the house, it being so hot and the house being small, but if not after the funeral, most had been there at some time during the week, and when they did come, it was always with food.

Southern folk bring food. They walk through the front door, platter or casserole in hand, and before they can find the kitchen, some white-haired, lightly powdered, lilac-smelling Southern lady swoops down and takes it away, while her compatriot at the front door writes down the name of the guest and a description of what they brought.

It had been a fairly typical white Southern funeral. Stoic, calm, and filled with stiff-upper-lip Anglo-Saxon hymns—"Onward Christian Soldiers," "Amazing Grace," and of course the Lutheran favorite, "A Mighty Fortress is Our God." Unlike the emotional relief of funerals in the black community, white society seemed to prefer internal bleeding. Children were told to be "strong little soldiers," and adults fought to maintain the proper decorum. Though many of the mourners were clearly moved by the death of such a young, exuberant little boy, only Lana wept with abandon. Will's internal bleeding was massive and untreated.

—◆ ◆ ◆—

Through the window, Will saw Eugene say something to Charlie Summers before turning to make his way through the dining-room crowd toward the porch. When the screen door opened and closed, Will moved from his place by the column toward the middle of the crowd.

"Eugene, you got a minute?" Will said.

The wiry, little man looked up out of hooded, asymmetric eyes. "I guess."

The deputy walked with Popper down the side steps of the porch and toward the dozen cars and trucks parked on the lawn. "You hear about Odell Grier's accident yesterday?"

Without looking at him, Popper said. "Yeah, I heard."

"You know anything about it?"

"How do you mean?"

"I gather you're doing some timbering work for John O'Neil. I just wondered if you knew anything that might be helpful."

"Well, first off, I ain't doing nothing for O'Neil. I'm renting some equipment to Curtis Transou and his boys. They're the ones doing the work for O'Neil."

"You know if they were working yesterday?"

"No."

"You been out there any?"

Eugene paused by the door of his truck and looked back at Will. "What the fuck you getting at, Deputy?"

"I'm trying to get at what happened."

"What happened is that Odell got his self plenty fucked up yesterday. You want to know whether the Transouses was working, go ask 'em. I ain't been out there. Weldon brung my 'dozer and skidder over a couple of weeks ago. He done some work for them boys but none recently. He's been with me at Pine Bluff all this week. You need to ask the Transou boys 'bout yesterday." Eugene opened the door to the truck. "That it? You got anymore sheriff questions?"

Will shook his head, "Not right now, but if I do, I know where to get hold of you."

"Yeah, you do that, Deputy." Eugene got in, slamming the door, and without looking back drove out of the yard and down Roanoke Street.

Ernie Tasker came up beside Will. "He didn't look too happy. What'd you say to him?"

Without looking at the sheriff, Will said, "Not much. I asked him about the timbering operation out on 521 where Odell had his accident. It's his equipment out there but he says the Transou boys are the ones doing the work. I wanted to know if he had been out there or knew anything about what might have happened."

"And did he?"

Will glanced at the sheriff and smiled, "What do you think?"

Ernie straightened his back and then leaned against the closest car. He looked at Will and said nothing for a few beats.

"Will, what do you think happened out there? I talked to Canipe and it looks to him like it was just a bad set of circumstances. You think otherwise?"

"I don't know, Ernie. I guess a dead raccoon thrown into Odell's yard, along with some of our more bigoted citizens blaming Hank for Paulie's death has my antenna up. I'm not against freak accidents, but like you've always told me, a good lawman never assumes anything. On first blush, this seems a little too pat. I mean, what are the odds?"

Ernie didn't respond.

"I had Robert Joyce go by the service station, and according to some of the boys there, Odell was on his way home."

"And . . . ?"

"And nothing, except they said he left at the same time every day, more or less. According to Robert, Rafe Grier, Odell's uncle, said that's the route Odell takes home every day. Rafe was supposed to be with him but got hung up at the Mack truck place getting some work done on one of C&R's big dumpers. Odell left without him. They only live a mile or so apart. Anyway, Rafe said that when he got to the station Odell had already gone."

"So where does that take us?" Ernie asked.

"If Odell went home the same way and the same time every day, then anybody looking to mess him up could easily arrange a 'freak' accident. One thing I learned in Vietnam, never take a convoy on the same route two days in a row. Ambushes are easy if you know where and when." Will pushed away from the car and turned to face the sheriff.

"Sheriff, we both know the way things are around here. With Paulie's death and all the loose talk about Hank being responsible, you can't tell who might be looking for some payback. I'll snoop around a little, but don't worry, I'll be discreet."

Tasker nodded. "Okay. Just don't drag it out. Keep me in the loop." The two men walked back toward the porch.

—✦ ✦ ✦—

As he neared the steps, Will stopped when he saw Mosby Foster coming out of the house. He stopped before going up the stairs again. When Mosby came down, Will put his hand on Mosby's arm.

"Mosby, thank you. It was a beautiful service. By the way, did you get it in Paulie's pocket?"

"You know I did."

"Thanks, I appreciate it. I should've given it to him years ago."

Mosby waited, then said, "If you don't mind me asking, what was it? I mean I know it was a knife but what was it? Where'd you get it?"

The deputy looked up on the porch. He breathed deeply for a few seconds to get hold of himself. "It was a Special Forces knife. My first sergeant gave it to me. We'd come back from a really nasty convoy, lost a dozen or so men. A really shitty op. One of the guys killed, an E-5 named O'Brien, had been with Special Forces for a tour. A real pro. In fact, he's the one who saved our asses, at least those that made it. Anyway, my first sergeant gave me O'Brien's knife. He said it was for luck. I've carried it since. Paulie used to ask for it every few minutes when we'd be out camping." He smiled.

"That boy really . . ." Will turned, his eyes full of tears, and walked away.

7.

Will drove north on Roanoke Street, then turned east on Tryon. Within a half-mile he made a right on River Road and headed south along the river.

His eyes ran ahead down the canopied row of live oaks that lined River Road and separated the massive houses on his right from the brown, acidic waters of the Roanoke River on his left.

Just past a large whitewashed brick column, Will turned into the circular drive of Cromwell House, parking after a few hundred feet in front of the herringbone-patterned brick walkway leading to the front steps.

On the grass beside the walkway and next to the driveway, stood a three-foot-high cast-iron statue of a smiling black boy holding his left arm aloft, an iron ring dangling from his fist. This antique hitching post had been used in the days when horse-drawn carriages frequented Cromwell. Will had never seen anything hitched to the little boy's iron ring, but his mother assured him that it had been used during Cromwell's storied past. It was the kind of artifact that carried little material value but spoke volumes as a symbol of ancestral wealth and position. This, at least, was Sarah Moser's belief.

He looked out over the intricately manicured front lawn and late-blooming perennial gardens and exhaled into the hot, sultry air that always seemed to hang over the yard. With hands on his hips, he looked up at the enormity of the house. Its dimensions could more accurately be expressed in acreage than square feet.

Cromwell House was the biggest in town—probably in the county. Four massive Corinthian columns, two per side, framed the ten-foot-high front door and fanlight above the entrance. No visitor could help but gaze upward along the fluted columns toward the tall dormer windows and expansive slate roof.

Behind the columns, a huge porch fronted by a three-foot-high white railing, ran the breadth of the façade. Ponderous white wicker furniture puffed with pink and lime-green chintz pillows were grouped for conversation. In keeping with Sarah Moser's love of horticulture, gigantic Boston ferns sat like Rastafarian sentinels atop metal plant stands along the railing. The house exuded undivided power, and had been Will's boyhood home.

Will struck the base plate of the large brass knocker twice, then pushed open the door and stepped into the brown silence of the entrance hall. It smelled of oiled walnut and African violets, with a hint of boyhood discipline and disapproval.

The paneling in the house, as well as all of the flooring, had been cut and milled by Moser Hardwood, most during the nineteenth century. The house was warmer than the air conditioning should have permitted, but then Sara Moser often complained of being chilled.

"Mother?" Will called, looking up the broad front staircase.

"I'm on the sun porch, William."

Will walked past the stairway toward the large glass-and-screened room at the back of the house. The sun porch, like the orangeries of eighteenth-century Europe, was a long room with sliding glass panels along the west wall. In the spring and fall, the glass was opened slightly, so that fresh air could flow through the screens and into the room. In mid-summer and winter, the glass was closed so that the air-conditioning could cool or the furnace heat the room. Today the air-conditioning was motoring along at a barely comfortable rate. Sarah Moser, fertilizing one of the Ficus trees at the far end of the room, had her back to Will as he came in.

"Mother, I missed you at Lana's house. When did you, or did you, come by?"

Sarah stuck her trowel into the base of the pot and turned, wiping small droplets of sweat from her forehead with the back of her hand.

"Actually, I decided to pass. I was at the funeral. Everyone saw me. I suspect that was enough. How many people were at the house?"

"I don't know, fifty or sixty at a time."

"Well, there you have it. I was right. Fifty people in that little house is entirely too many. I would have simply been perspiring like everyone else and accomplishing little. I'll see Lana and Grace tomorrow or Tuesday; besides, I assumed Lana would be sleeping."

Will shook his head, "All that may be true, Mother, but it looks bad when everybody else shows up and you don't."

Sarah walked over to the couch and sat down. "William, people here know me. They don't care whether I'm at Lana's or not. I was at the funeral and the cemetery, that's plenty."

While Will's relationship with his mother had never been as strained as that with his father, it also had never been one that reflected much warmth or intimacy. Sarah and William had had a child out of a perceived need to replicate themselves, but with her difficulties during pregnancy and her horror at losing her figure and tone, Sarah slammed the door shut on other babies after Will was born.

"William, please, sit down. You haven't been by in weeks. You come over to pick up food and leave. I hear more about what's going on from Mamie than from you." She wiped her forehead and gave him one of her mother-of-the-debutante smiles. "Why don't you go into the kitchen and get us some tea. Mamie made a pitcher just yesterday. It's your favorite, pineapple Earl Grey."

Will came out of the kitchen with two glasses of tea and sat down in the overstuffed chair beside the couch. He took a long drink from his tea and leaned back into the chintz pillows.

"How is that young colored boy who was with Paulie?" Sarah said.

Will rolled his eyes. "He, the young man to whom you refer, is still alive, if that's what you're asking."

Sarah paid no attention to his tone. "You know, it's a shame that young Reavis let that boy talk him into going into those woods on a day like that. I understand that he was quite a bit older than Paulie and more able to take care of himself. I just hope . . ."

"Mother, Henry Grier was exactly Paulie's age, and I'm sure Paulie was just as excited about going out to the creek as Hank. It's Hank that's going to have a lot of grieving to do."

Sarah's face showed no emotion. "Perhaps, but folks are talking."

"Now there's a surprise. Folks in Mussel Ford gossiping about something they don't know shit about. How unusual."

"No need to be crude, William. I only meant to indicate that people are aware of the incident and making comments. That's not unusual here or anywhere else, for that matter."

Will turned to look at Sarah, then nodded. "You're right. It's not unusual. It is, however, unnecessary, unfair, dangerous, and petty. However, what is not normal is when someone throws a dead raccoon into the Griers' yard late at night, yells threats, and then possibly tries to kill Odell."

"What are you talking about?"

"Yesterday, on his way home, Odell Grier's truck was crushed by a log falling from a work site above Highway 521. He's in the hospital and damn lucky to be alive. So it may be that some people are doing more than simply talking."

She had not expected this; thus, she had no ready answer or comment. Sarah blinked a few times and then looked across the room and out the windows. After a sip of tea she said, "Do you have reason to believe it was intentional? Something other than a constable's intuition?"

"No. Just a constable's intuition. But it's shared by a sheriff's intuition and even a bit of MP intuition. Have I left anyone out? Flatfoot, cop, John Law, Dick? "

She raised her eyebrows. "I see. We appear to be in one of our 'moods' today. Well, forgive me for speaking at all."

Will stood up and walked toward the window, then turned to face his mother. "I probably am in a mood, what with the death of one of my favorite people on this earth. You know how I felt about that little boy. But that has nothing to do with your incessant use of snarky terms like constable to describe your only son's occupation." He took a deep breath. "I'm a lawman. To be more specific, the chief deputy of Hogg County and eventually, I expect, the high sheriff. I know this has never thrilled you, but there it is. We each must choose our course in life—upholding the law is mine."

Sarah leaned back into the downy embrace of the pillows and stared at Will. After a brief silence she said, "We do not need to, yet again, discuss your choice of professions. You know how I feel about it, and I will not apologize. I have always felt that you had and have the potential to be anything you wish. You attended an excellent university and could have been a fine lawyer, or even a judge. It simply seems to me that being an ordinary police officer does not fulfill your . . . potential. The potential of being a Moser!"

Will laughed. "Well, Mother, we will simply have to disagree on what being a Moser is all about. Robber baron might be some folks' idea of success, but it's not mine. Let's drop it since we've never agreed on this."

Sarah nodded without acknowledging what her son had just said, then looked off into the distance again.

"Anyway, Mother, I do need you to try and stop the rumors about Hank Grier when you hear them. Such talk can only harm people that you will agree are good citizens and therefore of value to this community."

Sarah nodded. "Yes, I will try to prevent something from being said that is potentially harmful to the Griers. I realize that you are just doing your job of protecting them. I understand. On another subject, how do you think Lana is doing?"

"She's okay, considering. She's crushed; she's angry; she's . . . what anyone would expect. I'm going by to check on her as often as I can and I've got Dr. Velez checking on her as well."

Sarah got up and walked over to the Ficus tree again. She picked up her trowel and began to dig.

"It's all so distasteful. I'm sure your father would be outraged to see such behavior in a town that has been so civilized for so many generations."

"There's a lot that would outrage Father these days," Will said.

Sarah looked over at her son. "What do you mean by that?"

"I mean he would be outraged that I'm not running Moser Hardwoods, Inc. He'd be outraged that Oris Martin runs roughshod over this county. He'd be pissed that the Reavises have almost been decimated, at least the good ones. So you're right; he'd be outraged at such behavior." Will walked over to his mother and gave her a kiss on the cheek. "I've got to meet some of my deputies. I'll see you." He turned and walked toward the front hall. "I'll come back soon, Mother."

"You're wrong about him being outraged that you don't run the company, William. He only wanted for you to be the best you could be, at whatever you chose."

Will nodded and held up his arm without turning around. "Okay, Mother, then I'll be the best high sheriff Hogg County has ever had."

—✦ ✦ ✦—

Robert Joyce was sitting in Ernie's chair when Will came

into the office. Tommy Canipe was standing against the wall and looked up. Both deputies said at the same time, "Hey, Will."

"Gentlemen," Will said, "talk to me."

"I spent most of yesterday afternoon and early evening out at the O'Neil place," Robert said. "If anybody was out there at the logging site, nobody saw 'em. The work crew had left about forty minutes before Odell come by. Randall Transou was the last to leave and he's got a rock-solid alibi. They ain't the kind to do something like that, anyway. I asked him if anybody was supposed to be there after he left and he said no." Robert licked his lips. "As you would imagine, there was nothing real obvious out of place. Nothing that stuck out."

Will took off his hat and sat down. "You think it was just a piece of bad luck?"

"I don't know. It seems far-fetched. There is a pile of about a dozen oak logs stacked up at the top of that hill. They probably shouldn't have been stacked there but there ain't no law that says they can't be there, either. Just sloppy."

Will rubbed his mouth. "Could you tell where the log was that rolled down the hill?"

"Not really, but I think it had to be on top of the pile. There ain't no room in front for a log that big, so it had to be on top. But that don't seem right, either."

"How come?"

"The pile looked like it'd been held in place by a logging chain hooked to a come-along."

"And?"

"And when we got there the top length of chain wasn't attached to the come-along. That's why I figure that the log that come down the hill must've rolled off the top."

"How you think it came off the pile?"

"Good question."

"So, what's the answer?"

"Damn, Will. If I knew that, we wouldn't have a problem. I have no idea. Pushed, pulled, I don't know. Maybe the pile shifted some. No way of telling that I can see."

Will sat down in the captain's chair beside Ernie's desk and pushed his fingers against his temples. There had to be some logical explanation, but if not, then there had been a crime.

"Okay, listen up. I want to keep the site closed for a day or two while we poke around some more. I'm sure Curtis will be pissed, but that can't be helped. Let's see if anybody joins in on the pissing and moaning. Leave the pictures on my desk. I'll look at them in the morning. I'm tired now."

8.

Robert Joyce was already there when Will parked outside the yellow tape separating the logging site from the road.

"Morning, Robert."

"Will."

"Any problems?"

"Naw. Nobody's give me any trouble. Curtis was out here and I told him that at least for today the place is off limits. He wasn't too happy but said he understood. I told him it wouldn't be long. Maybe tomorrow."

Will walked along the side of the rutted mud track to the pile of logs stacked above the road. "Curtis is okay. You can't blame him if he's a little pissed. We can let him and his boys back in tomorrow." He stopped twenty feet from the logs.

"Okay, so we learn anything?"

"Not a lot," Robert said. He walked up to the right side of the pile. "If anybody was here and pushed that log off the pile, we'll never be able to prove it. Hell, look at the ruts and crosstracks.

This place looks like there's been a demo derby up here. I asked Curtis about the logging chain and come-a-long, and he just shrugged and said it should have been together. He wasn't the last to leave which means the rest of those boys were probably pushing like hell to get out of here once the boss was gone. We can look around, but I don't figure we'll come up with nothing."

Will took a deep breath and slowly blew it out between his teeth. "Shiiiiit. Well, let's not waste too much time. Talk to everybody that was out here working that day just in case something interesting comes up, which I doubt. Get their statements on the record and put all the photos in the file. I'll talk to Odell when I can and see if he remembers anything unusual." Will shook his head.

"But something don't smell right, Robert. Same as Paul's accident. Something's hiding out here and stinking up the place. I'm getting damn tired of workplace-accident folders." He turned toward his truck. "Make sure to tell Curtis to move those goddamn logs to the back of the site before he does another lick of work."

"Right. And Will, how 'bout I have the watch commanders schedule a few ride-bys every evening at Odell's place."

"Yeah, good idea, plus get the word out to everybody to keep their ears open for any loose talk, anything that might sound a little dangerous." Will turned around and took a few steps down the track leading off the hill, then stopped and looked over at Robert. "I gotta go by the office. While I'm there I'll dictate a brief alert notice to all deputies and get Sue to circulate it."

"You want me to meet you at the office?"

"Naw. I'm just going back to pick up some stuff. I gotta make a speech to the Democratic Women at their monthly luncheon." Will paused, raising his eyebrows. "Ernie has me doing this kindda shit these days. Says I better get used to it, but used to it don't mean lovin' it."

Robert smiled, "Well, when you're the big guy you gotta shake a lot of hands and kiss a lotta whatevers. By the way, how long you figure Ernie's gonna hang in there?"

Will shook his head. "I don't know, but lately he's been talking like a short-timer. I'm guessing he might even hang 'em up this term, but that's just a guess. Anyway, I'm making his speeches these days."

Robert smiled, patted Will on the back, and slogged across the logging yard toward his truck.

—✦ ✦ ✦—

The banquet room at the Golden Corral was full to overflowing. Counting the Democratic Women and guests, there must have been close to a hundred folks sitting or standing in the hall, including a smattering of husbands and party officials in the back. Will's speech took about twenty minutes, and based on the applause, was well received.

"Thank you ladies and . . ." Will looked at the half dozen men in the room, "you brave gentlemen as well. I appreciate the invitation and especially the fine lunch. At a time like this, I truly understand the old saying about singing for your supper." He stepped from behind the podium and moved back toward his seat. Before he could sit down it seemed like the whole room descended upon him. Everybody had an opinion along with their congratulations.

"Will, you're gonna make a fine sheriff. I know how proud your momma must be," said one woman, patting his forearm.

"Listen here, Will Moser, sheriff isn't the only thing you ought to be thinking about. A speech like that and I'm thinking congress. You study on it, Will Moser," said another, hustling off.

The noise level in the room became uncomfortable. Conversations jumped on top of other conversations and high-pitched laughter pierced the room like the stab of a fresh migraine. He could barely hear the person standing directly in front of him. Will smiled a lot and shook all offered hands.

It took about a half hour but finally the room emptied and

Will could gather up his papers and briefcase. It had been a good day. He'd made a positive impression on one of the most influential blocks of voters in Hogg County . . . certainly its most vociferous. The Democratic Women adhered to the philosophy that, "If Momma ain't happy, ain't nobody happy."

"William, that was one of the best speeches we've heard in many a year. You're an excellent orator." Will turned around to see Mrs. Dunbar Kaster standing behind him. She was beaming.

He nodded slightly and said, "Well, thank you, Mrs. Kaster. I surely do appreciate that. It was my pleasure to be able to address you ladies. There couldn't be a more knowledgeable audience."

Ruth Kaster was glowing. As dull and pedantic as Dunbar could be, Ruth was frequently the very opposite. She was a past president of the Hogg County Democratic Women and a longtime power in the state party. Will suspected that she'd harbored a few political ambitions of her own, but that they'd gone by the board long ago. She was smart, clever even, but such traits were unbecoming to a lawyer's wife in Hogg County. In any case, Will treated her with due respect—and not a small amount of suspicion. Ruth kept her ear to the ground.

She patted his arm and started to turn when something occurred to her.

"William, I played bridge with Sarah this morning. Always an interesting and stimulating game with your mother. Anyway, you really should have told her you were making the speech today. When I told her where I was going she seemed to be a bit disappointed that she didn't know about it. I asked Sarah to come but she said she had other plans." Ruth paused a moment for Will's reaction.

When he didn't register any, she said, "You know, she is very proud of you, William. You may not know it, but I do. Sarah hides things, as we both know, but I've known her for a long time and in a different way than you, so believe me when I tell you she is proud of you."

"Thank you, Mrs. Kaster," Will said. "I've often wondered

about that, so I appreciate your insight." Not a topic he wanted to pursue. He picked up his papers and backed toward the door. Ruth turned and walked toward the last group of women in the room.

When Will got outside he looked around the parking lot to make sure Ruth and the others weren't waiting. He threw his briefcase in the back seat, then leaned against the squad car for a moment. He'd have to get used to this when he became sheriff.

—✦ ✦ ✦—

Wallace watched as the local high school kids cruised up and down Main Street in their deep-throated pickups and muscle cars. He sat at one of the three concrete tables outside the Dairy Queen under the cover of a gargantuan blue-and-white umbrella growing out of the center of the table.

Wallace loved eating at the Dairy Queen. He would fantasize about being seventeen again, except in his fantasy he had a girlfriend, his own car, and friends . . . lots of them.

Wallace carefully turned the soft ice cream cone against his tongue so that none of the vanilla or chocolate topping dripped on his clothes. He was very careful about not looking messy or unkempt. Mrs. May had always made sure that her son looked proper.

It'd been almost four weeks since the state inspectors were at his farm, and still no word. Wallace figured his uncle had talked to the people in Raleigh, and there was nothing to worry about. He hoped so. Paulie's death had not only been very upsetting, but like Paulie's father's, it frightened him. He dealt with life simply, straight down the middle. To Wallace, people were either kind or mean, happy or sad, the subtleties of relationships were impenetrable, like a brick held in the hand.

He hoped Uncle John hadn't forgotten his promise to take him to see Lana Reavis. Wallace needed to tell her how sorry he was about her little boy. She had to know that he had nothing to do with the storm or the rain or the lagoon wall breaking.

He wondered if he'd ever have a little boy. He hoped so. They could do all the things he never got to do with his dad. He'd make sure not to die so soon. He took a deep breath, and amid the shouts from a truck full of laughing boys and girls, slowly let it out. Who was he kidding? He'd never find anyone to marry him. Still . . .

—◆ ◆ ◆—

He didn't hear Popper Winslow drive up and park even though it was hard to miss the loud growl of the diesel engine.

"Hey, Wallace. How they hangin'?"

Wallace turned to his right and saw Popper standing with one foot propped on the edge of his bench. He was smiling down at Wallace, and looking about as friendly as Popper could.

"Hey, Mr. Winslow. Uh, they're hanging fine, I guess. How are yours hanging?"

Popper patted him on the shoulder and smiled. "You mind if I get a cone and join you? It's mighty hot out here."

Wallace stood up and grinned. "Well, no sir, I sure don't." He looked around to see if anyone was looking. He wanted the other people at the Dairy Queen to see that someone had come over to visit with him.

Popper went inside and returned with a large butterscotch dip. "So, Wallace, my boy, how ya been?"

"Oh, I've been okay, Mr. Winslow. Them fellas from the state was down at my place a while ago looking around, but I haven't heard nothing since. I reckon they didn't find nothing. I hope not."

Popper Winslow made Wallace nervous. He was just like Wallace's Uncle John, always real serious and gruff; still he'd been nice to Wallace and given him a lot of work.

Popper had a small land-clearing business on the side, plus when he wasn't busy he'd rent out his equipment, like he was doing with the Transou boys. Weldon Goins, his man Friday, ran it for him. It didn't interfere with his farming or hog operations;

in fact, it was a good way to amortize the cost of some of his bigger equipment. He used contract labor instead of carrying a permanent payroll. Weldon did the day-to-day supervision and Popper just kept the books and made sure Weldon had the right directions. Weldon was reliable. While not a brain trust, he was quicker than Wallace by a long shot. But Wallace was the ideal contract worker: he was cheap, he worked hard, he was reliable, and he didn't ask any questions. The amount of time it took to explain things to Wallace was worth the extra effort.

"So, Wallace, I hope you're not worried about that accident. Everybody knows you couldn't help it. That storm was more than anybody's lagoon could handle. No matter how hard you try, you just can't keep some things from happening." He looked at Wallace to see if he was concentrating. "You remember how thorough those guys from Martin Farms were while you were building your sheds and lagoon, don't you? Man, they were all over the place, checking this and checking that. They didn't let a thing get by, did they?"

Wallace nodded, "Yes sir, I sure do remember them coming out to the farm while we were building. They made sure I was doing good, didn't they?"

"Man, they sure did," Popper agreed.

Lamont Edwards, one of the low-level field managers for Martin Farms had come by twice during the entire time that Wallace's feed sheds and lagoon were being built. The last time he was there, Wallace was pushing up the lagoon walls using one of Popper's bulldozers. Lamont spent about twenty minutes checking the base structure of the lagoon.

"This looks good, Wallace," the manager said. "I reckon we got enough clay in the base. Good enough at least for gov'ment work. I'll tell Oris and your uncle John that you're building a fine facility. Keep up the good work. I'll see ya." That was it. One man, two visits, and Wallace May had a qualified hog-waste lagoon.

Popper licked his ice cream and watched Wallace out of the corner of his eye.

"You know, Mr. Winslow, Uncle John didn't let me go to little Paul's funeral the other day. I wanted to go but he said it weren't a good time. But he said that he would take me by Mrs. Reavis's house pretty soon to tell her how sorry I was about her little boy. You think he'll still take me?"

"I'm sure he will, Wallace. He just wants to let a little more time go by. You know, so she isn't so sad and maybe angry."

Wallace shifted on his bench. He mumbled something to himself that sounded to Popper like "being so angry" or "seeming so angry."

"What was that, Wallace? Did you say you're angry?"

Wallace shook his head. "No, sir. I said I never did go by after her husband got killed. You remember that morning we were working out at your sheds and he come by. I felt kind of sad that he died so angry."

Popper dropped his ice cream in the wastebasket and stared at Wallace. "What do you mean, Wallace? What do you mean he died so angry?"

"Well, you know. When he come by and seen us leaving and got so mad at you for using his 'dozer. He was hollerin' and yellin'. You remember?"

Popper slid next to Wallace and in a low voice said, "Keep your voice down. Now listen. That was a long time ago and you and me had nothing to do with that morning. When you left, I told Paul all about using his 'dozer and he was just fine. You don't remember because you were gone by then. Isn't that right? You left when I told you to, right?"

Wallace nodded, "Yes sir, I had drove off, but I remember him being angry. I remember him yellin' and everything. I 'member . . ." Wallace remembered it all. It came back to him like being there again. He heard their words, their anger. He was transfixed but wanted to get out of there, too.

Wallace blinked a few times and rubbed his mouth. He was turning a little cold, shivering too. He glanced around the Dairy Queen to see if anybody was looking.

Popper said very slowly, "Wallace, listen to me. All that was a long time ago. You and me being at my sheds got nothing to do with Mr. Reavis, Wallace. You never talked to nobody about that morning, did ya?"

Wallace quickly glanced at Popper then back toward the street. He rubbed the flint arrowhead in his pocket and thought of what to say. "No sir," he finally said. "I never said nothing. But I was real sad when Mr. Cobb found Mr. Reavis dead. Maybe if we'd stayed there, maybe we could have helped him. Maybe . . ."

Popper put his hand on Wallace's shoulder to stop him from talking. "Listen to me, son; I fixed things up with Paul, Mr. Reavis, before I left. He wasn't angry anymore. Nobody knows we were there and I want to keep it that way. If they thought you were there, they might think that you ain't telling them all there is about young Paulie's death. They might think that you keep things from the law. You don't want that, do you? You don't want people like Will Moser snooping around, do you?"

Wallace shook his head, his eyes open wide. "You don't think he thinks I had sumthin' to do with any of this stuff, do you?"

Popper looked him in the eye and said, "Wallace, right now nobody thinks nothin', but you say one word and they might change their minds. If they do that, you might lose your farm. You might lose your pigs. And I don't know what they all might want to do to you. You understand me? Do you, Wallace?"

Wallace nodded his head. "I ain't goin' to say nothing. Not to Will or Sheriff Tasker, nobody."

Popper smiled, "Good boy, Wallace. Just remember that, and anybody calls you or comes by asking questions, you call me."

Wallace nodded, and a dollop of chocolate brick topping fell onto his overalls. He took a napkin and quickly wiped it off.

9.

"Drs. Jeffers and Newell, how can I help you?" Lana opened the steno pad beside her phone. "I'm sorry, Dr. Newell is on the phone right now, may I take a message?" She wrote down a number and short message. "I will . . . I'll tell her you called . . . Yes, just as soon as she can . . . Yes, all right . . . Goodbye."

Lana pushed her chair back from the desk and stretched. With her head back, she stared at the ceiling of the narrow inner office located between the doctors' private offices and the lab and examining rooms, then dropped her gaze to the right to make sure the door to the reception area was still open.

Carter Jeffers was standing in his office, his left hand on his hip, his right holding a small dictating machine. He had heard Lana on the phone and called out. "Lana, sorry about your having to answer the phones, but Ruth swears she'll be back tomorrow."

"Don't worry, I don't mind." She smiled at him. "I'll probably stay for a while tonight. I figure I can get a lot of my basic book-keeping done between calls."

Lana had joined Dr. Jeffers right out of community college, and except for the time she'd taken after Paulie was born, had been there almost every day. She enjoyed the work and liked having something useful to do. On occasion, she had brought Paulie with her to the office. He loved feeding and playing with the dogs and cats that occasionally boarded in the kennel. Once Dr. Newell arrived and they expanded the lab, Lana's importance to the practice increased fivefold.

Even so, she had had no intention of coming back to work so soon after Paulie's funeral, but the two doctors, especially Vicky Newell, had insisted, believing it would be better to keep her busy and out of her silent house.

Lana swiveled her chair and looked into Dr. Newell's office. "Vicky, you just got a call from Carl Ross over in Sessions County. Something about a problem with some of his boars. He said to call him at his office as soon as you can."

Vicky nodded and picked up her phone. After speaking with Carl, she rushed into Dr. Jeffers' office and closed the door. They talked for a few minutes, and when she came out, she hurried back to her office, waving for Lana to follow her.

"What's up?" Lana asked.

"Carl Ross has a serious problem with his big Duroc boar and some of his first years. I can't be sure what it is because I've only got Carl's description, but I definitely need to go out there and take a look. I know we were going to have lunch today but . . ."

Lana held up her hand. "Don't worry, we can have lunch another day."

Vicky looked serious. "I know. But . . ."

"But nothing. Stop worrying about me. I'm fine. You were right, being back is best. If I was at home I'd see them around every corner. I'd hear them outside talkin' about some new scheme. I . . ." She stopped talking and took a deep breath, tears welling up and spilling down her cheeks.

"I'm sorry, give me a sec."

She cleared her throat, then pulled a Kleenex out of her sleeve to wipe her eyes and blow her nose. She waited a few beats then said, "Vicky, I'm okay really. It's just that sometimes all of a sudden I get the feelin' that I'm completely alone. Like I've been swallowed by some huge black thing, some kind of alien creature. And then, like I'm gonna die inside it; feeling nothing, seeing nothing, hearing nothing. Just die alone."

Vicky came around the desk and put her hand on Lana's shoulder, slowly pushing her down into one of the two chairs in front of the desk while sitting in the other. After a few minutes, after Lana had calmed down, Vicky said, "Grief has a way of stealing your words, even your feelings, and to think of it as a dark alien creature is probably not too far off the mark. I'm obviously not a shrink, Lana, but I know that if you can focus on what's still out there, friends, family, work, you'll eventually find the light.

"You're a big part of this practice. A big part of our team, Lana. You're also a big part of this community. What the heck, you have a job with people who like and respect you and live in a town that has loved you since you were born! You have a mother and an extended family that needs you. You have . . ." Vicky looked to see if she could read Lana's emotional temperature. "You also have a fella who, it seems to me, cares very deeply for you."

With this Lana looked up and gave the faintest hint of a smile. Her gaze moved to the sunlight filtering into the room behind Vicky's desk, then through the plate glass window to the trees on the far side of the parking lot. Without looking back into the room, she said, "I think he does care for me, maybe always has, but I'm not . . ." She didn't continue, yet must have concluded her thought. Smiling, Lana looked back at Vicky and shrugged.

"How come *you* never got married, Vicky?" Lana said.

The doctor smiled. "No time. I mean, who would put up with my hours?"

"I bet lots of men would love being married to a successful vet." Lana said.

"I guess I haven't found the right one yet. Notice I said yet."

Lana regarded Vicky for a few seconds. "I should have been more focused on my education instead of getting married and trying to have a family right away. A profession is always there. You can't kill a profession. Professions don't drown. Professions . . ." Lana paused. A different expression came into her eyes.

"I should have been a vet."

Vicky looked a bit startled. "Well . . ."

Lana cut her off. "I know what you're thinking and I know it sounds silly, but I mean it." She looked down, and said, more to herself more than to Vicky, "I would be a good vet."

After a pause, Vicky cleared her throat. "So, let's get back to work, Dr. Reavis."

Lana roused herself. "Right, Dr. Newell, back to work." She stood and turned toward the door.

"I'll call you from the Ross place," Vicky said, as she pushed herself up and out of her chair.

But the call she placed was to Dr. Jeffers, not Lana. After he hung up, Dr. Jeffers walked over to the open door facing Lana.

"Was that Vicky?" Lana asked.

Dr. Jeffers nodded, then said, "If you're up to it, we're gonna need your help. Dr. Newell isn't exactly sure what the problem is, but after describing all of the observable symptoms to me, we've decided to send tissue and blood samples to Raleigh as soon as possible. Maybe even a live pig. She's calling Dr. Evans at the N.C. State Veterinary School. He's one of the people DEHNR will go to if they need to get involved."

"It's that important?" Lana asked.

"Based on what Vicky's seen, it doesn't look good." Dr. Jeffers walked over to the doorway of the laboratory. "You know when Sylvia's back?"

Sylvia Reily was the office lab technician responsible for growing cultures, taking samples, doing blood and urine analysis, and any other basic science.

Lana shook her head. "She shouldn't be long. She went to the DMV to renew her license."

Dr. Jeffers nodded and said, "Sylvia needs to get together some petri dishes for tissue samples, some tubes and sample vials for blood work, and maybe, no definitely, an ice chest. And a crate for transporting a live animal."

The phone rang but rather than answer it, Lana got up and walked to Dr. Jeffers' open door. Dr. Jeffers picked up the phone, said a few words, then paused, waiting for the caller to find something. When he glanced over at Lana standing in his doorway, she mouthed the words, "What's the favor? You never said."

He shook his head, held up a finger, and after writing down some numbers hung up.

"We need you to drive over to the Ross farm, deliver the stuff we'll get together, then wait for the blood samples Vicky is sending to the folks in Raleigh. I've got to go out to the Happenger place. They've got a horse down."

She turned and glanced up at the clock . . . noon. It was forty minutes to Sessions County, and at least an hour from there to Raleigh. Plus another hour-and-a-half back to Mussel Ford.

Dr. Jeffers was on the phone again and when he finished, he walked over to Lana's desk. "That was Vicky. She'll meet you at the entrance to the Ross farm and get the supplies you're bringing. You'll have to wait on the road outside the farm until she collects the samples. It shouldn't take too long. We've decided that to be safe, we need to quarantine the place for at least forty-eight hours. If the samples don't show any contagion, we'll lift the quarantine; if they do, well, we'll have to go from there."

Lana's expression changed from passive to focused.

Dr. Jeffers smiled. "Hey, I wouldn't send you on a job that could be dangerous. No matter what this thing is, it's not dangerous to people, only to pigs."

Lana held his eyes. "That for sure, Carter? No weird strain of influenza or bubonic plague or something?"

Dr. Jeffers laughed, "Well, bubonic plague I hadn't thought of, but no, no dangerous disease."

"So why do you look so worried?"

His smile faded. "I'm worried that maybe hog cholera is back. We haven't had a case in the U.S. for over ten years, but the symptoms Vicky described to me sound an awful lot like cholera. I hope to God not." He pursed his lips and looked at the door to the lab.

"I hope to God not," he repeated.

"What if it is?" Lana asked.

"Then we call the feds, the state, the county, and anybody else who's on the list. We quarantine Carl's farm. We . . . basically we tell Carl that he's out of the pig business."

Lana shook her head. "I guess we better pray it's not cholera."

"You got that right."

—◆ ◆ ◆—

Oris Martin leaned back in the red leather chair and switched his phone from speaker to handset. "Hold on, Eugene." He looked up and said to the men sitting at the conference table in his office, "Gentlemen, I'm sorry, but will you excuse me for a few minutes. I need to take this call." His three financial managers smiled and quickly left the room.

"Okay, shoot."

"Oris, we need to talk."

Oris hated the way Popper made such a big mystery out of everything.

"Well, talk."

Popper paused a beat. "Maybe we need to talk in private."

"We are in private. Nobody is in my office. Where are you?"

"At Pine Bluff, but I don't have people listening in on my conversations or standing outside my door."

"For Christ's sake, Popper, nobody is listening in on my conversation. What is it?" Oris said dismissively.

"I had a conversation with Wallace May that concerns me," Popper said, lowering his voice.

"And," Oris said as he shifted the phone to his other ear.

"And," Eugene said, "I'm concerned. As a matter of fact, you might wanta be, too."

"Why," Oris asked, trying to be as civil as possible, "are you concerned? What happened?"

"I was going by the Dairy Queen yesterday and I seen Wallace by himself outside. I stopped to see how he was doing, what with all the shit coming down about young Paulie's accident. He was a little shaky, as I figured, but what made me really nervous was when he told me his Uncle John wouldn't let him go to the boy's funeral. He said how sorry he was about his death and how he wanted to tell Paulie's momma that. I said John would probably take him by Lana's soon enough and he says something about not going by after Paul's death, either.

"Then he says how he was sorry Paul died so angry. I asked him what he meant and he starts talking about the fight we was having that morning."

"I'm assuming," Oris said, "That he wasn't there when Paul had his accident."

"He wasn't," Popper said. "At least I'm pretty sure he wasn't. I asked him if he left when I told him to and he said he did. I believe him."

Oris put his head back on the chair, the phone resting against his shoulder. After a few moments of silence Eugene said, "Oris. You there?"

Oris shook his head. "Then what's the problem?"

"The problem is that the official story says Don Cobb found Paul's body. That he was the first person at the site after the accident. I was never there. Wallace was never there. Am I going too fast for you?"

It was becoming harder for Oris to hold his temper. "Eugene, I understand what you're saying. I'm just not sure what you want me to do about it."

Popper glared at the phone. "I'm not sure either, that's why I'm calling you. But you better be thinking about it because what happened that morning at Pine Bluff affects us both."

"Yeah, well, it affects some of us more than others. I recall that I got the news of Paul's untimely death while I was entertaining some foreign hog producers at my farrowing operation in Chatham County."

Eugene was waiting for something like this. "Oris, you may not have been there, but you've known about my fight with Paul for over a year and ain't said nothin'. That kinda puts you in it. Or do you think the law will figure that knowin' about an accident and saying nothin' is okay?"

"Don't threaten me, Popper, or my memory about what I was told that day might get mighty dim. In any case, I can prove for a fact that I wasn't there. I also don't believe that 'accident' would be what they put on the report. Try 'murder' or at the very least 'manslaughter.'"

Popper took a deep breath. "Look, we ain't gettin' anywhere with this. Let's just get to what we can do to make sure Wallace don't come unglued. He didn't see me hit Paul but he did see us arguin'. He could say he and I was there. What we need is for John Keaton to keep him away from Lana Reavis for now. He might get emotional about Paulie and tell her about Paul. We need to wait until this whole thing with his lagoon blows over, so I need you to call John and get him to delay going over to Lana's."

"How you want me to do that?"

"How the fuck do I know, Oris? You're the educated part of this team. You're the one who always has the answers. You figure it out."

"Okay, I'll figure out a way for John to delay his and Wallace's trip to Lana's, but you've got to get a handle on Wallace. If he'd said anything to Will Moser or Ernie, we'd have heard or seen something by now; so we can assume he's only made the comment to you. You need to keep it that way. Did you tell him to call you if anything came up that he didn't understand?"

Popper rolled his eyes and answered with thinly veiled annoyance, "No shit! Of course I did. You're not dealing with some rube, Oris!"

"Whatever."

With that, Popper exploded. "Listen, hot shit, I'm not asking you to do nothin' but call John Keaton. I can handle the rest. I always have. Don't worry, you won't have to get your lily-white hands dirty."

Oris could, in his imagination, see the veins starting to stand out on Popper's neck. "I'm sorry, Eugene, it's been a long day. I didn't mean anything."

The blood slowly started to recede from Popper's face and he calmed a bit. "Oris, it's just that he's so unpredictable. I did scare him pretty good about what might happen if he talked. Maybe . . ."

Oris interrupted, "Popper, you got any work for him to do? You got any 'dozer driving coming up?"

"Uh, I don't know. Nothing really. I might . . ."

"No, wait. Wait a minute." Oris started to tap his pencil on his desk, a sure sign that his energy level was rising. As he tapped out random tunes, he started talking to himself.

"We're adding to a facility down in Charter County, maybe we got some work there. We need to keep an eye on Wallace, at least until everything settles down. I don't think he's got any feeder stock right now. I'll make sure we have some guys out at his place working on that lagoon. We can keep him going with some loans and stuff, but we need to keep him occupied, at least for a little while. Once his lagoon's okay, we'll ship him some feeders. We can't let him freak out." He suddenly remembered that Popper was still on the line.

"You get that?"

Popper leaned back in the old wooden chair and nodded. "I'll take care of it. I'll get Weldon to hire him on for a while. If you got the work, we'll figure out the rest."

"Okay," Oris replied, "I'll call you in a few days. By the way, I heard about Odell's accident. I assume you heard the same as I did?"

Popper didn't say anything.

"Popper? You there?"

"Yeah, I'm here. I reckon I heard what you heard."

Oris paused a few beats. "Shame about that. Bad luck seems contagious these days. I understand Rafe was supposed to be in the truck. That right?"

Popper rubbed his chin. "I heard the same thing. 'Course, I don't know whether Rafe was supposed to be there or not. I ain't talked to Rafe since you and me had our little conversation with him a few weeks ago. Not since he got it up his ass to threaten us."

Oris didn't say anything, only rubbed his chin and looked around the room. Popper kept waiting for a reply, then said, "Sounds like you might think I'm the kinda guy who might do somethin' to someone who threatens me. And if that's what you think, you could be right. I don't like threats, but of course I don't know nothin' about Odell's accident. That was a real shock."

Oris started to say something about threats, but given Popper's current mood, he decided saying nothing was best. "Okay. If anything comes up you think we need to talk about I'll be here. I'll let you know what John says and I'll call you about the work in Charter County. You got anything else now?"

"Naw."

10.

Lana stood beside the Ford econoline van and watched as Vicky Newell got out of her truck.

"You look beat, Doctor."

Vicky nodded, "You could say that. Thanks for coming." She leaned against her truck's tailgate and took a few deep breaths, stretching her neck. She was a solid woman with hard hands and none of Lana's slim softness, but then practicing large-animal medicine in a small rural community was no place for a woman who wasn't fit or was finicky about dirt.

"Our friend Carl's got a heap of trouble. Six of his boars, two of the old ones and four of his next-year breeders have got the shakes and convulsions pretty bad. I'm sending one of the young boars to State with you. I'll pack him in the crate and put a tarp around it. He'll probably urinate and defecate on the way there, but just open the window and stick your head out." She walked to the back of the van and opened the two doors.

"Good. Carter covered everything with plastic. Where'd he get the van?"

"He borrowed it from the sanitation department in Mussel Ford. Sylvia put all of the stuff you asked for in those two coolers. I've got four bags of ice in the big red cooler. That enough?" Lana asked.

"That's fine," Vicky said. "It only needs to keep the samples cool until you get them to Raleigh. Dr. Evans will put everything in the refrigerators at his lab."

Lana got out of the van and walked around to the back. "Just out of curiosity, Vicky, how cold does this stuff have to be?"

"Above freezing, at about a normal home refrigerator temperature. It can stay viable for quite a while if it doesn't warm up." She pulled the animal crate out of the van and asked Lana to grab the two sample coolers. They walked back to Vicky's truck and put everything in the bed. "Okay, you wait here for about thirty or forty minutes and I'll be back."

In less than thirty minutes, Dr. Newell returned with all the samples and one squealing ninety-pound pig. She backed her truck up to the van and stopped. Lana got out and walked back to the rear of the van and opened the doors. The two women grabbed the sides of the tarp and slid the crate in along with the ice-packed coolers of blood and tissue samples. Lana shut the back doors and Vicky handed her a hand-drawn map.

"I know where the vet school is. Right across from the state fairgrounds."

"Right," Vicky said. "But this will also show you the door where you need to deliver the stuff. I just talked to Dr. Evans and he'll be waiting for you. Now listen. When you get there, Evans will have another van for you to drive home. They're going to wash this one down with bleach and other chemicals just to be safe. Someone from the school will bring this van back to Mussel Ford and pick up the one they loaned you." She bit her lower lip as she tried to think of anything else that Lana needed to know. "I can't think of anything else. See you at home."

"Listen," Lana said. "Do I need to be careful about breathing any of this crap in? I mean how lethal can this thing be?"

Vicky turned around and smiled. "Don't worry. Even if it happened to be cholera, it's not catching to humans. The virus of whatever this thing is will most likely be in the urine, stool, and blood of the animals. Sometimes it's airborne, but they aren't contagious to people, in any case. But the reason Carter told you to wear clothes that you can throw away is you need to throw them away. Dr. Evans, at Raleigh, will let you shower at the school and then you can change into your other things. You did bring other clothes, didn't you?"

Lana nodded.

"In a sealed bag?"

Lana nodded again.

"Okay, when you change into your new clothes, the school will destroy the ones you're wearing. Okay? Everything copacetic?"

Lana opened the door to the van. "I don't know about copacetic, but I know what to do." She hesitated for a moment then looked back at Vicky. "What in the world could have brought the virus back? Carter said it hasn't been around here for years."

"I don't know, Lana. This bug can hook a ride on lots of things; clothing, any kind of equipment, other animals, all kinds of ways." She reached to pull the van door shut. "But we'll find out soon. See you back home."

Near Tarboro, Lana's traveling companion decided to void his entire intestinal tract. Lana heard it first; then the foul stench crept forward and slapped her in the face. She rolled down the driver's side window and took a deep breath.

I can't believe I've got sixty more minutes with this animal. Think about something else.

As she frequently did these days, she thought about Paulie and Paul the way an amputee thinks about a missing appendage. So she made herself think of something else—Dunbar Kaster sitting on the couch in her living room wringing his hands and shaking his head. She should never have said anything to him, never bothered asking him for anything.

"Lana, dear, your lovely son was the victim of an act of God.

You know, a force majeure. It was no one's fault really. Trying to force some legal settlement will be to no avail."

Bullshit, you can't take the case because Oris won't let you off his leash.

She tapped a tune on the steering wheel and watched the passing cars, her eyes wide and fixed on the headlights coming toward her. Random thoughts flew in and out of her head. Everything was relevant and nothing was relevant.

Loss of power, financial loss; that would get Oris's attention. He and his gang'd understand that. My loss doesn't matter to them, but power does. Their power. Power to control.

She thought of Will and how she had ached for him when they were young. How she had fantasized about being Mrs. William Moser. Then he left. Went off to college and then to the army without looking back. She knew why, but that didn't make it any easier. Every time she saw his father she would ask how Will was doing, and every time he'd smile and say, "Fine, I guess."

When Will married that girl in Raleigh, Lana knew he'd never stay with her. She knew from talking to her sister who lived in Raleigh that Shelby Moser was nothing but a spoiled brat, a gold-digger, and when she met Will in Raleigh after his divorce, she saw he still cared. But she had moved on, with her own problems to work through.

When Paul Reavis finally asked her to marry him, she had accepted without any hesitation. After all, they had been friends since grade school and, along with Will, had been a threesome always together. Paul had his own set of problems but had tried to be a good father and husband. Maybe that's all one can expect.

A sign whizzed by, then another—"Danger Zone, Caution: Men Working." She laughed, then yelled into the reeking stench of the van.

"Danger Zone, Caution: Women working. Women can be dangerous too, asshole! And pigs, so can they."

Her heart was racing; heat spread across her face and chest. She'd never contemplated being dangerous, at least not actively dangerous. But then she'd never imagined a pain or hatred so strong that she'd be willing to harm or even kill another human. Nothing could ever take away the pain of losing a child, but maybe, just maybe, justice would triumph. Not Will's kind of justice, but a mother's justice, God's justice, ancient justice . . . an eye for an eye. She shivered at the thought.

Forty minutes later, she turned into the entrance of the NCSU Veterinary School.

After a shower, the exchange of clothes, swapping out the vans, and ten minutes of small talk with Dr. Evans, she was headed back to Mussel Ford. Her new ride was much nicer than the heap from the Mussel Ford Sanitation Dept. It smelled better and it had leather upholstery and a reasonable sound system. By early evening she was parking in front of the veterinary office and letting herself into the reception area. Carter and Vicky were in Vicky's office.

Carter smiled at her. "Congratulations. I see no symptoms of bubonic plague are present, but then it's still early in the incubation period." Vicky cocked her head with a quizzical look. Carter said, "Lana asked if we were sure that you hadn't found something like bubonic . . . never mind. Glad you're back, Lana, and thank you."

"You're very welcome. It wasn't a bad trip once I got that awful pig out of the van." She sat down in front of Vicky's desk and looked at Dr. Jeffers. "Dr. Evans told me to tell you that he'd be back to you soon . . . a couple of days. When I asked him how this could happen and what caused it, he said that there could be lots of ways but that whatever the case, Vicky was the chief investigator for now."

Vicky looked at Carter and smiled. He nodded in her direction and said, "As a matter of fact, we were just discussing the whys and wherefores."

Vicky looked at the ceiling. "I have asked Carl to try and remember everything he's bought over the last few weeks; who has been to his operation; anything that might be a means of introducing the virus. Other than feed and a visit from his accountant, the only thing he could think of was some pharmaceutical supplies he got from two other farrowing operations. Some medicine for the scours from John Keaton's operation in Sessions County and some antibiotics from Oris Martin's facility here in Hogg County."

"Is that the one Eugene Winslow is partners in?" Lana asked.

"Sure, him and Oris."

"So could he have gotten infected antibiotics?" Lana asked.

"Almost impossible." Carter replied. "Antibiotics are in sealed, sterilized bottles. Somebody would have to intentionally sabotage the container and that would be almost impossible to do."

Lana leaned back in her chair. "So now what?"

"So," Vicky replied. "We've been sitting here thinking about every possible way a virus could have gotten into Carl's operation. We have covered food scraps from humans, clothing, feed, other animals, birds . . . everything."

Carter shook his head. "There're a boatload of possibilities, strange as they may be, but I can't think of a way of proving or disproving any of them right now. Let's go home and cogitate and reconvene tomorrow."

Vicky nodded and looked at Lana. "Let's go grab something to eat and call it a day."

Lana smiled. "Okay, but not for long. I'm really bushed—especially my overused olfactory system."

"I'll lock up," Carter said, smiling.

The women walked out into the parking lot. "What say we go to Denny's for the special?" Vicky said.

"Okay by me. I'll meet you there."

—✦ ✦ ✦—

Seated with Vicky at Denny's, Lana said, "Long day."

"Tell me about it. I feel like I've been at the Ross farm for a month. That poor son of a bitch. I have to tell you, I'm betting a thousand dollars that he's got hog fever."

"I thought it was cholera," Lana replied.

"Same thing. Cholera is the proper name but it's so scary a word that the industry uses hog fever instead."

"Why is it so scary?" Lana asked.

"Because it has a bad history. Human cholera has been around for a long time and is very dangerous, thus any mention of the word carries bad vibes. The human variety, which is not dangerous to pigs, is rare these days but where there are outbreaks, it's usually fatal. Kind of like that bubonic plague you mentioned to Carter. Both human and animal varieties cause death in a matter of days, even hours. The pig variety is for pigs just as bad. Death comes quickly when the outbreak is acute."

"What if it isn't acute?"

"Then it's slower. Still dangerous but not as quick, and it could even pass and the hogs recover."

Lana appeared to be only half listening. She twisted her fork around in her food as if she was trying to find the words she needed. "Vicky, you remember our conversation this morning when I said that I should have been a vet?"

"Of course."

"You think I'm dreaming to say that, don't you?"

Vicky drew back with a surprised look on her face. "I think you can be anything you want to be. It would be hard and a long haul, but you could do it. You've been thinking about this for a while, haven't you?"

"Yes. As a matter of fact, I was thinking on the way home from Raleigh that I don't have any responsibilities now, not, you know, any family stuff. I could get my B.S. in two years. I've got enough credits for the first two years and even though it's been twelve years since college, I'm still only thirty-four. I bet working for a veterinarian practice for so long will help, and knowing Dr. Evans in Raleigh can't hurt either. I could . . ."

Vicky held up her hand, "Vet school *is* tough. You'd have to take a lot of chemistry, math, and biology to even qualify for the program. I'm not trying to talk you out of anything, but you need to be realistic about the journey. Should you decide that that's what you want—we're here for you. I hope you know that."

She looked closely at the woman across from her, studying Lana's face and listening to the urgency in her voice. The face, alabaster smooth with piercing blue eyes, was staring straight at her, her earlier question lingering in the air between them. Vicky realized that she was in the presence of a human being who had been pushed by grief to a new level of awareness. She was observing a woman in the process of discovering the person her DNA intended her to become. A person set aside by the care of family, but now struggling to be seen and heard as she really was, perhaps for the first time.

"It can happen. If you're realistic and set objectives and time schedules you can keep, it can happen."

Lana smiled. "A week or so ago Will and I were talking when I mentioned I needed something in my life. I needed a goal. He said what I really needed was enough time to heal. I told him I would never totally heal. I could only harden the scab, then the scar. He went on about letting go of the past, but he doesn't understand.

"I like Will, maybe even love him, but he can't understand. Nobody can, really. It's like I said this morning. Like some dark beast has swallowed me. Like I'll die inside it with no family, no love, just darkness." Tears were rolling down her cheeks, so Vicky patted her arm and said, " Shhhh. Don't talk. Let's eat and breathe and when we can we'll talk some more."

Lana wiped her eyes and nodded. After a minute or so, she cleared her throat and whispered, "I'm gonna get through this. I'm gonna heal, but I'm never gonna be so dependent on others that I lose myself inside the dark beast when they're gone."

11.

The covey flushed from somewhere in the field off to his right, probably frightened by the sound of his car or the school bus in front of him. Will watched as an old cock bird, his white throat flashing in the early morning sun, led his family of young quail across the road and toward the protection of Mitchell Creek and the blackberry jungles on its banks.

He smiled, watching the birds pitch into the tangle of blackberry and scrub brush beside the creek. This was what Hogg County was all about, why he was here. The smell of morning in the mists of a creek bottom, a school bus stopping on a country road to pick up excited youngsters, and quail calling to each other from their daybreak feeding, everything seemed right today, normal. Even Lana seemed to have a renewed purpose. He wasn't sure that normal could be used quite yet to describe her life, but at least it seemed to be acquiring a pattern more akin to normal.

Lana Reavis made Will happy. She had always had a sense of self that he envied. Even with the horror of her recent life, she seemed to be reaching a level of acceptance; to be gaining a focus. She was starting to find her laugh. That wonderful laugh that could infect a room, actually a belly laugh with manners. He was in love with her and always had been. Were he completely honest with himself he'd admit that she was one of the reasons he'd returned to Mussel Ford. But that kind of honesty was painful, her being the wife of his best friend. Yet it was a truth he couldn't ignore, try as he might.

He knew that all of his hunting about for self-realization had simply been an effort to cover up occasional laziness, a habit of insecurity, and more than a modicum of self-pity. He wasn't good enough for her. She was better off without him. His father was disappointed in him. No one understood him. On and on it went until Will finally realized, probably while in the army, while an MP, that he was meant to be a cop. When he accepted this, his life stopped bailing and righted itself.

He did a double take.

My God, that's Henry.

Will stopped behind the slowing school bus and honked his horn. The black boy standing on the far side of the road looked over. Will put his head out of the window and yelled, "Hank, it's Will. When did you get home?"

The smiling boy hollered back, "On Saturday. Momma had me stay with Aunt Lovie in Charlotte for a while; leastwise until she could get Daddy home and back on his feet. Daddy said for me to get on home 'fore I missed too much school, so I guess things is about back to normal."

Will nodded his head and yelled, "I'm glad you're home. You take care. I'll be by to see you. We'll go fishin'." Henry Grier waved his hand and ran across the street to the waiting school bus.

—◆ ◆ ◆—

Will decided to take the whole weekend off, and promised

himself that, come hell-or-highwater, he wasn't going to the office on Saturday or Sunday. No sir, this weekend was for fishing.

—✦ ✦ ✦—

Odell waved as Will pulled his truck and boat trailer into the yard. "Morning, Will. Some kind of morning, wouldn't you say?"

Will nodded, "Tailor-made, Odell, tailor-made. It's what God intended a Saturday in October to be." He parked the truck and walked over to the car that Odell was working on. "Man, for a fella that was vying for pancake of the year, you sure do look mighty spry! You feel like fishing?"

"Can't, Will. Promised my Uncle Rafe I'd fix his car. I'd love to go, but I promised Rafe."

"You're a good nephew, Odell."

Odell nodded then turned his head toward the house and shouted, "Henry, Will's here. You goin' fishin' or not?"

"Momma says I got to clean my room and brush my teeth first. I'll be right there. It ain't much to do."

With that Nancy Grier responded, just as loudly, "Not much to do, my foot! You haven't seen that boy's room. He's going to need a bulldozer just to get to the dirty clothes. Grab a seat, Will, and I'll bring you a cup of coffee. You got a few minutes?"

Will laughed and waved, then sat down on a stump beside Odell.

"So, how's he been since he got home?"

"Pretty good. He still has dreams about that day, but I think he's starting to get past 'em." Odell took his head out of his uncle's car and looked at Will.

"He misses Paulie, you know. Those two were mighty good friends. I sometimes wonder what . . ." He smiled and shook his head and went back to work.

Will looked over at him and said, "Wonder what?"

Odell didn't reply.

Nancy came out of the house with a mug of hot coffee and handed it to Will.

"I forgot about cream."

"No thanks, black's fine. Four years in the Army teaches you two things. Keep your head down, and take your coffee strong, hot, and black. Well, maybe three things."

Odell looked up, "What's the third?"

"Never volunteer for anything," Will said, smiling.

Odell moved his cane off the radiator as he stepped around the car. "I reckon you forgot that one."

Will liked listening to Hank and Nancy arguing about what clean your room meant and how long brushing your teeth was. It was a great day. He looked back at Odell leaning into Rafe's car and realized how lucky Odell was to be alive.

"Odell, you really okay? I mean you got any pain?"

"'Bout like you, I imagine."

"Good. You can live with that."

Odell looked up. "Anything ever come of your investigations out at 521? The O'Neils and all?"

"Nope. Nobody saw nothing, so all I got are hunches." He paused a moment and then said, "Odell, the whole thing smells to me, but it could be that you were just unlucky."

Odell looked back up. "On some things, but," he looked toward the house, "mighty lucky on others."

Will turned his head toward the house then back to Odell. "You had any more incidents at night. Anything I ought to know about?"

"No, not really. I hear the occasional truck slow down and I get a little nervous but nothing out of the ordinary."

The deputy straightened his back. "The night someone threw that dead raccoon in your yard, you see the truck or hear anything?"

"Nothing that stands out. 'Course I didn't know anybody had thrown anything until after midnight. I went out to just check around. Saw it then. Somebody yelling something out the window, you know, you don't really think about it or what they said until later and then it's hard to remember exactly."

"Anything about the voice or truck that makes any difference. Anything unusual?"

Odell looked up from the motor. "Naw, just, you know, an engine." He paused a few beats. "Probably a diesel engine. It sounded loud."

Henry came running out of the house like a boy on a mission.

—◆ ◆ ◆—

Will pushed the bow of the aluminum boat off the bank and carefully walked down its center until he got to the forty-horse Mercury bolted to the stern. Hank was sitting on a cushion in the middle of the boat talking a blue streak.

"I heard a fella caught a twenty-pounder this year, Will. I hear there're more Stripers in Lake Gaston than has ever been. I bet we catch a big one today. You think we'll catch a twenty-pounder?"

He went on and on. The joyous chatter of a boy on his way to Striper heaven. Will smiled as he cranked up the motor and headed south to his favorite part of the lake. The parking lot at the boat ramp was full. They weren't going to be lonely today.

Will yelled over the motor, "Tie your life vest up, Hank, and make sure to sit in the middle of the boat. We're going to run flat out. And yes, I think from what I hear we're gonna catch a boatload today."

Hank's smile defined the day.

The water was on the cool side, just right for fall Stripers. After a twenty-minute trip, Will cut the motor back and turned on the fish finder. Hank straddled the metal seat and watched as Will adjusted the screen.

"How deep is it? You see anything?" Hank couldn't sit still. "What are all those little lines?"

Will was concentrating on the screen. The boat moved north from the end of a small wooded peninsula toward open water.

After a few minutes, Will smiled and pointed at the screen.

"Okay, sport, look at all those lines at twenty feet. You see them?

"Yeah, I see 'em."

"That's a school of shad, and those bigger lines just behind them are Stripers. Let's drop some goodies down there."

Hank grabbed his spinning rod and reached for a live shad in the bait well. Before Will could even pick his rod up, Hank was fishing. He let the lead sinker take his line down until Will said, "That's deep enough. Try it there." Will smiled as he watched the boy's eyes fixed on the water.

"I think," said Will, "I'll try one of these Chartreuse buck tails. Maybe I can jig one of those . . ."

Hank let out a yell. The six-foot rod bent double and the line surged off the reel.

Will hollered, "Loosen your drag, Hank. You don't need to pull his lips off." The boy turned down the drag, and with that the line simply flew off the reel. The next ten minutes were full of whoops and excited prattle. Hank had a big fish on, and it gave him all the fight he could handle. Finally Will lowered his net into the water and scooped up the ten-pound Striper. Hank was shaking as much as the fish.

"Look at the size of him, Will! Can we keep him, huh, can we?"

Will's grin was as big as Hank's. "Of course we can keep him. If we don't, your daddy wouldn't ever believe us." Will put the Striper in a cooler as Hank re-baited his hook, only to repeat the same process within minutes.

By noon both Will and Hank had aching arms and hands.

"Yo, Hank." Will said. "How about a break? My arm hurts, and my stomach thinks my throat's been cut."

"Okay. I'm a little hungry, too," Hank replied.

Will rummaged through the cooler. "We got Coke, Sprite, a beer or two for Uncle Will, and some water. Don't tell me: A Coke."

Hank smiled, "Yes sir, a Coke for the Hank Man."

Will stopped searching in the cooler and looked up. Hank

had a startled look on his face. As if a shadow had passed over him, he looked at Will and tears started to roll from the corners of his eyes. His shoulders shook with sobs and he buried his head in his hands. The Hank Man was what Paulie had always called him—especially when they were out on one of their adventures, like today. He hadn't thought about what he was saying until it came out, and then it was too late, Paulie was in the boat with them. Will moved forward and put his arm around Hank's shoulders.

"Hey, that's all right. We had to think about him sometime today. Me, I been thinking of him since we left this morning. I just couldn't bring myself to say how much I miss him." Hank took the towel that Will had draped over his shoulder and wiped his face.

"I'm sorry, I won't cry no more."

"I don't know why not, Sport, there's nothing wrong with missing our buddy. I've cried a lot since he . . . left us." Will didn't want to choke up in front of Hank so he took a drink of beer. "Here, Hank, here's your Coke." The boy took the soda and the bag of Cheetos Will passed forward. After a few minutes, Hank turned around in the boat and said, "Will, you think Paulie can see us catching all these fish?"

Will smiled, "I think the reason we're catching all these fish is because Paulie is up there making them take our bait. He's probably laughing every time you lose one!"

"Well, don't laugh too hard, Paulie!" Hank yelled up in the sky. "I've seen you lose just as many." That moment had to come. Will expected it would return many times in the months and years ahead.

Hank looked in the cooler behind him and found a smoked turkey sandwich and another bag of Cheetos. "Did a lot of people come to Paulie's funeral?"

"The church wouldn't hold any more."

"Did they say lots of nice things about him?"

"You'd been real proud, Hank. They got it right. I talked to the minister for a long time about Paulie, and I told him a lot of the things that the three of us did. He used some of it. Your mom and dad came. They sat with the family, where you'd have been if you could have come."

Hank thought about this for a few minutes, then said, "You know, Will, I dreamed I was there. One night in the hospital, I dreamed I was at Paulie's funeral. You and Dad was sitting next to Miz Reavis. There was flowers all over the place, and we were in this huge church. I don't know where it is. I never been to it before, but it was beautiful."

"There was this big stained window behind the preacher. It was a picture of Jesus and the disciples, I think. I was standing with Momma. She was wearing that pretty blue dress I like. Next to the coffin was Paulie's dad and that man he was arguing with the day he got killed. The preacher was just singing away. I wonder if the night I was dreaming was the same night Paulie got buried." Hank took a bite of his sandwich and leaned back in his seat.

Will didn't move. Hank had just described the sanctuary of the Fairview Baptist Church, the Reavises' church, the church where Paulie's funeral was held, a church into which Hank had probably never set foot. There was a stained glass window behind the pulpit depicting Jesus and his disciples. Nancy Grier had worn a blue dress.

He told himself it could be a coincidence; Hank could have been in Fairview before, but it didn't seem . . .

"You think the night I was dreaming was the same night, Will?"

Will shook his head and looked at Hank. "I don't know, Son. I suppose that anything . . ." He stopped in mid-sentence. Beer sloshed out of the can he was holding and ran down the center of the boat. Will stared at the back of Hank's head for a few minutes. As nonchalantly as he could, Will said, "What do you mean, 'the man he was arguing with the day he got killed'?"

Hank leaned forward but didn't turn around. "Nothin'. There

was a man, but I don't know who he was. He was just a man."

"A man in your dream or a real man?"

"Will, can we come fishing more times this fall?"

"Hank, Son, turn around. We need to talk about something."

The boy slowly swung his legs over the metal bench and faced Will, but instead of looking at him, he stared out over the blue-green water of Lake Gaston to the narrow tree line.

"Look at me, Hank, not the water." Hank slowly raised his eyes. Will saw the concern and confusion.

"How long have you known me?"

"Seems like all my life."

"And in all that time, did I ever tell you something that wasn't true? Did I ever treat you wrong?"

"No sir, never."

"And I'm not going to now, Son. But I need to know what you meant about that man that Mr. Reavis was arguing with. What did you see, Henry, the day Mr. Reavis died?" Hank dropped his gaze, then looked back at Will. It was obvious that something had happened and it was equally obvious that Hank was nervous about saying anything.

"Uncle Rafe told me to never stick my nose in other people's business, 'specially not white men's. I reckon that Mr. Reavis's accident is none of my business."

"Your uncle is mostly right about that, but when somebody gets killed or even hurt, it's everybody's business. And it's especially the business of the sheriff's department. No matter what you think or what Uncle Rafe thinks, what is and isn't meddling is for me to decide. Our conversation will go no further than this boat—you have my word."

Hank squirmed on his seat cushion. The boy looked uncomfortable, and maybe scared. Finally he looked at Will. "Uncle Rafe told me not to say anything to anybody. He said arguments between white men was trouble that we didn't need. I ain't never . . . haven't ever, said nothing about this to nobody, 'cept Uncle Rafe."

"I understand, Hank, but I'm your friend—in addition to being the chief deputy of Hogg County. Paul Reavis was my best friend when we were boys, just like you and Paulie were best friends. I just want to help my friend. Now, tell me what you saw, Hank—please."

Hank frowned, then looked Will in the face, "Uncle Rafe gave me a job last summer working with him on the grain trucks. He let me come along to shovel up the spills and to help with the augers. It wasn't but for a month or so. I had to be at his place by sunup every day, and it's a pretty good piece from my house to his. I'd get up before dawn and ride my bike over to his place. I'd go down 264 and turn onto Pine Bluff Road. After a while Pine Bluff crosses Cane Creek. It's near a big curve in the road. You know where I mean?"

Will nodded, breathing shallow.

"Anyway, I was crossing the bridge over Cane, and I heard some equipment running. Sounded like a bulldozer. When I got to the clearing past the creek, the one that looks through the big pine trees, I could see across Mr. Winslow's bean field all the way to his and Mr. Martin's hog sheds. It's a long way across, but it was enough light to see. I stopped my bike to see what was going on.

"There was this man driving a bulldozer and looked to be pushing dirt in a hole. There was another man standing by a truck watchin'. Anyway, the guy on the 'dozer finishes then pulls up in front of the pickup, turns off the 'dozer and gits down to talk to the fella watchin'."

" 'fore they could say too much, another pickup comes flying down the road to the sheds and Mr. Reavis gets out."

Will raised his hand for Hank to stop, "How do you know it was Mr. Reavis?"

"Well, I don't exactly know, but it was a white pickup, and it had big red letters on the door. I just guessed it was Mr. Reavis. It was still kinda dark. The sun hadn't got full up yet. Anyhow, this man, Mr. Reavis, comes running over to the other two fellas and starts yelling at 'em, especially the one who'd been standin' by the truck. The other man, the one who'd been driving the 'dozer, he walks off and gets in his truck, or somebody's truck."

"Mr. Reavis didn't try to stop him. I guess he was too mad with the other fella. I wanted to stay but the sun was near 'bout up, and I had to get on to Uncle Rafe's; so I took off down the road.

"I told Uncle Rafe about it when I got to his house, and he told me, like I said, that white men's fights ain't none of our business. I'm sorry I never said nothing, but I figured it didn't make no difference. Does it?"

Will was staring out over the lake, searching the far shore for answers.

"Will? Does it?"

"I don't know, Hank, maybe. Could you tell who it was driving the bulldozer?"

"No, sir. He was bigger than the other two, but you know, it's a long way from the road to the hog sheds."

"Could you tell what kind of truck the man was driving?"

"A blue one, maybe a Chevy. It was blue; I know that."

"Light blue or dark?"

"Kinda dark. A Duke blue, and it had a white tool carrier on the back.

Will rubbed his upper lip with his thumb and index finger. What the hell was going on? The two men working at the sheds had to be Popper Winslow and Wallace May. After all, it was Popper's farrowing operation, his and Martin Farms. But why was Popper out there so early? He never said anything about being out at Pine Bluff that morning. Don Cobb had reported the accident. And why would Wallace be driving Paul's bulldozer—if it was Wallace who was there? It had to be. Who else drove a dark blue pickup with a white toolbox? This didn't make any sense.

"Listen, Hank. Did the two men who stayed at the bulldozer get into a fight?"

"I don't know. I had to get to Uncle Rafe's."

"Come on, Son. You had to be curious—I would've been. You looked across the field even when you rode off, didn't you?"

Hank nodded. "I could hear them yelling, but I couldn't tell what they were saying. The man who drove up, Mr. Reavis, was mighty hot, though."

"Was the other man, the one who was standing by the truck, Mr. Eugene Winslow?"

"I think so, but like I say, it was still kinda dark."

"What did the truck, the one that was still there, look like?"

"It was black and big, real big," Hank said.

"So what happened then?"

"They kept yellin' and Mr. Reavis, the bigger man, starts pushing the other fella away from the truck. Anyway, I couldn't see 'em after that, but I could still hear 'em and I know they was mighty mad with each another."

Will smiled then shifted his gaze. It was getting a bit too intense and Hank was starting to look worried. "Well, it may be nothing. I just wanted to know if there was anything that, you know, could help us. When somebody dies and there are no people around to say what happened, well, the sheriff's department is always interested in anything new. But Hank, our talk is just between us. I'm not going to tell anybody that you've told me this, and I don't want you to mention it to anybody, either, including your Uncle Rafe, okay?"

Hank looked relieved. "Okay, Will. I won't say nothing.

12.

The sun shone through the remaining brown and yellow leaves of the poplar in Lana's front yard and bathed the porch in a soft glow. Will swung slowly back and forth on the old swing, his right arm draped along the back, his left holding a cup of extra strong Columbian. Lana was in the kitchen fixing breakfast. The Sunday edition of the Raleigh *News and Observer* was scattered on the floor in front of the swing, with the usual pile of auto dealer ads, K Mart come-ons, classifieds, and pages of drugstore specials. He was reading the Living section.

"I'll be damned."

"What?" Lana called from the kitchen.

"Shelby Hopkins and her senile husband threw a party last night for the Raleigh Symphony Guild. La De Dah. 'The Hopkins house was radiant and reflected the elegant charm of the new Symphony season.' Do tell."

Lana looked through the screen door at Will. "Sounds like a little bitterness seeping through, Mr. Moser."

"No, no bitterness. I'm over it. Actually I'm glad she finally found someone rich enough and lazy enough to indulge her ego.

I sure as hell wasn't." He quickly turned the remaining few pages and threw the section down.

"Bitch."

"Will, no bitterness? Best I recall, 'bitch' is not exactly a term of endearment."

"I know, I know, but see, it really is. I used to put about twenty adjectives in front of it, now I'm down to just 'bitch.' "

Lana came out onto the porch, carrying a full tray and set it down. She glanced at Will with a smile.

"You married Shelby half a lifetime ago, William. All we need to say now is that it wasn't one of your better life decisions."

"Perhaps my worst."

Will kept his eyes on her as she moved to a chair on the other side of the small table.

"No, not your worst."

"You're right. My worst was when I left you. What a jerk. Off to prove something to Father and the world. All I proved was that I . . ."

Lana wasn't looking at him but staring across the yard. Will picked up his cup of coffee.

"Whatever," he said. She smiled again and looked over at him.

They sat for a while, neither one wanting to talk. Will glanced up now and then and smiled between bites, but that was all.

"Lana," Will said wiping his mouth, "When Paul got the job out at Martin Farm's farrowing operation, who hired him? Who gave him the contract?" He shifted his gaze to the front yard.

"Eugene Winslow, I think. Why?"

"No reason, just curious. Did he ever say anything about the job, ever mention any kind of disagreement with Eugene over the job? You know, how it was going. Was he on schedule and . . ."

Lana put down her coffee, "What do you mean disagreement? You mean argument or disagreement?"

"Either."

Lana cocked her head. "I don't remember. Why?"

"I just heard recently that maybe there was some bad blood

on the job. Nothing specific, just, you know, talk."

"Well, so what'd you hear?"

"Just what I told you, maybe some bad blood."

"And what if there was?"

"I don't know. I'm just curious."

Lana put the paper down and stared at Will without blinking, her jaw set. "Before you start to ignore me and change the subject, who told you about an argument?"

"I didn't say argument. I said bad blood, you know, general disagreement. Anyway, it's just talk. I'm not sure it's reliable, just checking it out. You know, doing my job." He flipped the sports section to the floor and picked up the business pages. Lana continued to stare at him.

He looked over at her. "Don't look at me that way," he said. "I'm just doing my job."

She wasn't looking at him, she was looking through him. She was looking all the way to Pine Bluff and Eugene's hog pens.

—✦ ✦ ✦—

Ernie Tasker, leaning back in his chair, his feet propped on his desk, was reading the *News and Observer.*

Only a skeleton crew worked in the sheriff's office on Sunday afternoons. Not much happened in Hogg County on Sundays. Most of the good ole boys were still in church or suffering hangovers.

"Afternoon, Ernie. Thanks for coming in, sorry for ruining your Sunday."

Ernie put down the paper and stood up. "No sweat. I was just messing around trying to decide whether to watch Atlanta get the shit kicked out of 'em. I got all the time you need. Let me get some coffee first."

Armed with a fresh cup of black coffee, Ernie sauntered back into the office. But instead of the wooden swivel chair behind his desk, he plopped down on the red leather couch that took up most of the opposite wall, his ego wall, covered with dozens of eight-by-tens of him with various luminaries.

Few people alive in Hogg County could remember when Ernie Tasker wasn't sheriff. Ernie was a legend as the first eastern North Carolina boy to make it in the major leagues. He pitched with the Braves, the Cardinals, and the Red Sox, where he had a perfect game and four shut-outs.

Will was sitting to Ernie's right, in the matching red leather wing chair. The sheriff put his feet up on the table in front of the couch, took a sip of coffee, and with his eyes cocked toward Will said, "Shoot, Major."

Will looked at the sheriff and smiled. Ernie Tasker was honest, smart enough to know when he needed help, and the most perceptive politician in the county, maybe the whole state. On top of owing him a lot, Will admired the sheriff and trusted his sense of justice.

"Ernie, I found out something yesterday that may shed some new light on Paul Reavis's death. Let me tell you what I heard, and you tell me what you think we ought to do, okay?"

Ernie nodded and took another sip of coffee. The sheriff was not a man given to random conversation. He believed that since he had two ears and only one mouth listening was twice as important as talking . . . an unusual trait in a politician.

Will stood up. He could think better on his feet, plus he could work off his nervous energy. He started pacing.

"Ernie, someone saw an argument take place at Popper's farrowing operation on the morning Paul had his accident. That the argument took place is a fact; who was involved is an open question. My source was quite a distance away and isn't positive about the identities of the men involved, but from what he saw I'm guessing that the argument was between Paul and Popper.

"But back to the facts. First, someone was driving Paul's bulldozer before sunup. The driver was using the 'dozer in the middle of what is now a parking lot, while another man, standing beside a large black pickup, watched him.

"Second, just as they were finishing, a man in a white pickup with red letters on the door drove up and got out of his truck. He walked over to the fellow who was standing by the black pickup and started yelling at him. When they started yelling at each other, the guy who'd been driving the bulldozer got in another truck and drove off.

"Now, I don't know what the result of the argument was; I don't know for sure that it was Popper and Paul arguing; and I'm not sure who was driving the bulldozer. What I do know is that three men were there, someone other than Paul was driving his bulldozer, and it was probably Paul who drove up, since there were big red letters on the door of the white pickup. Paul's white pickup with RGC on the door was at the site when Don Cobb found him that morning. I also know that the man driving the 'dozer drove off in a dark blue pickup with a white tool box on the back, a pickup like the one Wallace May drives.

"Now, several things seem obvious. First, if Paul was in an argument, then why didn't anyone mention it? Second, what were the other two men doing at the hog sheds before sunup? Who were the men? How come no one said anything about being at Pine Bluff before Don got there? And most important, could this have something to do with Paul's accident? Why . . ."

Ernie held up his hand. "One thing at a time, Will. Those are all good questions, however; 'could have been,' 'perhaps it was,' 'he sort of looked like,' bring us back to the reality. First, who saw all this?"

"I can't say."

"Why not?"

"Because I promised I wouldn't. It was a condition."

Ernie held Will with his gaze as if deciding what to believe and what to question. He stood up, walked over to his desk, pulled open the top drawer for his pack of Winstons, and lit up. With his first inhale, he sat down and rocked back. Will moved to the couch opposite the desk and sat while Ernie thought.

Looking up through the smoke, Ernie said, "Will, if you trust your source, then there are a bunch of serious questions to be asked, not the least of which is why no one came forward with the fact that they were at Pine Bluff that morning. Logic would say that it's because it had something to do with Paul's accident, which might mean that it wasn't an accident. You mention any of this to Lana?"

"Not what I've told you, but yes, I mentioned I had a hint that there might have been a disagreement on the job."

Ernie nodded.

"You gotta be careful on this. You've got good instincts, Will, but you might be too close to this thing. You might look like you're trying to get some sort of revenge. Everybody knows how close you were to Paul and his boy. I'm not saying this isn't important but let's just be real careful. Your questioning of Wallace May and the folks at Martin Farms ruffled a few feathers. We both know that the collapse of a hog-lagoon wall is nothing new. It happens all the time. So correct me if I'm wrong, but why am I getting the distinct feeling you're trying to tie the two accidents together?"

"I don't know, maybe because I'm starting to think of them together. I don't think they have anything to do with one another. It's just that . . . I don't know. I guess it's the same family in both cases and, like you said, I'm real close to it."

"Just be careful, Will. We don't need folks getting all bent out of shape."

"Folks like who?"

"Like Oris Martin and John Keaton."

At the mention of Oris and John, Will blurted out, "What the hell difference does it make what those two think? Fuck them." He was hot, and the idea of pressure being put on Ernie to stop him questioning anybody he wanted to made his blood boil. "As a matter of fact . . ."

Ernie cut him off before he could finish, "Just you wait a minute, hot stuff! Let me tell you what difference those two, and others like them, make. First, if you go around asking questions about an accident involving two young boys and then start pulling in an incident that happened over a year ago as if they were connected, people got a right to be confused and even annoyed. They don't see any connection between the two events. In fact, neither do you apparently. You can't accuse somebody of murder just because you lost a friend and his son.

"Will, I didn't bring you back to Mussel Ford to be crucified in your first election. I told you when we met in Raleigh that you had the potential to be the next high sheriff. I told you I'd support you when the time was right. Well, my friend, the time's about right, and you don't win elections by getting in the face of two of the most respected and powerful men in the region.

"Until notified differently, the job of sheriff is decided at the ballot box. Maybe that's a stupid way to do it, but that's the way it is—live with it. This ain't the Raleigh police force, Will. You're not a civil servant appointed by the chief here. Here your friends and neighbors elect you. When they do, they're saying that they trust you to protect them, and they say that on Election Day. You owe them your honesty and your commitment to be fair and impartial. If you can't do that, then you let me know and I'll back somebody who can." Ernie lit another Winston and leaned back.

As the sheriff exhaled toward the ceiling, Will said, "Sheriff, you saying you don't want to investigate this new information because it might piss off Oris Martin or John Keaton?" Ernie narrowed his eyes. Will could see the muscles tighten in his jaw.

"Open your ears, Will. I didn't say nothing about pulling a punch. If that's what you think of me after all these years, then something is wrong. You're here because you're a lawman. At least that's what you've always told me. You're a lawman who wants to be the head lawman. You want to stand for something."

Ernie paused then looked out the window behind his desk. When he turned back, he froze Will in his glare. "And one more thing—you better goddamn well know that I never whitewashed an investigation in my life!" Ernie Tasker didn't lose his temper often, but when he did, it was out there for God and all the world to see.

"You want to start questioning Eugene Winslow or Weldon

Goins or, for Christ sake, that poor May boy, then think real hard about whether you're really investigating or just plain castrating. Just remember, they don't have to tell you shit, and you got nothing substantial enough to make 'em."

"Ernie, don't ever think I'd question your honor or sense of justice. I'm sorry if it came out that way. And yes, I do have a lot of personal feelings tied up in this. Paul's death was hard. It was pointless, it was tragic, and it's still suspicious, now more than ever. You know it and I know it. But you're right, I need a lot more before we can put together a murder theory. You're also right that Paulie's death was undoubtedly an accident. An accident that kills my soul, that I can't forget and won't forget, but it also has nothing to do with what I just told you. I promise I won't force the two together, but I need to shine a light."

Will sank back into the couch and stared at his hands folded on his knee. After a few minutes, he looked up, "I won't chase Paulie's death. I'll just use it to keep me focused on Paul's. And if you want me to tell you that I'll be impartial, then I'll tell you I will. Take that for what it's worth. I am a professional. And for the record, I know that getting elected sheriff is political. Shit, I ought to, I've made enough damn speeches in the last six months to know that."

After another pause, Will said, "Back to what we were talking about in the first place. You asked me if I trusted my source—I do. I believe that Popper and Paul had an argument before Paul's accident. I figure that if they did and it resulted in Paul's death, then the reason we didn't know anybody was out there before Don Cobb is pretty clear. But as you always say, believin' ain't knowin'. I'd like to dig deeper on this, Sheriff. You tell me what you want me to do and I'll do it, but I think with this new information we need to ask some appropriate questions. I won't embarrass us or the department."

"I know you won't. Just be real careful and don't be obvious. It was over a year ago and digging it up now might seem real odd; plus, I don't want to tip off Eugene if there is something there. Let me think about this some more and we'll discuss it again tomorrow."

13.

Lana's breathing was returning to normal. She had crept on her hands and knees from the stand of alders where she'd parked to a patch of scrub oak beside the Pine Bluff farrowing facility. That fifty yards of mud and gravel had seemed like ten thousand in today's heat and humidity. Adding to her discomfort, a cloud of mosquitoes swarmed around her face and hands as she crouched in the bushes. Though late, it was still too light to cross the last hundred yards undetected. She needed to wait until Weldon Goins decided that he'd done his Sunday duty and leave.

Sunday was down time for every business in Hogg County, hog operations included; still, no day could pass without at least one inspection of the animals. Pigs in confinement were vulnerable to too many problems not to check them every day. Weldon had been at the facility for about an hour and would soon be headed home to catch the NFL game of the week.

When his taillights finally disappeared around a bend in the road, she took a final look around, then left the bushes and mosquitoes and headed for the building complex. She didn't bother with the office trailer, figuring it had an alarm system. Instead she headed for the entrance to the main building that held the first several hundred sows. The front of the building would contain the feed and supply rooms as well as the freezer she knew had to be somewhere on the grounds.

She slid back one of the double doors that fronted the building. The smell became increasingly vile the closer she got to the animals. Pigs may be some of the smartest of domestic animals, but God Almighty, they stink. It was dark inside the building even with the fading light outside. She squinted, looking for a light switch, and turned on the solitary overhead light bulb. Besides the smell, the room was filled with what felt like a fine mist, a tangible cloud of dust or mold, something noxious. Working in such a place had to be disgusting. Perhaps that's why Popper was so fond of it.

She opened a wooden door to her right and found bags of lime, fertilizer, and some unrecognizable chemicals stacked against the walls. The augurs for the feed silo were to her left just below the giant metal hopper. Past the augurs, she saw two shower stalls and a small changing room. The room had two metal benches and a dozen cabinets full of disposable overshoes, head nets, and what looked like hospital gowns. Popper and Don took sterilization seriously.

Through the changing room was the entrance to the first breeding shed with its two or three hundred noisy, smelly sows. As another security precaution, a ten-foot-high double chain link gate cut across the concrete walk. A huge padlock held the gate secure against cement posts on either side. Lana looked around the room for something that might speak to her, that might say, "Hey, look at me. I know what happened. I'm the smoking gun." But nothing leapt out.

She walked over to a small side door, opened it and looked outside. Except for the trailer that served as the office, all she saw were other hog sheds. The boars were kept in the far building. Vicky had said that Popper kept antibiotics in a freezer, so one had to be here somewhere and the office didn't seem a likely place. She noticed what looked like a metal container beside the shed. A container like those hauled cross-country by giant Sea Land semis, a sort of corrugated metal box without the wheels.

She walked to the double doors and pushed down the lever on the right door. It swung open with little effort. Inside was a door that looked exactly like the walk-in freezer door in her office. An unfastened padlock hung from the handle. She took it and put it in her pocket, then pulled the handle and opened the freezer door. A switch plate to the right of the door had a small, recessed red light below the switch. If the red light was on, the inside light should also be on.

She flipped the switch and looked inside. Metal shelves lined the side and back walls. The shelves on the side were three or four feet wide while the back ones were much narrower. Dozens of small vaccine-like bottles filled the back shelves while boxes of tubing, needles, and what looked like Tupperware containers filled the sides. Next to the side shelving and on the floor were huge bags of dog food. Don and Weldon were using the freezer to store their personal items.

She inspected the contents of the freezer, but nothing stood out as suspicious. Lana didn't really know what she was looking for, though. She narrowed her focus. What's in here that can help me? What doesn't belong? What calls out? But no call came; plus, she was starting to shiver.

Lana left the freezer and was about to close the door when she heard a car or truck door slam. She froze. Had Weldon forgotten something? Tiptoeing to the front of the container, Lana looked around the door. Her heart leapt to her throat. It was Eugene Winslow. The angry little man had parked beside the office trailer and was walking toward the building she had just left. He must have seen the open door and the light on inside. Lana looked around the container. There was no place to hide and the open ground between the container and the trailer or the other sheds was too wide for her to run undetected. Popper was now in the building beside her. She could hear him cussing at Weldon as he stalked around. She started to slip out of the container and head for the woods when she heard him grab the handle of the side door.

"Son of a bitch, Weldon! Are you so stupid that you leave all the fucking lights on and doors open? Goddamn idiot."

She quietly pulled the container door closed. By now her breath was rapid and exaggerated—fear constricted her chest. She couldn't get enough air. Desperately she looked around the container for somewhere to hide, something to get under or behind, but saw nothing. The freezer was her only option. She flipped off the light in the freezer and stepped back into the frigid room. She dared not pull the door shut because it would make too much noise, so she slowly pulled on the inside emergency plunger and hoped Popper wouldn't come in.

Inside was total darkness. She felt on her left and touched the bag of dog food sitting on the floor. Her best chance of avoiding detection was to slide onto the bottom shelf and pull the bag of dog food in after her. Dear God, please don't let him come inside the container and freezer. No need to shut my eyes, open or shut is the same. She heard the container door open and Popper cuss again.

"Weldon, that's it! Tomorrow you're through. Lights on, freezer door unlocked. What the shit were you thinking?" He turned on the light and pulled the door open. Lana pressed her mouth against the dog food bag and held her breath. She tried to concentrate on not shaking, not making noise of any kind, but it was becoming impossible. Her heart was pounding and she needed air. Just as she exhaled, the freezer compressor came on, providing enough noise to cover her gasp. She kept pressing her mouth against the bag of dog food so as not to exhale any mist. She dared not look up or move a muscle. Popper was so close she could have touched him.

"I can't believe this shit. What the hell were you in here

for anyway, Weldon? Goddamn moron," Popper mumbled to himself.

After what seemed like an eternity, he walked outside, turned off the light and pushed the door closed. She could hear him looking for the padlock, then heard him swear again and walk out of the container. She didn't dare move, not until she was sure he had left. She started to move the dog food bag and at least get off the lower shelf but as she started to, she heard Popper return to the container. It sounded like he was putting something into the hole that usually held the arm of the padlock. Then silence.

Lana waited for as long as she could before sliding out of her hiding place. Careful not to touch the door with her ear since it would stick to the sub-freezing metal, she listened to find out if Popper was still nearby. She heard nothing, but knew that having found so many doors open and lights on, Popper would be checking all the other buildings. She'd wait some more.

But she was starting to go numb and shaking uncontrollably. Her thought processes were slower and it was hard to focus. She leaned against the round knob of the emergency plunger and pushed. Nothing. She knew the plunger was for just such an occasion; a way to open the door from inside if you were accidentally shut in. She felt the padlock in her pocket and knew that the door couldn't be locked. Why wouldn't the door open? Popper must have put something into the hole that normally held the padlock. What did he put there?

Lana was shaking so hard she couldn't think, and her fingers, whenever she touched the door or plunger, were sticking to the cold metal. She couldn't see anything and didn't recall seeing anything in the freezer that she could wrap around her hands. Where was the door, which direction? Her mind was starting to play tricks on her. She put her hands in her pockets to warm them, but that didn't help. Then she felt something in her back pocket, a small memo pad from her home office. She remembered thinking that she might need something to write on. Not a pressing need at present.

She took it out and felt around for the door. Again she touched the plunger attached to the outside handle, but this time she placed the memo pad between her hand and the flat surface. Her mind was starting to wander. She could barely feel the pad. She needed to push but with something besides her hands.

Her hands were too cold and she couldn't get enough power just by leaning against the knob. Her shoulder, she needed to use her shoulder. She needed to hold the pad against the plunger and crash into it with her shoulder. She started to count but forgot what the next number was. Her feet were a shoulder's width apart. No need to count, just do it. She threw herself against the plunger with all her strength, and the door opened with a crunch.

Lana fell out of the freezer onto her knees, scraping her hands on the metal floor. It didn't matter. She felt warmth, heat, the moist air of eastern Carolina. She lay there, half expecting to look up and see Popper Winslow standing over her with a gun, but nothing happened. Her senses slowly returned and she listened for any sign of another person in the building. All she could hear were the grunts from a thousand sows and boars. She was, for the first time in her life, happy to smell the porcine stench that engulfed her. She was happy to smell anything.

Lana got to her feet, rubbed her hands together to get the circulation working, and cautiously walked to the container door. Looking around the yard, she didn't see or hear anything. She stood there long enough to satisfy her fears before she turned and inspected the freezer door. Popper had put a small wooden dowel into the lock keeper; so, when she smashed her shoulder against the inside plunger, the door handle cut the dowel in half. She picked up the two wooden pieces, thinking how lucky she was that he hadn't found a large nail.

Lana needed to find out where Popper had gotten the dowel because she needed to replace it. She went back to the room where the bags of fertilizer were stacked and found a box of assorted bolts and nuts and, thankfully, some dowels the same size as the one Popper used. She returned to the container and shut the freezer door, securing it with the replacement dowel. She put the lock on a shelf outside the freezer, hoping Popper would assume he had missed seeing it.

After making sure nothing was out of place, she left the container and headed back to the patch of alders hiding her car, grateful that she could even walk. Will had been right. What did she really expect to find, the ghost of Paul Reavis meeting her in the yard and showing her what had happened? Still, it was somehow cathartic to finally be at the site of her grief. A feeling of calm came over her as she walked out of the yard. Lana was safe. Somebody or something was looking out for her. To hell with caution. She was glad she had come. Next time, she'd find what she was after.

14.

Grier Exxon was packed. The service bays were full, and cars stood at every pump in the station.

"Hey, Will. Out chasing bad guys?" Odell Grier walked up to the squad car from the middle service bay.

"No, no bad guys, but I was about to chase Doris Cleveland away from your pump. What the hell is it about women that makes them decide to put on lipstick and make-up in the busiest places at the busiest times?"

Odell smiled, "I don't answer any 'women' questions. I flunked that course."

"So," Will said looking around as he put the pump handle into his gas tank. "Looks like you're doing okay."

Odell nodded, "Not bad. I'm about a day behind on service work, and the store, for a Tuesday, is doing all right. Weekends are the big time for retail. Beer and junk food don't really start moving til Friday or Saturday."

Before Will could reply, Odell added, "Before I forget, thanks for the other day. Hank hasn't stopped talking about his big fish. At this point, I'm not sure why you didn't harpoon it. A fish that big almost calls for harpooning."

Will laughed, "No true fisherman lets a fish die. Each catch develops a life of its own. Even after death, they just keep on growing."

Odell nodded, "I think Hank was a little nervous about going without Paulie, you know, afraid that things would feel . . . different. But it worked out okay."

"Odell, you should have been there. I've never seen that many fish on a fish finder. It looked like a school of Blues off the coast in September. We were in 'em from the time we got there to the time we left. You've got to come next time."

Odell switched his cane from his right hand to his left and slowly moved closer to Will. When he was about two feet away, he looked around and lowered his voice. "How you think Hank is doin'? I mean really. Anything bother you?"

Will thought for a moment. "No. He's doing real good as far as I can tell. Why? You been seeing anything?"

"Not really. He did seem somewhat distracted when y'all got home. Nancy and I try to notice anything different about him."

Will finished filling his car and put the handle back in the pump. "What do you mean 'distracted'?"

"I don't know, kinda distant. Like he was thinking about something, but didn't want to tell us. Not that a ten-year-old shares much, anyway."

Will smiled, "I think I told Nancy about when Hank referred to himself by a name that Paulie always used . . . the Hank Man. He got real upset when he said it, but he got over it. We can't shield him from his memories. He'll learn to put them in their proper place." Will paused, sorting through his own memories. "He's a good boy. You and Nancy should be real proud."

"We are," Odell said with smiling.

Will handed Odell his credit card and started to walk into

the store when he heard a large diesel truck pull into the station. He turned around and saw Weldon Goins behind the wheel of a massive dump truck pulling a D8 bulldozer on a flat bed. The two vehicles were almost too big to get into the parking area. Odell had his diesel pumps separated from the regular gas plaza for just this reason. Weldon pulled the truck up to the pump and got out. As the truck was filling up, Weldon walked toward the store. When he was about six feet from Will, he nodded, "Deputy."

Will nodded back. "Weldon, how's it going?"

"Pretty good, I guess."

Will stayed outside while Weldon went into the store for coffee and a pack of cigarettes. Will waited until Weldon had lit a cigarette, then said, "Where you taking the 'dozer?"

Weldon didn't look at him but replied, "We got a job at a Martin Farms facility over in Charter County. I'm taking it over there." Will paused, and as nonchalantly as possible added, "You doing the work?"

"Yeah, me and Mr. Winslow."

"I mean you doing the driving?"

Weldon looked at him. "Probably not. Why do you wanna know?"

"Just curious. Is Wallace May still working for you?"

Weldon seemed a bit annoyed. "I reckon so. Why?"

"No reason special, but you know how upset Wallace has been after his lagoon busted. I just didn't know if he was up to it."

"Seems to be. At least that's what Popper thinks and he's the one who calls the shots."

"Yeah. Anyway, I hope Wallace is okay. I like him. It's a shame he's had such a bad run of luck." Weldon didn't say anything.

"He's done a lot of driving for you guys over the last couple of years, hasn't he?"

Weldon took a deep drag on his cigarette, blew it out then drank some coffee. "Yeah, he's done right much for us. Couple of years' worth, I reckon."

"He's a good man. I feel real sorry for him. I just hope he can get over this thing. Driving for you and Popper means a lot to him, I expect. He can make some money while his feed operation is down." Weldon didn't say anything.

"He do the work for you guys last year out at Pine Bluff?"

Weldon looked at the pump to see if it was almost through, then back at Will. "Paul Reavis did the work at Pine Bluff."

"Yeah, I know, but who did the work after Paul's accident?"

"I did."

"Not Wallace?"

"No."

"How come?"

"How come what?"

"How come you did the work and not Wallace?"

"How the shit do I know? Popper told me to finish the job. How come you're asking all these questions? Why don't you talk to Popper? He's the one who owns the equipment. I just do what he says."

"I have talked to Popper. I talked to him last year, but you know I never talked to you about the day of Paul's accident. You know us law guys, we stay curious. Anyway, when did you get to Pine Bluff that day?"

"I don't know. After eight some time, I reckon."

"That your usual time in?"

"I guess."

"I didn't see you when I got there that morning."

Weldon shrugged his shoulders.

"Don Cobb's only at Pine Bluff a couple of days a week. When does he usually get there?"

"Whenever he wants, I guess. I don't know. It's Popper's business."

The pump stopped so Weldon started toward his truck, Will walking right beside him. Weldon squeezed the handle to top off the tank and then put the pump handle back in its cradle. "Listen, Deputy, I gotta go. You got any more questions?"

"Not really. Maybe just one more. How do you think Paul could have been so careless? I mean, you know 'dozers as good as anybody. How do you think he could have had such an accident?"

"I really don't know, Deputy. Bad luck, I guess."

"Uh-huh. Real bad luck. Anything like that ever happen to you? I mean you ever have a 'dozer slip a clutch?"

Weldon opened the door to the truck. "Naw. Nothing like that."

"You ever heard of it happening to anybody but Paul?"

Weldon started the truck. Over the roar of the motor Will could see but barely hear him say, "Nope, never heard tell of it."

—✦ ✦ ✦—

Weldon pulled the giant truck and 'dozer into the asphalt parking lot at Pine Bluff. He turned off the truck motor and looked around to see if Popper was nearby. Not seeing him come out of any of the farrowing sheds, Weldon headed toward the double-wide used as the office.

As he walked into the trailer he yelled out, "Popper, you in here?" From the bathroom he heard a muffled "Yeah, I'm here." Weldon figured he might be here a while since Popper was known to be an acute hemorrhoid sufferer. He flopped down in the old metal chair in front of the rusty, dented desk. Oris and Eugene were nothing if not thrifty. After another ten minutes Weldon heard Popper slam the door to the bathroom and start down the hall.

"You got everything for Charter County?" Popper asked.

"Yep, I got it. I'm supposed to meet Wallace out here so he can follow me to the site. It's only about fifteen miles, but you know Wallace. He's scared he might not be able to follow my directions well enough. I told him to meet me here."

Popper said nothing, just harrumphed and walked around the desk, sitting down in the old wooden chair on the working side. Weldon picked up a copy of *Sports Illustrated* and started reading. After a page or two, he said, "You know, that Will Moser is a nosy bastard." Popper made a low guttural sound and kept on reading his breeding records for the month. After a minute or two, he looked up as if Weldon had just said something and said, "What do ya mean?"

"Huh?"

"What do ya mean Will Moser is a nosy bastard?"

"Oh, nothing, I was just filling the truck over at Odell's, and Will was there and starts asking me a whole lot of questions. That's all."

"What kind of questions?"

"Just stuff like where we're working now. Where I'm taking the 'dozer. Am I doing the work. Stuff like that."

"What did you say?"

"I said we're doing a job in Charter County."

"That it? That all he asked about?"

"Mostly. He did ask if Wallace was still working for us."

"And?"

"And I said that he was."

"That it?"

Weldon rubbed his chin. "Uhm, he asked something about whether I finished the job out here after Paul's accident or did Wallace. He asked what time I got here in the morning. And uh, he asked if I had ever had a clutch slip on me." Weldon twisted his mouth a bit then finished with, "I said I never had."

Popper got up from the desk and walked around to stand in front of Weldon. His eyes bored into him. "Weldon, what exactly did you say about that morning and your part in fixing the parking facility?"

"What I told you. I said that I ran the equipment after Paul's accident. I told him I got here after eight that morning and that Don had already found Paul. And I told him to call you if he had any more questions. I told him I just worked here."

Popper thought for a minute. "You didn't tell him that I called you that morning and told you to go by the store for me, did you?"

"No. Fact is I forgot about that."

Popper walked to the front door and opened it to look out.

No one was in the parking lot. Weldon's truck was alone out there. Without turning around, Popper said, "Weldon, what time did you leave yesterday?"

Weldon put down the magazine. "I don't know exactly, about five, I reckon. Why?"

"I'm just curious," Popper said as he turned around and looked at Weldon, his voice rising as he did, "Why didn't you close the door to the fucking freezer when you left?" Weldon's face turned white. Startled, he was edging toward angry.

"I never opened it, Eugene."

"Then why was it open when I got here? And why the fuck was the lock out of the door?"

Weldon's face went red. "I ain't got no fuckin idea, but I never went into the freezer and I never took the lock out of the door. I ain't never left that door open in all the years I been here, you know that!"

Popper pulled at his nose as he thought. Weldon wasn't acting like a man who was covering something up. He was pissed instead.

"You didn't see anybody or hear anybody the whole time you were out here yesterday, right?"

"I'd of told you if I did. I didn't see or hear nobody." He got up from his chair and walked over to the door. "You think somebody was out here?"

"I don't know, it's possible."

"Who would want to sneak into a pig shed?" Weldon said making a face.

"When was the last time Dr. Newell was out here?"

"You think Dr. Newell was out here yesterday?"

"Just answer the question, Weldon."

"Uhm, a week ago, I reckon. She come to deliver some needles and medicine. I put it in the freezer."

"She give you anything? A pen, pad of paper, anything from the vet?"

Weldon thought a second. "Not that I remember. She might have but I can't recall it. Why?"

"Nothin.'" Popper moved back around the desk and sat down. He opened the drawer and took out the pad of note paper with Jeffers and Newell printed at the top left corner. He looked on the back and brushed off the dust. "Weldon, if Will asks any more questions about anything out here, I don't want you to say a word. You tell him to call me. You got that?"

"I got it. I didn't like him asking me stuff, anyhow, and I already told him to call you."

"Okay, just don't forget, and when Wallace comes, make sure to get me before you go. Okay?"

"Yeah."

—◆ ◆ ◆—

The two men stood on the porch of the trailer waiting for Popper to come out. Wallace was almost a foot taller than Weldon and several years younger. He was a strong man and could pick up two fifty-pound feed sacks like they were just bags of potato chips. Weldon was more compact, about five nine and average weight. He was a cocky and arrogant sort when he was around someone like Wallace but reverted to more of a sycophant around Popper. He was wary of Popper. Not that Popper had ever done anything bad to him, but Weldon knew Popper was only gonna take care of one person and it damn sure wasn't Weldon Goins. Waiting for Popper made both men antsy—and cautious.

"What's he want?" Wallace asked as he shifted his hat from one hand to the other.

"How the fuck should I know, Wallace? I look like I got my mind-reading hat on?"

"I didn't mean nothing, Weldon. I just figured you already been out here and might know what he's thinking."

"He's probably gonna tell us about the job and remind us to not say nothing about it to nobody. He already slammed me for talking to Will Moser."

Wallace looked over at Weldon. "He done the same to me last week while I was over at the Dairy Queen. Will been asking you questions, too?"

"Yeah. Too many."

Before Wallace could reply, the door to the trailer opened and Eugene came onto the porch looking kinda cranky.

"How you doin', Wallace? You ready to do some work down in Charter County?"

"Yes, sir. I . . ."

Popper turned to Weldon. "Make sure to talk to Bernie Hopkins down there before you start doing anything, okay?"

Weldon nodded. "Right. I'll get our schedule and job plan all laid out before we start anything."

"Okay, and call me tonight to give me a report."

"I'll do it as soon as I get back," Weldon said.

"Wallace, you think you can remember how to get down there tomorrow?" Popper asked.

"Yes, sir. I'll remember."

"Okay, you guys take off. But first, Wallace, let me talk to you a minute." Popper looked at Weldon and jerked his head in the direction of the dump truck and D8. Weldon nodded and backed off the porch. Popper looked at Wallace. "You had any more questions about young Paulie's accident?"

"No, sir. Nobody asked nothing."

"Will Moser been asking anything about anything? Either Paulie's accident or anything else?"

Wallace started to say something but Popper put his hand up. "Before you say no, which you were about to, think. Be real sure. I'm asking this because Will was asking some questions of Weldon today and it's making me a little angry." Wallace stood still and thought. When he figured he'd thought enough, he said, "Mr. Eugene, ain't nobody asked me nothing about nothing. Like I told you before, I ain't said nothing 'bout last year to nobody, and I ain't gonna."

Popper smiled and patted him on the back, "Okay, Wallace,

you and Weldon get on down to Charter and do me a good job. You get it done right and on time and there will be a little something extra in it for ya."

Wallace grinned and took a leap off the porch, then waved and headed toward his truck.

15.

Slouched down in his truck, Popper watched the Dairy Queen across the street. Will Moser and Wallace May would never notice him in the car-wash parking lot, especially with other black pickups coming and going through the building. Popper's left eyelid started to twitch.

Will was leaning against one of the tables while Wallace licked the side of a large vanilla cone. Will was keeping it low key. He said something, waited a minute, then said something else. Wallace didn't look at him, attending to his ice cream and occasionally nodding his head.

Wallace finished his cone and wiped his mouth with the handkerchief he always carried in his back pocket. He was starting to fidget. His eyes darted from the parking lot to the front door of the Dairy Queen and back. He shifted from one foot to the next then began to suck his lower lip. Will watched as Wallace reached into his pocket and pulled out an arrowhead and began rubbing the small grooves on its side.

"What you got there?" Will asked.

"Nothin', just a piece of rock."

"Looks like a rock that somebody worked on." Will knew he needed to change the subject. Asking Wallace a lot of questions had gone on long enough. It also wasn't getting anywhere.

Wallace looked up. "It's a arrowhead. It was in the field below the lagoon."

Will smiled. "I didn't know you collected arrowheads, Wallace. I collect 'em too. Can I see it?" Wallace handed Will the piece of flint.

"I'll be darned," Will said. "It's a Clovis head. These are really rare, Wallace. You got a good eye."

Wallace reached out his hand to take back the arrowhead. He hesitated a few seconds, then said, "Actually, I didn't find it. It was give to me."

"Well, it's a nice gift."

Wallace glanced back at Will. "The young Reavis boy give it to me last spring. He was on my place huntin' for 'em and give it to me."

Will looked at Wallace, then down at the arrowhead.

"Him and his friends used to play down at the creek. Before the day the lagoon busted. I never told you that, that I seen them there before."

Will smiled and shook his head. "It don't matter, Wallace. I figured they'd been down there before. Don't worry."

Wallace rubbed the arrowhead harder. "I guess I should've run 'em off, but they weren't doin' no harm." He put the flint point on the table. "It's pretty, ain't it? Must of took them Indians a long time to make somethin' that pretty just using other rocks."

Will looked at the stone and nodded.

"I was up at the sheds one day and I seen somebody down in the bean field next to the woods. You know ain't nobody 'lowed near hog sheds, so I yelled down, 'Hey, what you doin' on my land?' Young Reavis—but I didn't know it was him then—waves at me. I couldn't hear what he yelled, so I walked down into the field. When I got near, I seen it was young Paul."

"Young Paul, you ain't supposed to be walking near hog sheds."

"I'm sorry, Mr. May, but I was just huntin' for arrowheads and scrapers."

"Well, that's okay, but you'd best call so I know who's down here."

"I will, I promise. Next time I'll call. That is, if it's all right."

"It's okay. Just 'member to call so's I know."

"You know anything about arrowheads and Indians, Mr. May?"

"Well, some, but not too much."

"Look here at this arrowhead, Mr. May. This here is a Clovis point. They're the oldest arrowheads around. Over a thousand years old. You ever heard of Clovis points?"

"No, not as I remember."

"They're the daddy of all arrowheads."

"I never heard of Clovis Indians."

"They wasn't the Clovis Indians; Clovis is a place. It was where they found the first one of these arrowheads. I reckon that any head that looks like the first one is called a Clovis."

"Where'd you git it?"

"I got it from my uncle, Will Moser. He's a deputy, you know him?"

"Uh-huh. I know him."

"You know the best time to find arrowheads, Mr. May? The best time is right after a rain. The water washes away all the dirt around the rocks and the arrowheads and scrapers are left sittin' on top of little towers of dirt. Like this here. This here is a chip. A piece of rock that the Indians knocked off another piece that they was making into a arrowhead. These here are all over the place. I found lots of 'em."

"I seen 'em before, but I never figured they was from no arrowheads."

"Mr. May. I'm sorry we didn't call. Here, you can have this

here Clovis point. It's for letting us look on your place. I feel bad we ain't never called or nothin' and besides, I got more of 'em."

"Young Paul, I can't take this from you. It was give to you by your uncle Will."

"He's not really my uncle, I just call him that. He and my real daddy was best of friends, now he's more like another daddy. My real daddy is dead. Besides, we'll find some more. We go out a lot. Maybe when we're fishin' or huntin', or maybe we'll just be out walkin' and looking for stuff. You're busy and might not find a Clovis on your place, so now you'll have this one."

—✦ ✦ ✦—

Wallace licked his lips and swallowed hard. He re-focused on Will then said, "Will, young Paulie was a real special little boy. He gimme this point and told me it had come from you. That it was real old and from somewhere named Clovis. I never heared of Clovis but the Indians that lived there must have been pretty smart to make a arrowhead like this. He said that you was more like a daddy to him than an uncle, even though he called you Uncle Will. He was a real nice boy and smart, too. Most boys around here just call me Wallace . . . and other things. Young Paul always called me Mr. May." Wallace's eyes were wet and lined in red.

"The worst thing that ever happened to me was for that little boy to git killed on my place. I ain't been able to tell his momma how sorry I am, but my uncle John says that he's gonna take me to her house so I can tell her. I . . . uhm . . . I don't . . ."

Will, whose own voice was shaky, put his hand on Wallace's shoulder. "Wallace, don't worry. She knows it wasn't your fault, but if you like, I'll make sure to tell her what you said. And Wallace, she'll be real proud of what you had to say about Paulie. She'd be proud of how polite he was to you, just like I'm sure your momma's real proud of the man you've become."

Wallace smiled, "Thank you, Will. I hope she's proud, and I hope that my daddy would be too, if he was here."

"I know he would be, Wallace."

Wallace nodded. "I bet bein' a daddy is hard. There ain't no place to learn it. Just one day you're a daddy."

Will looked at Wallace. "Someday you'll be a daddy, Wallace, and when you are you can remember what your daddy was like and what talking to Paulie was like, and you'll know how to be."

Wallace looked at Will then down at the ground. "I got to first find somebody that would want to marry me."

"Oh, you'll find somebody. A good lookin' man like you . . . a successful hog farmer."

Wallace smiled. "I hope so. I'd like to be a daddy, no matter how hard it'd be."

Will looked at his watch. "I've got to go, Wallace. Thanks for lettin' me talk to you, and thank you for telling me about your time with Paulie."

Wallace got to his feet and nodded. Then he reached into his pocket and took out the arrowhead. "Will, I reckon you oughta have this. You give it to young Paul in the first place."

He held it out. Will smiled and reached over and closed Wallace's fingers around the arrowhead.

"I wouldn't think of it, Wallace. Paulie gave it to you, and you need to keep it. Someday you can give it to your son."

Wallace nodded and put the Clovis back in his pocket. "Thanks, Will, and I enjoyed speakin' with you."

—✦ ✦ ✦—

Popper shifted his Ford into first gear and started toward Martin Feed Mills. Oris had called that morning and told him to meet him at the mill. He was concerned about the cholera scare in Sessions County and what effect it might have on his operations, especially at Pine Bluff. Popper had told Oris about their hog shrinkage problems at Pine Bluff. He told him there were a number of scoured hogs plus a few dozen flu deaths, but he said it was nothing to worry about, he had it under control. Oris maybe had some idea it was more than scours, but he didn't ask too much.

Deniability was always important if you were looking to nail blame somewhere else or on someone else. So far the state boys seemed to believe the cholera problem was confined to Sessions County and specifically the Ross farm. They hadn't gone crazy with inspecting other lots unless they had direct business with the Ross operation, and no Martin Farms places dealt with Carl Ross, at least none that would admit it.

Popper also was pretty sure the supplies Don Cobb had sold to Carl last year hadn't been the cause of Carl's problems, but he didn't need to tell Oris about any of that. Cholera was the biggest boogieman in the pig business, so everybody lost their perspective when an alert was sent out.

Oris was already at Martin Feed Mills when Popper arrived. He'd parked in the back, staying out of the bustle of the harvest season, which had the mill surging with activity. Harvesting had started in the east and grain was pouring in from the surrounding fields and farms. The hammer mill was pounding away inside the old wooden plant; the pigeons wheeled and darted in and out of the open vents at the top of the building. The air was thick with pale yellow dust from pulverized grain, and the plant reverberated with the voices of men yelling over the clanging of ancient milling equipment. Dump trucks belched black diesel fumes out of their stacks as they rumbled into and out of the mill yard.

Oris looked up from his seat at the table as Popper, looking sullen and raspy, walked into the room. "Hey, Eugene. What's up? You look like somebody who needs a friend."

"Trouble's up," Popper groused. "And it's gettin' a lift on the back of Will Moser."

Oris put down his mug of black coffee and took off his drugstore half-frame reading glasses. He watched Popper snatch a chair away from the table and plop down on the seat. Eugene wore emotions on his face the way a soldier wore battle ribbons on his chest—clearly visible and in your face. His mouth was pinched and tight, and his eyes simmered with anger. Oris knew this was no time to rib Popper, and it damn sure was no time to discuss disease-fighting procedures at Pine Bluff.

"What kind of trouble, Popper?"

"I just seen Will talking to Wallace May over at the Dairy Queen. I don't know what they were talking about, but it can't be good. The sum-of-a-bitch is running around asking questions all over the place. Just the other day he corners Weldon at Odell's station and starts firin' questions about where he's working, whether Wallace is still doin' work for us, shit, he even starts asking him about last year and where he was the day of Paul's accident. Hell, Oris, he come out here and put you through the ringer over Wallace's problems. I don't know what he's doin' but it's startin' to piss me off."

Oris stared at Popper. "What do you suppose got his dander up about Weldon and last year?"

"How the hell should I know? Weldon says that Will and him was just passing niceties and Will starts talking about Wallace and how he likes him and how he's had a run of bad luck. Stuff like that.

"Then he says something about who did the work out at Pine Bluff last year. Weldon says that Paul did the work, then Will says, no, after Paul.

"Anyway, Weldon told him to call me if he had any questions about work at Pine Bluff and Will says he already talked to me, but he never talked to Weldon.

"Weldon says that he wasn't out there and didn't know nothing about it. Then Will asks when he got there that morning and is that his usual time."

Popper was now up and pacing around the room. "You see what I mean, Oris? All of a sudden he's asking a lot of weird-ass questions. I don't know what kinda bee he's got up his ass, but it's starting to sting me."

Oris leaned back in his chair and let Popper breathe a little bit. "Eugene, maybe Will's just uptight about Wallace and his troubles. It don't sound like anything other than a harmless fishing expedition."

Popper looked across the table. "Listen, Oris, I'm not a fucking airhead. I know about fishing expeditions. What worries me is that Wallace is pretty shallow water and eventually, he keeps it up, Deputy Moser might hook somethin'."

"Yeah, but you got a handle on Wallace, don't you? You said you've already scared the shit out of him. He ain't gonna say anything, and if he already had, Will would be acting totally different. I wouldn't worry."

"I'm glad you're so optimistic, Oris," Popper said, "But I'm not so sure about Wallace. That's what I've been trying to tell you. I happen to think that Wallace can break wide open. I don't give a shit if Wallace saw me hit Paul or not. It's enough that he was there. In case you don't recall, our story is that Don found Paul, and I got there a half hour later . . . shocked at what happened. That's what Don thinks, that's what Ernie thinks, that's what everybody thinks except you, me, Wallace, and now maybe Will Moser."

Popper didn't tell Oris that Weldon might also have a clue that everything reported about Paul's death wasn't totally true. No need to introduce something that Popper wasn't even sure of himself.

"And something else. I came out to the office last Sunday to get something and I find the lights on and the freezer door open. At the time, I thought Weldon had been careless, leaving the lights on and the door open, but he swears to God that he was never in the freezer or the container. The padlock for the freezer was on a shelf beside the freezer and I found a note pad on the floor."

"What kind of note pad?"

"One of those three by fives that Carter Jeffers gives out."

"So what. I must have fifty of the damn things," Oris said.

"Yeah, so do I, but I don't got 'em on the floor of the freezer."

"Maybe one of the docs dropped it when they were out there last."

"Could be. Dr. Newell was there a few weeks ago but I don't remember seeing one on the floor. I . . ."

Oris cut him off. "Look, Popper. You ain't in the freezer every day. A pad could've gotten there lots of ways. What difference does it make?"

"Who the fuck opened the freezer, Oris? How come the damn door was open and the lock sitting on a shelf?"

Oris shrugged his shoulders. "Maybe Weldon was lying to you. Maybe he opened it and forgot to close it. Maybe he told you he didn't do it so you wouldn't chew his ass out. Why the fuck you think he'd admit to it with you in his face?"

Popper stood quiet for a minute, turning his head slightly so he was looking at Oris out of his good eye. "Could be. But I don't think so. I know Weldon pretty good. He's lied to me before and this didn't seem like his way to lie."

Oris stood up and pushed back his chair. "Look, you're suspicious, fine. Will Moser is asking a lot of questions. Wallace May is rattled about all the commotion at his feed lot. Everybody's a little on edge. Like I said, if Will had anything concrete he'd have said or done something more substantial than ask a lot of random questions. Just relax and let's see what's what."

Popper slammed the chair against the desk and stepped up to the corner. He looked like he was trying to contain himself but having a hard time of it.

"'Just relax.' That's what you say, 'just relax.' I got this retard about to come unglued and shoot his mouth off about how sorry he is that Paul died so angry and I'm supposed to just relax? We got a lot riding on this situation, Oris, and just relaxing ain't gonna get it done!"

Oris started putting on his windbreaker as if nothing had happened. He almost smiled. "Eugene, I have already called John Keaton about delaying his trip to see Lana Reavis. In fact, we discussed that a while ago. He is going to wait for a month or so. He says that Wallace is okay with that.

"Now, there's nothing more I can do right now. I think you may be overreacting to what's going on; however, in case you have forgotten, let me remind you of something." Here Oris leaned over the table, his eyes boring into Popper's. "You see, I didn't fucking lose my temper last year and kill somebody. Accident or not, the sheriff looks on such things with a jaundiced eye. We're partners in that operation and friends for a long time, but like I've said before, I wasn't at Pine Bluff last year, you were.

"I was in the company of several dozen feedlot operators, all of whom would verify my presence. No one is asking me questions. Now, if you believe that Wallace represents a risk to you, then talk to him. Give him guidance. Pray with him. I really don't give a shit. If Will is suspicious, make him un-suspicious, act normal, don't let him see you agitated.

"And if you think somebody's been snooping around, find out who and persuade them that it's unhealthy to trespass. Handle the problem, Eugene."

With that, Oris zipped up his windbreaker and walked out of the room. Popper's left eye started to twitch again and his mouth pulled up into a tight, hard pucker.

16.

Dr. Newell came out of her office and turned off the light. "Lana, I'm going home."

Lana laughed, "Be still, my heart! The workaholic is actually leaving before seven or eight o'clock."

"Actually, I should do more work on these tissue samples, but I'm tired and don't think I can do the work justice."

"What samples?"

"I brought back tissue samples from Raleigh. Dr. Evans and I are doing some preliminary research on this particular strain of cholera virus. The docs in Raleigh think it could be a new strain. I did a lot of research on cholera when I was at vet school. In fact, they've asked me to be part of the teams checking the hog operations around here."

"Isn't it dangerous to have that kind of stuff here?"

"Not really. I have it in our walk-in. It's marked with a skull and crossbones so Sylvia can't possibly mistake it for anything else. I only take it out in our sterile room and then destroy any tools or materials I've used. No one except you and Dr. Jeffers, has access to the fridge and you don't look like you want to do cholera research anytime soon," Vicky smiled. "Anyway, things will slow down now, what with the fire and all. Not much left to inspect. I'm just real sorry for Carl."

"What fire?"

"At Carl's. Sorry, I thought I told you. Sometime early this morning Carl's hog sheds, his storage shed, his office, everything burned down. He got a call from the fire department and got to the sheds within a matter of minutes, but by then his whole operation was up in flames."

"You think somebody set the fire on purpose?"

"I don't know. Could be. Somebody might be afraid of being connected to Carl. Sheriff in Sessions County is on it."

"That guy really has had bad luck."

"Actually this may be good luck."

"How come?" Lana asked.

"Insurance covers the fire, but I'm not so sure that if the state burned the place down because of the cholera, that he'd be covered."

"Would they have burned everything, office included?"

"Maybe, but if the state did it, they would have spared his records. Now they're all lost. I hope he has copies, plus I hope he has a lawyer."

"Why would Carl . . . ?" Lana said, then answered her own unfinished question. "Gottcha. You mean for the insurance money?"

"Right," Vicky said. "Ah, well, life goes on. Speaking of which, I start a new artificial breeding program at Martin Farms in a few weeks. Meaning we've finally got a client we can bill and be sure of collecting from."

"And don't you worry about that," Lana said, "Martin Farms is one client that will get billed fully and promptly." Lana turned off her computer. "But just out of curiosity, I thought all Martin Farms operations were off-limits until notified otherwise."

"Only the ones in Sessions County," Vicky said. "The quarantine is for Carl's farm and any farm within five miles. Martin Farms has a few contract feeders over there, but no farrowing operations. The work I'll be doing is in the farrowing sheds and nurseries. Martin has set up sterile nurseries at each facility. We're trying to breed clean pigs in order to create a more efficient farrowing operation. It's all pretty complicated, and," she smiled, "expensive to do.

"DEHNR and USDA are still around," she went on. "But our program won't involve anything that poses a threat. We won't be transporting pigs for a while. Anyway, Oris is anxious to move ahead. He has a bunch of contractors to keep supplied with feeders, so he wants to proceed as fast as possible. The delay is, or has been, with the state and Federal boys; they're making sure no signs of cholera are around before they'll let any pigs be moved. Anyway, by the time we're finished, the transportation ban will probably be lifted."

Lana looked at her watch and then glanced out the windows in the waiting room.

"Let me guess. Dinner?" Vicky said.

Lana smiled and shrugged her shoulders.

"Well, have fun. Where you going?"

"Cody's."

"Too bad. I wish my cheapskate dates would spring for a good place occasionally." She smiled and winked. "Tell Will I said hello."

—✦ ✦ ✦—

Will was late. "I'm sorry, Lana, but I had to edit a speech, and I didn't finish until thirty minutes ago."

"That's okay. Vicky just left."

She smiled as Will held the car door open. "This is quite a treat. I think Vicky's jealous. She says her dates don't spring for something as nice as Cody's and I told her she needed to upgrade her dates. Maybe you could help."

Will laughed, "I'll think about it."

—✦ ✦ ✦—

Their table was, as he had requested, at the far end of the restaurant. It had a beautiful view across a lake lined with cypress trees. They sat next to the bay window at the south end of the room so they could see the failing sunlight reflected off the glassy water and against the pines and cypress trees lining it. A large flock of Canada geese, having already eaten their fill of corn in the fields to the north, flew over the restaurant and landed far out on the dark gray water.

Will ordered a bottle of chardonnay and for a long time they didn't speak, only watched the gradual close of day. Their silence felt open and relaxed, allowing them to drink the cool chardonnay without the temptation to say something trite and pointless.

As the light disappeared, Lana looked over at Will. "So, now that we've had a little wine, watched a beautiful sunset, and resisted tripping down memory lane, let's talk some trash. What's up in Hogg County, Deputy?"

Will smiled. "Actually, I was going to ask you the same thing. What's the juicy gossip from Vet Land?"

"Nothing much," Lana said, "Just the cholera scare in Sessions County, and I told you about that."

Will nodded, so Lana continued.

"The state agriculture guys are hysterical, but the farmers seem pretty calm. Of course, no one wants cholera, but everybody seems convinced that it was just an isolated case. Vicky Newell has been talking to the doctors in Raleigh about how it could have occurred and what to do. Who knows? Oh, here's some news. I found out a few hours ago that Carl Ross's feeder sheds and office burned down, raising the obvious questions of how and why—and who."

"Who told you that?"

"Vicky. She said that sometime early this morning Carl's whole operation went up in smoke. He's afraid the insurance company will think he did it. Probably with good reason. Vicky thinks somebody might have been trying to eliminate their connection with Carl. It's so tragic. He's had so much on him. Poor man."

"Actually, I heard there was a fire, but I didn't pick up on it being at Carl's. Anybody hurt?"

"Not that I know of."

Will looked out the window, then back at Lana. "Do you know if Carl saw or heard anything? Did . . . ? Never mind, I'll call Sheriff Wilson tomorrow." Will poured himself another glass of the chardonnay, then re-filled Lana's glass.

"Anyway, as soon as we can, Vicky says we're starting an artificial insemination project at Martin Farms. This could be a big deal for us. We might even become known as the veterinarians who created the super herd . . . the swine from Krypton!"

Will signaled to the waiter for menus. "What do you mean by 'super-herd'?"

"I mean," Lana said, "that Oris is trying to breed a strain of super pigs. He got twenty or thirty boars from some company in Germany—must be 'Aryan' pigs that have superior market traits: longer bodies, leaner profiles, faster weight gain, that sort of thing. He wants to breed them to the same species of gilts, virgin sows, at his farrowing operations. What he eventually wants is not only pigs with better market traits, but a herd of disease-free breeders. Animals raised in a sterile environment without any of the bad bugs. No bad bugs means they can't pass on any. Their litters are bigger, healthier, and have less shrinkage."

"Less shrinkage?"

"Less mortality in the litter," Lana said. "Or, to quote Dr. Newell, 'fewer dead pigs.' It seems that swine mortality at the nursery level is fairly high in most operations. It's usually from things that are fairly benign, like scours or influenza, but sometimes they get something really scary, like this hog cholera possibility. It can wipe out an operation in days. Since pigs in these new mega operations are raised so close together and in such large numbers, any airborne disease, like hog cholera, spreads like wildfire. Just like at poor Carl Ross's. That's why farmers usually try to cover it up at the first sign, by getting rid of any sickies before they become acute."

Will pursed his lips and leaned back.

"Vicky says burying the dead pigs before anybody can see them doesn't always work because the virus can still be on the ground. They're not supposed to bury the pigs without notifying a vet, but good luck on that! Anyway, it looks like Carl Ross is out of business.

"Vicky says his insurance will probably pay for a lot, but she doesn't know if he's got the heart to start all over again. I kind of know how he feels." She stopped talking and turned to look out the window. She reached for the wine but Will was already holding it up to pour her some.

"Thank you," she said, looking at him. "And thank you for inviting me out to dinner. It's been a while! Paul and I came here a few times just before . . ." She took a sip of wine and pressed her lips together. "We . . . sorry."

Will said nothing, just sipped.

After a minute Lana looked up from her glass and smiled. "You know, it's funny how the mind works. One minute you're tripping along thinking about your job or schedule or just, you know, errands and stuff, and all of a sudden this terrible pressure surrounds you and grips you until you almost can't breathe. You think, this can't be true, this can't be my life. But it is. Everything's gone. Yesterday seems like it never happened and tomorrow vague and like it will never come." She sat there shaking her head in small quick movements, her lips pressed together.

Will gently put his hand over hers. "Shhhh. You're okay. You're with someone who feels your loss almost as much as you do. I do know the feeling you're talking about."

She looked at him and nodded. "I'm glad you understand."

Will smiled and picked up his menu. "Okay, down to business. I hear the sirloin steak with Portobello mushrooms is sensational."

—✦ ✦ ✦—

The ride home seemed quicker. Will pulled up in front of Lana's house and stopped at the bottom of the front steps. He started to get out.

"That's okay, Will, I can manage, but I appreciate the gentlemanly gesture."

Will smiled and leaned over to give her a kiss before she opened her door. "You know me, Mr. Gallant."

Lana smiled and kissed him warmly on the lips, then again. "Yes, I know you, Mr. Moser. You are a gentleman and a friend. My very best friend. I . . ." She stopped speaking.

"I, what?" Will said.

"Uhm, I just want to thank you for a wonderful dinner, and evening, and . . ." She shook her head slightly, "and everything else." She opened the door and got out. Will waited until she opened the front door. When she did, she turned around and blew him a kiss. He waved, blew her a kiss, then he slowly drove onto Roanoke Street and toward home.

—✦ ✦ ✦—

Except for the backyard light and the municipal street lights on Roanoke Street, her house was dark inside and out. She hadn't been home since leaving for work that morning. Lana took her keys out and flipped through the ring for the right one. The front door swung open easily.

She turned left and found the switch for the front hall light. It didn't come on. She moved it up and down. Still no light. How strange, she distinctly remembered the light working last night. She pushed up the switch for the front porch light. Again nothing. Both lights burned out at the same time? Lana walked onto the front porch and looked to her right, toward Mrs. Maynard's. Lights were on both inside and outside her house. The same for the houses on the left and across the street.

She went back inside and found the light switch for the living room. Again nothing. There hadn't been a thunderstorm, so she must have blown a fuse or a circuit breaker. She wished she'd let Will walk her inside. So much for being the independent sort. Where was her flashlight? Upstairs, of course, on the bedside table.

Lana was not normally afraid of being alone, but now she stood in the hallway and looked up the stairs into the dark hall, with, she knew, a very dark room at the end. She recalled the freezer at Pine Bluff, and a chill crept over her. Her breathing raced, becoming shallow. She left the front door standing open on the vague promise of providing an escape route and a tad of light. She climbed the stairs to her bedroom, chuckling at how far her imagination had taken her.

But halfway up the stairs, as she was in mid-stride, she heard a door close. Her head jerked to the right and downward to where she thought the noise came from. The kitchen, it was in the kitchen, or the dining room. Now she stopped breathing, her foot poised to gain the next stair. Heat replaced the chill of moments before. She gasped, having to work at getting air into her lungs. Suddenly she was racing up the stairs and down the hall. She grabbed the door frame of her room and slung herself into the blackness. Her eyes blinked repeatedly until she finally processed the small amount of light coming into her windows from the street light out front. She pulled herself along the bed to the nightstand and the flashlight.

Where is that damn thing. It's not in the drawer. Goddammit. What did I do with it?

She felt it at the back of the drawer. She took it out and started to turn it on. What if someone is in the hall? What if . . . ?

She took two steps to her left, felt for the dresser then slowly opened the top drawer. She felt the rough-knurled handle of the .357 magnum lying on a pair of Paul's socks. She took it out of the drawer and, holding it in wildly shaking hands, backed toward the window and the light from the backyard. She tilted the gun down so she could see the cylinder. It was loaded. She tried again to slow her breathing but imagined it could be heard in Sessions County by now.

Deep breaths, Lana. Breathe through your mouth. Slowly, more slowly.

She listened for any new sounds of movement in the house. Maybe what she had heard was the wind blowing something closed. Yes, except there was no wind tonight. Maybe the front door being open had created a type of vacuum, thus pulling some door at the back of the house closed.

Call Will. The phone is right there, call him. And say what? That you thought you heard something. Come save me from the wind. No way. Use the flashlight. Go check the circuit box.

—◆ ◆ ◆—

Lana turned on the flashlight. Shining it on the floor, she started toward the door when it occurred to her that maybe something was out of place in the room. Maybe someone was here. With her back toward the dresser and the gun held chest high, she moved the light slowly across the room. Everything seemed in place; the door to the bathroom was open and nothing inside seemed disturbed. The closet door was as she remembered it that morning. Her nerves began to gather themselves. Shoes where they belonged. Laundry was piled on the floor beside the bathroom door. Her chair was pulled out from her desk. Nowhere else to hide. She shined the light under the bed, just in case.

Okay, nobody here so . . .

Open mouthed, Lana began to take short shallow breaths.

What was that on the desk? What was sticking up in the middle of her desk?

She focused light on the papers and books scattered about. *Maybe it was her pen set that . . . no, her pen set was at the back of the desk.*

She inched away from the dresser and slowly moved toward the desk, stopping every few feet to flash the light around the room and listen for strange noises. When she got to the foot of the bed near the open doorway, she leaned out and pushed the door shut, then quickly turned the deadbolt to secure it.

Leaning against the back of the locked door, she tried to calm herself. Her throat felt like it was beginning to close. She could hardly breathe. Sweat poured down her face. She squinted at the object. A knife!

A hunting knife, one of the folding kind. A large pocket knife. She squinted her eyes. Something was around the knife or impaled by the knife. It was a cloth or fabric. What was it . . . ?

A pair of her underpants. The knife was stuck through a pair of her underwear and into the desk.

She moved closer and shined the light on the desk. A large pocket knife was stuck through her underwear, into a memo pad from the office, and then into the wooden desk.

A pair of her underpants from the pile of dirty clothes had a knife jabbed through them. Who would do such a thing? Why?

She could feel her heart pounding in her throat and temples.

She reached out to pull the knife from the desk then suddenly pulled her hand back. There was something smeared on her pants. She carefully lifted them and saw that they had been soaked in the crotch with red paint or dye, maybe even blood. She let them drop and felt her stomach begin to contract. She felt sick. Her chest began to throb, she felt dizzy, and finally she vomited on the floor while backing toward the bed.

Jesus, Lana. Bloody pants on a knife in your bedroom! Who the hell would do something that sick? In my own Goddamn bedroom. Call Will.

She reached for the phone.

"Hello, Moser here."

"Will, you have to come back. Someone was in my house! Maybe still here. I don't know. They, they put a knife . . ."

"Lana, where are you?"

"Upstairs. I'm in my bedroom. I have a gun. I think I heard . . ."

"Stay where you are. Don't move and don't open the door. You do have the door locked, right?"

"Yes."

"Don't move. I'm on my way."

She heard the siren in what seemed like a few seconds, certainly not even a minute. Before she got to the bedroom door Will's car skidded into her drive and he was out of the car and racing up the stairs.

"Lana, it's me. You all right?"

She pulled open the door and without saying anything threw herself into his arms, her gun still gripped in her hand. They stood there clinging to each other for what seemed like an eternity. Will absorbed her sobs and simply stroked her hair. They parted only when another car sped into her driveway and slid to a stop.

"That's probably Robert. I called him on the way over." Will stood back and looked down at her. "You okay? You want to come downstairs with me?" Lana nodded and followed him to the stairs.

"Will, you in here?"

"We're upstairs, Robert. We're coming down." When they got to the bottom of the stairs, Will said, "Robert, give me your flashlight and wait here with Lana." He took the light and walked to the back of the house, his gun in hand. Within a few seconds the lights came on. Lana went to sit in the living room in the large wing chair, the .357 on her lap. Will walked over, kissed her on the forehead, and carefully picked up the gun.

Speaking to the deputy while still looking down at Lana, Will said, "Robert, check the house, then come back in here. And Robert, be very careful not to disturb anything, especially in Lana's room upstairs."

"Right."

While Robert was inspecting the house, Lana recounted exactly what had happened from the time Will dropped her off until she called. Will didn't ask any questions, rather he just let her get everything off her chest. She seemed surprisingly calm, considering what had just happened.

Robert came back. "Will, everything looks normal except, of course, Lana's bedroom. You need to go up and take a look."

Will looked at Lana and said, "That okay with you? Mind if I leave for a second?"

Lana looked up at him, "Not if you let Robert stay here."

"He's not going anywhere."

Will left the room and Robert stood at the door. After a while, Will came back into the room.

"Robert, I want you to take some pictures then close the door to Lana's room. We'll go over it with a fine-tooth comb tomorrow. I'm taking her to my house for tonight," He looked at her, "Okay with you?"

"You're not gonna get any argument from me."

Robert went out to his car to get his camera and Will put his hand out to Lana. "Let me get a few things," she said.

"Okay, but don't touch anything in your room that you don't have to, okay?"

"Okay."

—✦ ✦ ✦—

Will handed Lana a short glass of bourbon and poured himself one as he sat beside her at his kitchen table. "You want to talk about it?" He said.

Lana took a sip and looked at him. She took a few deep breaths before speaking. "Okay, Deputy, fire away."

"Just tell me what you think. Start with who and why, if you can."

"Who, probably Eugene Winslow or Weldon. Why, because I guess they think I was trespassing at Pine Bluff."

Will stared at her, his glass suspended between the table and his mouth. Lana took another drink and said, "Well, you asked."

He took a sip and put his glass down. "I did. So, did you go out there?"

"Yes."

"Why?"

"Because I hadn't been before and I thought that I might find something or feel something. I don't know, I wanted to go." She took another sip. "I told you I wanted to go out there. It shouldn't be any big surprise."

"I guess it isn't a surprise, but that doesn't mean I'm not disappointed. You told me you wouldn't go out there."

"No, I didn't. You said not to go. I didn't say anything."

Will looked into his glass and slowly poured in some more. "You want a splash?"

"Please." They sat for a while and didn't say anything. After a while Lana looked up. "Will, it was stupid. You were right. I don't know, I just needed to go. I won't do anything that dumb again. I'm sorry."

Will watched her speak. There was no point in getting mad. She knew. Better to find out why she thought Popper or Weldon may have taken the risk to come into her house and scare her.

"Okay, what happened?"

It took her about ten minutes to tell him the whole story, including what she was thinking and how scared she was. When she finished, Will made sure to let everything sink in before he spoke.

"So, you think they probably found the pad you dropped in the freezer and figured somebody was out there. Why you? Why not Vicky or Carter?"

"Vicky or Carter wouldn't be sneaking out there on a Sunday, and even if they did, they wouldn't be in the freezer. Besides, I'm the one who cares enough to take that chance. Popper found the freezer open when I was there, but when I left I know I locked it, and locked it with a piece of wood just like he did. Look, I don't know how they thought it was me.

"I don't know if it was them that broke in here. You asked what seemed the most logical. So, here's what seems logical. One, I know I left the freezer closed. Two, I know I didn't pick up the pad after I used it to open the door. Three, I'm guessing they probably found the pad on the floor. Four, I'm assuming they discarded the docs as their off-hour visitors. Five, I know that someone put a knife through my underwear and stuck it into a memo pad from the office just like the one I used at Pine Bluff. Where do you come out?"

Will nodded. "The same place you do. The question is do we have any proof that can tie them to the break-in. The answer is that we aren't going to know that until we take prints and investigate your room and house. I'm not counting on finding anything, but you never know." He paused. "If it was Popper, then he's mighty nervous about something."

"What?" Lana said.

"A bunch of things. I don't have any hard proof, but I have some ideas."

"You gonna share with me?" Will looked at her for a moment. "Not yet, but soon. Right now you need some sleep. I think the guest room is made . . ."

She shook her head, "Bullshit. You're not sticking me in some other room. I just hope you don't snore."

17.

As he struggled to move the last of the hogs off the livestock trucks and into his feeding sheds, Wallace kept his eyes on the mountain of dark gray and black clouds moving toward his farm. Even more concerning was the oily green light reflecting off the darkening sky, for this was the sign of a nascent tornado. November was a dangerous time—the end of hurricane season but the beginning of the fall northeaster season. A cold front banging into warm air from the Gulf meant trouble. He hoped he could get all the new pigs settled before the storm hit.

On his first day with a new group of pigs after the awful storm in August, Wallace couldn't believe that another storm was coming. Please God let it be a short one.

The last Martin Farms delivery truck was pulling into the turnaround in front of his third shed. He raced out into the dust-laden wind and motioned the truck toward the loading doors. "About ten more feet!" Wallace yelled to the driver. "Keep coming, keep coming, okay stop!" The truck's air brakes wheezed and the driver cut the diesel motor.

"Open the doors and put the ramps in place," the driver yelled as he got out of the semi's cab. "I'll start 'em out once you're ready."

Wallace raced into the shed and gripped the side of the ramp. He wished Buford, his part-time helper, was here. There hadn't been anything to do over the past month, so Buford had gotten a job on a farm down the road.

Wallace bent down, keeping his back straight, and then stood up with what little power he had left in his legs. Lifting the metal ramp was about all he could do. He glanced back toward the trailer, wondering how he was ever going to get the ramp in place.

"Need a hand?" He couldn't look around, but recognized Eugene Winslow's voice immediately.

"Yes sir, Mr. Winslow, I surely do." He smiled over his left shoulder as Popper grabbed hold of the other side of the heavy metal ramp.

"Oris told me," Popper yelled, "that he was sending you a load of pigs. I came by to congratulate you and see if I could help. Looks like I got here a little late."

"No sir, Mr. Winslow, you got here just in time. I handled these things for the first few loads, but 'bout now they're gettin' mighty heavy."

Wallace and Popper dropped the ramp's metal hooks into the slots on the back of the truck. As soon as they were sure that everything was stable, Wallace waved to the driver to begin moving the pigs out. The immature feeder hogs started down the metal ramp, their hooves tapping a nervous beat on the rough steel. They passed through the outside doors and down the hundred-foot-long center aisle of the shed.

Even though the overhead lights were on, it was gloomy in the facility. The approaching storm had plunged the farm into darkness; plus, in anticipation of the wind, Wallace had already dropped the plastic side panels to protect the pigs from the weather. Pigeons fluttered out of the way as the young feeders trotted down the center aisle. All he needed was another twenty minutes.

Popper stood at the far end of the feeding facility making sure the proper number of pigs went into each holding pen. When each pen had the right number, he closed the gate and moved to the next one. They worked rapidly until the last of the pigs were penned.

The rain started just as the truck pulled out of the feedlot yard and toward the paved road. The wind and water battered the farm for about thirty minutes, then slowly moved north to blow and rattle other farms and farmers. Wallace and Eugene came out of the office trailer next to the feed room and looked around the now-muddy feed lot. The lagoon was fine; the sheds were all secure, side panels in place, and none of the new pigs seemed particularly agitated.

Wallace let out a huge sigh of relief. "Thank you, Mr. Winslow. I was kind of nervous. I wanted to be sure everything went just right. Buford that used to help me got another job when I couldn't pay him, what with the lagoon problem and all. I was about tuckered out hauling that big metal ramp all over the place." He was relieved, and it showed on his face. Laugh lines reached up to meet the smiling crow's feet beside his blue eyes, and his straight white teeth shone in the changing afternoon light.

The weather channel predicted more storms for the evening, but at least the first test was over, and Wallace's new hogs were safely in their proper places.

"Wallace, you did a good job, Son, congratulations." Popper had his right arm around Wallace's shoulder and was patting him on his chest with his left hand.

Then Popper winked his eye and said, "This calls for a celebration. What say we go over to Lolly's and have us a little drink?"

Wallace was all smiles. He was back in the pig business and the world was looking up. "I'd love to go with you to Lolly's, Mr. Winslow," Wallace beamed. "Thanks."

"Okay," Popper said, "I need to pick something up at Rufus Austin's, then I'll be right over."

Wallace nodded and replied, "Well, I gotta make sure everything's okay here; so, I reckon I'll be a little while myself."

—✦ ✦ ✦—

Albert Lolly had bought the old Kriner place over twenty years ago. What had been an infamous liquor house became a more respectable restaurant and beer bar. The clientele were farmers and average folks from around Mussel Ford. The food was country and the service the same . . . waitresses who popped gum and called everybody "Hon."

Albert had installed a rooftop neon sign that proclaimed "Lolly's Pop" in two-foot-high iridescent blue letters. It was a kind of inside joke since Albert called bottles of beer "pop". Oris, Rufus, Charlie, and Eugene were regulars, as was Ernie and to a lesser extent Will. It was a good place to find out what was going on in Hogg County. If you wanted to have an ear to the ground, Lolly's was the place to put it down.

Wallace, even though he was over thirty, had never been a regular at Lolly's. He had a hard time keeping up with the conversations, and always felt that the regulars were laughing at him in some way. It wasn't that he didn't like the place, only that he never felt comfortable going there alone. When he did, he would usually end up listening in on everybody else's conversation and then leaving the way he'd come . . . alone. But tonight was different; tonight he'd been invited to join Eugene Winslow and his buddies for a few beers—the perfect ending to a hard but successful day. He checked the locks on the last hog shed then headed for the office. As he shuffled across the windy parking lot, Wallace smiled to himself and started to sing a few lines from a Waylon Jennings song. "Let's go to Lukenbach, Texas, with Waylon, Willie, and the boys . . ." He shook his head, then laughed aloud.

—◆ ◆ ◆—

Wallace pulled into the dirt and gravel parking lot at Lolly's and looked for Popper's black Ford pickup with the row of yellow running lights up top. It was parked right next to the front door. In fact, the huge dualie took up two full spaces.

He parked his blue Chevy behind Popper's truck, turned off the engine, and stepped out into the humid, breezy night. The wind blew an empty cigarette pack across the hood of his truck and some oak leaves onto his front seat. The air smelled like approaching rain and the sound of distant thunder ricocheted off the doors and windows of Lolly's. Lyrics from a Dolly Parton song squeezed through the cracks on either side of the front door and rode the wind to the cars and trucks beyond. Wallace smelled his armpits and blew into his hands to make sure his breath was okay, then adjusted his John Deere cap and brushed off his jeans.

The inside of Lolly's was noisy and full of smoke. Dolly Parton was ending her plaintive ballad and the accumulated conversations of the Friday-night crowd surged. Wallace squinted through the haze at the neon beer signs on the wall behind the bar. Rachel Chambers, the manager, leaned across the bar and with a mighty laugh kissed Dewitt Tompkins on the lips. Dewitt turned two shades of red and almost fell off his barstool. He was a shy man, not given to loud talking or public displays of emotion, so the kiss was all the more hilarious to the regular crowd. In all probability, somebody put Rachel up to it.

"Wallace. Wallace May, over here."

Wallace turned to his right and spotted Popper sitting at a table with Rufus Austin and a man he didn't recognize. Popper motioned to Wallace to join them. He smiled and slowly walked toward the men sitting around the red Formica and steel table.

"Hey, Mr. Winslow. Thanks for invitin' me. Hey, Mr. Austin. Good to see you." Wallace looked at the other man and nodded, not holding his gaze too long.

"Wallace, this is Bill Cheany. He's the Caterpillar rep for

these parts. I been thinking about trading my old D-8 and gettin' a new one." Eugene turned to Bill.

"Wallace May is the best 'dozer driver in these parts, Bill. I'll put him up against anybody you boys can think of."

Bill looked up and put out his hand, "Good to meet ya, Wallace. I'm always glad to know a pro."

Wallace took his hand and smiled. "Good to meet you too, Mr. Cheany, but I reckon that they might be somebody better."

"I doubt that, Wallace," Bill replied. "If Eugene says you're the best, then you're the best."

Wallace nodded and sat down. After a few minutes Weldon Goins came in and pulled up a chair. He patted Wallace on the back and said, "Hey, buddy, hear you got a feedlot full of hogs. Way to go."

Wallace looked up and smiled, then looked around the room to see if anybody else heard what Weldon had said.

It didn't take long for the table to be covered with empty beer bottles. Popper found out what everybody liked and kept 'em coming. Wallace ordered a Miller Lite, but Popper said, "Aw, bullshit, Wallace. Lite is for pussies. You need a regular Bud. This is my pay, so you got to drink what I say." Wallace wasn't about to argue with him—after all, he was paying for the beer.

Rachel brought a bowl of mixed nuts and another spilling over with hot popcorn. Somewhere along the line Popper ordered a couple of plates of baby back ribs and some hush puppies. New beers showed up almost before the old ones were finished. Everybody was laughing and talking at the same time. They went from farm prices to the cost of new equipment to politics.

"D'you read 'bout what ole Wiley Hoots did the other day in Washington?" Rufus yelled. "Sombitch tole that commie asshole in Cuba to kiss his butt. We ain't taken his convicts, so stop sendin' 'em over! Goddamn Wiley's a sure-fire 'Murcan.' " Everybody nodded and agreed that Wiley Hoots, the senior senator from North Carolina, a Republican, was certainly a true American.

Wallace pounded his fist on the table and hollered, "Damn straight."

Popper leaned back and through cold-sober eyes studied Wallace's reactions. He watched him drink his beer to see if he was spilling any. He studied how long and how direct a route the bottle took to his mouth, and he watched to see if Wallace would occasionally close his eyes for longer than a blink. Popper reckoned that Wallace had already drunk seven or eight beers; it was time for him to be getting sleepy. Popper noticed a couple of guys leave Lolly's only to come running back in soaked from the rain.

"Must be a nasty night out," Popper mused. "Holy shit, it's eleven o'clock. My ole lady's gonna kick my ass." Everybody laughed.

"Yeah, me too," Rufus chimed in.

"Not me," Bill said. "My ole lady's asleep in Raleigh and has no fuckin' idea where I am." The usual suspects slapped their legs and laughed again.

Wallace lived alone in a house given to him by his uncle John. It was a small but attractive place about a mile or so from Wallace's hog pens, a place originally built for one of John Keaton's farm managers. Wallace had decided that he'd never find a wife if he still lived with his mother; so, just after he bought the property from John, he moved into his own place.

"Yeah, I'm getting kinda sleepy myself," added Wallace. "I reckon I'll git on home, too." Wallace was as drunk as he'd ever been. He usually had one or two beers when he came to Lolly's, but tonight he'd had a lot more than that.

Popper and Rufus pushed up from the table and, after getting their bearings, headed toward the front door.

"See you boys!" Popper yelled to Wallace and Bill. "Don't close the place down. Tomorrow's a workday, Wallace." He waved and walked out into the wind and rain.

Bill Cheany and Wallace were still sitting at the table, laughing and licking their fingers after dragging them through the barbecue sauce from the ribs.

"Wallace, I gotta go," Bill said getting to his feet. "It was good to meet ya." He stuck out his hand and Wallace took hold as he got to his feet.

"Good to meet you, too, Bill," Wallace replied, then patted him on the back and waved to Rachel. "See ya, Rachel. Have a night!" He chuckled to himself as he stumbled toward the front door. The rain hit him in the face like a cold slap. He shuddered and pulled up the collar of his jean jacket. "Jesush, what cruppy weather."

When he finally located and got into his truck, Wallace fumbled for the handkerchief in his back pocket. After wiping the water from his eyes, he gazed intently at his key chain to find the right key, then aimed it toward the ignition switch.

The truck started with a roar, made louder and longer by Wallace's heavy foot. Looking over his right shoulder, Wallace slowly eased back into the open space behind him. He again pressed the brake and shifted into drive. He never was sure which drive to use. He knew that the D with the circle around it was for big roads, and the plain D was for little roads, but who was to say which road was big and which was little?

Wallace looked both ways and then pulled out onto the blacktop. The rain was coming down so hard he could barely see past his low beams. He leaned forward on the wet seat with both hands gripping the top quarter of the steering wheel, and squinting to see the road.

Just go slow, Wallace. You only got a few miles to home. Make sure you stay inna road.

After about a mile, the rain slacked and the wind seemed to shift to the west and die down a bit. Wallace flipped on his high beams and felt some confidence return. He was only a few miles from Mitchell Creek and then only a few hundred yards from his turn-off.

What a great night. Them fellas were real nice and I . . .

Headlights flashed in his rear-view mirror. They got closer and brighter until Wallace couldn't see without moving his head.

Damn guy. Put yer lights on low, you dumb bunny.

The car or truck moved to within a few feet of Wallace's rear bumper. He glanced in the mirror to see if he could tell who it was. It was too dark, and the rain made everything look blurry.

Looks like a truck . . . lights on the roof. So bright. Who are you?

Wallace found the brake pedal and slowly depressed it. Maybe they would go around him if he slowed down. No such luck. The truck slowed down, too, then moved back so that its lights were full in his mirror.

"What the hell is goin' on? What do you want?" Wallace yelled into the mirror. He took his foot off the brake and jammed it down on the accelerator.

Maybe I can leave 'em. I'll turn in at my house and they'll go away.

The truck in the mirror accelerated right along with Wallace. Wallace went sixty; the truck went sixty. Wallace went seventy; the truck went seventy.

"Leave me alone!" Wallace screamed. "Go away!" He started to cry.

This wasn't supposed to happen . . . not tonight.

He felt a jolt and then another. The truck was so close that it'd bumped him! Not hard enough to damage his truck but enough to make sure he knew they were still there.

Wallace wiped the tears out of his eyes with his sleeve then turned around and yelled at the speeding vehicle, "Stop hitting me. Go away. I don' wanna play."

As he leaned left over the back seat yelling at the mysterious truck behind him, his right foot pressed down on the accelerator. It was a natural reaction; the torque of his body forced his weight to his feet.

He turned back around, his eyes wide with fright and desperation. The front windshield was blurred with the sweep of his wipers, and the haloed yellow lights from the guard rail reflectors confused and disoriented him.

Wallace didn't realize that his truck had left the road and was hurling through the air until the noise inside the cab changed. Everything was quiet except for the roar of the motor pulling against thin air. He sat frozen at the wheel, understanding at last what had happened.

He thought about his new pigs; about how proud his dad would have been that he had his own farm, and he thought about his mom, Cornelia.

The huge cypress tree at the bottom of the creek embankment only registered with him as the front of his truck slammed into it at over seventy miles an hour.

Death put its arms around Wallace May quickly and without prejudice. At long last he was at rest.

—✦ ✦ ✦—

"Base to unit two. Base to unit two. Come in, Major Moser. Please respond."

Will ran back to his car. Two trucks from Duke Power had just arrived, and the men had already replaced Will's flares with flashing lights. There was no longer any reason for him to stand outside in the rain waving cars away from the downed power lines. He opened the driver's side door and quickly slid behind the wheel. The dispatcher came on again. "Base to unit two. Please . . ."

Will picked up the hand mike and answered. "This is two. Go ahead, base."

"Will, we've had a call from an individual reporting an accident on Mitchell Creek Road. Only one vehicle involved. Reported as a dark-blue late-model Chevy pickup, license number alpha, romeo, tango, one, one, three, niner. Vehicle registered to a Mr. Wallace Keaton May."

Will closed his eyes and swore. "Goddammit. Goddammit. What the hell, Wallace?"

"Anyone on the scene at present?" he asked.

"Negative . . . at least not at the time of the report. Individual made the call from a pay phone located at Albert Lolly's place. He . . ."

"How many people in the truck, base?" Will started the patrol car.

"The caller saw only one, Will. He reported going down the embankment in order to turn off the vehicle's ignition. Sounds like Wallace was in the truck by himself." The radio went silent. "Will? Major . . ."

"I'm here, base. Did the caller give an opinion about whether the subject was alive or dead?"

"The caller said he thought the subject was dead."

Will shook his head.

"Subject was headed south on Mitchell Creek Road," the dispatcher continued.

"It looks like the truck went off the road about fifty to a hundred yards from the bridge. It hit a big cypress tree head on. The truck's totaled. We've dispatched an emergency vehicle from County Hospital."

Will pulled into the middle of Highway 261 with his emergency lights flashing and his siren on. "Base," Will replied, his voice cracking, "I am approximately five miles from subject. Any other units in immediate area?"

"Negative, two. You're the closest."

"Unit two in route. ETA five minutes or less." Will threw down the mike and gripped the wheel til his knuckles turned white. It was just past midnight and the roads were empty.

—◆ ◆ ◆—

The rain was falling harder as Will parked on the side of the road above Wallace's truck, stepped through the shattered guardrail, and hurried down the muddy embankment as fast as his gimpy hip would allow.

Son-of-a-bitch, Wallace, what the hell has happened to you, Son?

The pulsating blue-and-white light from the top of the patrol car flashed against the mangled blue truck, giving it a spectral quality, while the reflected light from Will's headlights bathed the whole tragic scene in an eerie white glow.

Will shined his Maglite on the steaming wreck and slowly approached the driver's side door. The engine block was pushed diagonally into the cab on the passenger side. At first glance, Will thought that perhaps Wallace could have survived. He reached inside the cab and felt for the carotid artery on the side of Wallace's neck. No pulse. He looked at Wallace's blood-matted hair and contorted body and felt sick.

—✦ ✦ ✦—

"Captain. Captain Moser." Lieutenant Pratt was fifty yards down the road, yelling through the monsoon. "Captain, my RTO's dead. I can't call fire support, Captain!"

Will Moser looked away from the wrecked truck and into the night. The wind blew his wet hair back, and the rain stung his face. He remembered. He remembered the rain, the wreck, and Specialist James. He remembered the convoy on the road to Swan Loc.

Carne. Come on man, talk to me. No answer. Specialist James was dead. The monsoon had hit them before they could get out of the rubber plantation. A mine had blown the jeep backward into a ditch at the side of the road. Will had checked on Carne, but it was too late. Shrapnel through his helmet. Will's legs hurt. They were like weights pulling him down. Who was that yelling?

"Captain. Are you all right? Will!" It was Lieutenant Pratt, but where was he?

"Lieutenant! Tom," he heard himself yelling. "How many men you got? How many can shoot?"

"We're okay. I got six shooters. RTO's dead. We're getting fire from the sheds a hundred meters out. Looks like gooks at nine o'clock."

Will looked to his right, out into the rubber trees. There were four or five small buildings scattered about in a clearing seventy-five or hundred meters from his position. He could see muzzle flashes coming from all the buildings.

"Tom, keep 'em out there. I'll see if my radio works." *Will crawled over to the jeep but saw in an instant that the radio was destroyed.* Shit. I hope battalion's got this.

"Lieutenant, the radio's out. Keep . . ." *The wind was drowning him out. He knew Lieutenant Pratt couldn't hear him. He could barely hear himself. Will found his M-16 and crawled into the ditch.* Okay, Will, at least help out. *He aimed at the flashes coming from the near shed . . . nothing. The rifle was so caked in mud and slime that it wouldn't shoot. He pulled his .45 out of his shoulder holster.* We're in big fucking trouble now. I hate this fucking gun.

Men started running out of the buildings toward Lieutenant Pratt, who was firing everything he had. Will saw V.C. moving to the left. He fired until his hammer locked back. They didn't even notice him. He put another clip into his pistol and tried to steady his aim. Goddamn rain. Can't see shit. Easy, Will. Take your time. *He fired at the lead soldier.* Did ya get him, Will? *He wiped his eyes with his sleeve.* Goddamn water.

The V.C. soldier fired at Lieutenant Pratt. Will watched Tom's head jerk back.

You sons-of-bitches. *He was on a knee firing at the shadows as they closed in on his men.* "Lieutenant!"

—✦ ✦ ✦—

"Major. Major Moser."

Will shook his head and looked up at the EMS driver standing on the road above him.

"What's the truck look like, Major? Do we need the Jaws?"

Will paused to get his bearings and then yelled back. "I don't think so, Ronnie. The driver's side door is functional. The problem's Wallace. I can't find a pulse. I think he's gone. You better come see for yourself, though."

Will knew EMS wouldn't find any signs of life, but no reason for him to play doctor with people around who knew what they were doing. Will shined his light back into the cab of the truck.

Wallace's neck must be broken. His body was splayed across the front seat. His left arm was under his chest and his right lay across his stomach. Will moved the light across the seat and floor. Something caught his eye. Shining gray and white under the mag light's beam, it was wedged between the floor mat and the bottom of the door. Will leaned into the truck and picked it up. It was the Clovis point. He groaned.

Resting his forehead on the window frame, Will stared at the flint stone. When he heard the EMS team slogging toward the truck, he raised his head.

"You okay, Will?"

"Yeah, fine." He wiped his eyes with his sleeve and crawled up the bank to his patrol car.

—✦ ✦ ✦—

"Unit two to base."

"This is base. Go ahead, Major."

"Base, EMS is on the scene. What is the status of additional personnel? Also what is status on the wrecker?"

"Sergeant Joyce is almost to your location. Wrecker maybe ten minutes away."

"Roger, base." Will wiped his face with a towel and waited for Sergeant Joyce. Within a few minutes he noticed flashing blue lights in his rearview mirror. He got out of his car and signaled Robert to pull in behind him.

"What's up, Will?"

"It's Wallace May. Truck's totaled and I'm pretty sure he's dead." He looked down at the truck below the road and the EMS personnel working around it. "Unusual behavior for Wallace. Don't think I remember him even getting a speeding ticket."

Will looked back at Robert. "I want this whole area checked out with a magnifying glass. Put some flares up so there's no traffic on the right lane from," Will turned and looked up the road away from the bridge, "say, a hundred yards up there, all the way to the bridge. I want to know if Wallace knew what was about to happen to him."

Robert Joyce nodded and started back to his car.

Will called after him. "Robert, I'm going up the road to Lolly's. The man who reported the accident called from there. Could be somebody there knows somethin'. Maybe somebody saw Wallace go by. Anyway, be thorough. I don't want to miss a thing on this one." Will opened his car door and then turned, "Robert, assume this could be anything from a DUI to a homicide."

Sergeant Joyce stood in the road and stared after the departing patrol car.

18.

Lana looked at the clock beside her bed. Two-thirty in the morning. Who the hell could be ringing her doorbell? She took her gun from under the pillow and put it in the pocket of her bathrobe, then unlocked the bedroom door and leaned over the railing. "Who is it?"

Will shivered as a light breeze blew across Lana's porch. "It's Will, Lana. Turn off the alarm."

She stepped back into the bedroom and deactivated the front alarm. After her recent incident, Will had insisted on installing a security system over her entire house. All of her windows and doors were wired and motion detectors monitored the halls. Lana had never considered a security system necessary but her recent encounter convinced her otherwise. She gathered her robe around her and hurried down the stairs, unlocking and opening the front door. Will was standing in the middle of the doorway wearing a camo hunting jacket over his damp uniform. "Jesus, Will, I hope the other guy looks worse."

Will walked past Lana and headed toward the kitchen. "Mind if we talk in the kitchen? I could really use some hot coffee."

Lana closed the door and followed him down the hall. "No, of course not. You sit down, and I'll fix the coffee."

Will took off his coat and sat at the table in one of the oak ladderback chairs. His shirt was damp from the early-morning rain and he shuddered as he hung his coat on the back of the chair. Lana looked over at him as she started to fill the coffeepot. "Looks like you've had a long night."

Will nodded but didn't speak, then slowly raised his head. "Wallace May is dead. His truck ran off the road at Mitchell Creek bridge. Smashed into a big cypress tree. Based on the distance the truck went, he had to be going over seventy. He probably died on impact."

Lana finished spooning coffee out of the bag and set two coffee mugs on the counter while Will sat with his elbows on the table and stared vacantly out the window. When he finally spoke, his voice was quiet, barely above a whisper.

"It doesn't make any sense. Wallace never drank, at least never got drunk at a place like Lolly's. I talked to some of the folks out there and they said this was the first time in a long time that they remember seeing him there. And clearly the first time with a group of men. They were drinking pretty hard and Wallace was laughing and acting like the life of the party. Something's just not right."

Lana turned around, her eyes fixed on Will's pallid face. "Why do you think that?"

"Because everything points to it. Wallace's past actions don't add up to a simple DUI. I think somebody ran him off the road. I think somebody killed him."

Lana stiffened.

She took a deep breath and slowly exhaled as she watched Will grip his coffee cup in both hands.

"Will, you need to warm up and relax. How long you been up?"

"All night."

"You look like hell and you're going to catch your death. I'll wash and dry those, and bring you some clean things."

Will nodded and slowly got up and walked toward the bathroom in the downstairs hall.

Lana went upstairs and started pulling hangers across the wooden rod in the hall closet across from her bedroom. She took a pair of Paul's worn jeans and a stretched-out cotton sweater from the closet and held them to her nose, then closed the door and walked slowly down the front stairs, her hand nervously gripping and releasing the banister as she went.

Will hung his uniform over the towel bar, and dropped his wet T-shirt and boxers in a pile beside the sink. He put his weight on his left leg and leaned, stooped over, against the porcelain wash basin, his hands on either side. He looked into the mirror above the sink, and slowly rubbed his hand across his face. His bloodshot eyes locked deep into their reflection.

—◆ ◆ ◆—

The casket was open and the pale-gray visage of the young boy stared up into the room. Lana was kneeling beside the grave and weeping. Will, standing ramrod straight in his deputy's uniform, patted her on the back and shoulders. Paul's pale face held them there unmoving.

The body bags were piled two and three deep at the edge of the clearing. Will pulled Lieutenant Pratt's bag off the deuce-and-a-half and carried it to the chopper as if crossing a threshold. It seemed heavy, Tom's body, but then it wasn't him. He'd gone leaving his ride behind.

"Your father's funeral was magnificent, William. There were hundreds of people there, as you would expect. The governor sent his regards and regrets, assuring us that only state business could keep him away. I'm told it was the largest funeral procession eastern North Carolina has ever seen. As his wife, I was very proud."

He closed his eyes and gradually lowered his head. With hands muffling his sobs and the occasional tremor, Will Moser wept.

Lana watched from the hall. Though not intentionally, she didn't breathe for a long time, and it was only when she finally inhaled that Will knew she was standing there. His back straightened, and he put on his MP face . . . calm, resolute, and in control. Slowly he turned to his right and looked at Lana standing in the hall.

"Sorry, it's been a long night." He paused, "Actually, it's been a long couple of months. Tonight was simply another installment . . . but you know all about that."

Lana nodded, and with tears slowly running down her cheeks, she pushed open the bathroom door. Dropping the jeans and sweater to the floor, she put her arms around Will's neck and her head on his shoulder. With the extension of her arms, the red paisley robe opened and her now exposed pale flesh pressed against Will's damp, scarred body.

"I'm sorry, Will. I'm sorry for everything that's making you cry, and for Paul and for my beautiful little Paulie." She wept convulsively, her arms wrapped around his neck in a desperate grip. She shook against him as he enveloped her in his arms and kissed her gently on the neck.

"I'll be all right," Will said. "I'm just having a small meltdown right now. Finding Wallace in that truck was more of a shock than I was prepared for. It brought back so many others. Where does it end? Tonight I stood there beside Wallace's truck holding his head and looking down on that poor young man. A sweeter, more innocent, loving soul never traipsed this earth. Lana, I just . . ."

She loosened her grip and pushed away from him, her streaming eyes searching his face and her index finger pressed against his lips. Without a word, she took him by the hand and led him from the bathroom, into the hall, and up the stairs to the warm-quilted double bed in her room.

Without impatience or impulsiveness, they slid onto the cool sheets and beneath the rumpled quilt comforter. Their arms and legs wrapped around each other, and each breathed in the comfort and security of a lover. Tears continued, finally subsiding. There was no rush, only deliberate and purposeful movement. They kissed, their tongues pressing and darting around the other. Will moved his mouth down her neck, his lips massaging the tensing muscles below her ear and kissing the hollows where her chest and neck joined, his tongue leaving a cool damp print as it moved back and forth.

Lana ran her hands through Will's hair, pressing and pulling rhythmically as he began to suck on her nipples. Her thumbs kneaded the tense knots on his shoulders; her fingernails furrowing the pale flesh of his back. All the while she rubbed her damp pubic hair against him . . . slowly up and back until at last he brought his mouth back to hers.

Will remembered the first time they'd made love. They were seventeen and in her bedroom. Her parents were out for the evening, and they had sneaked back to the house from the movies. It had been awkward, and as with most young lovers, defined by an urgency and clumsiness that left a sense of guilt and inadequacy. It had been over quickly. This time was different. He knew they were grasping each other out of a desperate longing for another human being, for companionship at its most basic level, a sign of warm life. Today, passion served them well.

—✦ ✦ ✦—

Lana lay in Will's embrace and rubbed his arm as the sun started to fill the room. He slowly stroked her breast and stomach. Every few minutes he would turn his head and kiss her.

"Will?" Lana said at last.

"Yeah."

"Will, I've got to tell you something."

"So, tell me." Will said, his eyes closed and his head resting in the down pillow.

Lana sat up in bed and moved slightly to the side.

"No, sit up and look at me."

Will opened his eyes and leaned up on his elbow. "Okay."

Lana blinked a few times then looked away. She rubbed her hand over her mouth and then looked back at Will's chest, then his eyes.

"Will, you remember the time I came to Raleigh almost eleven years ago now?"

"Yeah."

"The time Paul and I had that big fight about his uncles and such? I called you. You, the hot-shot detective of the Raleigh police force?"

"Lana, what are you trying to say?"

She shook her head, "Please, just go with me. I'm trying to tell you something and I want you to remember back then. I want you to be there again."

"I'm sorry. Go on."

"Paul was just impossible. You remember. He was arguing with his family, if that's what you call that back-stabbing bunch, and he was bringing it home to me. You remember?"

"Yes."

"I decided to get out. To go to Raleigh to see my sister. Remember, I called you and said that I was coming and that I wanted to see you."

"I remember."

"It was a wonderful time. You were so nice, so understanding. You gave me my confidence back. You gave me a reason to . . . to believe in myself again. But you also gave me something else. You gave me the most wonderful gift the world has to give. You gave me," her voice cracked. "You gave me a son, Will."

Will didn't move. He stopped breathing and his face went hot, his skin clammy. He didn't need for her to repeat it. He didn't play dumb and say something stupid like "What did you say?" He just stared; first at Lana, then at the picture of Paul, Paulie, Lana, and him that sat on the bedside table. Of course. He had known it all along. There had been so many hints, so many times when down in that part of himself that had no Latin name, no spot on any anatomy chart, the truth revealed itself and he just knew . . . knew that Paulie Reavis was his son, not Paul's.

He didn't know what to do, what to say. He couldn't pretend or suppress anymore. He simply looked at Lana as tears started to form in his eyes and roll down his cheeks. He cried for his lost son, his lost friend, the friend whom he had betrayed, and his lost life with Lana. Perhaps even for his lost opportunity to tell his own father, William, that he had had a grandson.

He moved his legs to the side of the bed and sat next to Lana. He didn't look at her. He didn't ask why she had never said anything. He knew why.

"When you went home. When Paul called and said that he was sorry and that he needed you. Did you know then?"

"Yes. I knew the way a woman knows, knows in her body."

"Did you ever think of, of . . . "

"Of terminating the pregnancy? No. If you remember, I had had a miscarriage a year before. That was another thing that me and Paul had to deal with. I guess I wanted to pretend that when we were back together, after I got home here, that I was really pregnant by him, but I knew it was really you."

Will looked at her. He held her face in his hands. "I'm so sorry. I loved that little boy. You must know that I loved him like a son."

"I know you did. But what has always bothered me, has in fact haunted me, is whether Paul ever knew. I don't think so, but I don't know. I only know that if he did he never let on. He never treated me or Paulie any differently. We were his family and as far as I'm concerned he was ours. Maybe he would have eventually known. I don't know."

Will wiped his eyes. "I'm glad. I'm glad he had the family he deserved. He should've had a friend worth his trust."

Lana patted his arm. "He did have a wonderful friend. What we did in Raleigh was foolish, but all we can do now is understand why we were weak then. I don't want to beat myself up any more, and I don't want you to, either. It happened and it produced a wonderful little boy and a happy father, so let it be. You can't change anything. Besides, I'm the only one that needs to feel any guilt. I let my little boy die."

Will put his hand over her mouth. "Stop. You know that's not true. Boys become young men. Young men believe they're bulletproof. Paulie made his own decisions that day—decisions contrary to what you told him. All little boys do that sometime—and more than once, Lana." Will stood up and looked around. "I need something downstairs. I'll be back." Will said, leaving the room.

"What's so important?" Lana called after him.

Will came back into the room and sat on the bed. He held out his hand, opening his fingers. In his palm was a chipped three-inch piece of gray-white flint. Lana looked at the flint with a quizzical expression, then up at Will.

Will smiled. "It's an arrowhead, but not just any ordinary arrowhead, this is an anthropomorphic vessel. Think of it as a soul holder. I gave it to Paulie last year while we were on a camping trip. Want to know who gave it to me?"

"Who?"

"Paul Reavis Senior. We were on an overnight camping trip and our scoutmaster, old Mr. Evans from Troop 20 at Centenary Methodist, decided it was time to find some Indian relics. They were his specialty and his love. Paul found this one afternoon in a fallow bean field. Mr. Evans couldn't stop talking about it for the rest of the weekend. The civilization that produced this is ranked as one of the oldest in North America. The first point that looked like this was found in Clovis, New Mexico, thus the name. Anyway, Paul, in a fit of camaraderie, gave it to me. He called it a friendship gift.

A few years ago I found it in an old shoebox full of miscellaneous stuff I saved over the years. I remembered when Paul gave it to me and thought it might be fun to give it to his son." Will looked at the three-inch-long piece of flint as he rubbed his thumb in one of its grooves. "Or maybe I was subconsciously giving it to my son?"

Lana looked up from the Clovis. "Maybe. Do you remember

what you were thinking at the time?"

"No, not really. In any case, I gave it to Paulie one day when we were on a camping trip. I remember telling him about the time his dad had given it to me and that Paul had said that it was a friendship present. I told him that it was only right that I give it to him. I told him that by rubbing the side grooves of the Clovis you could put some of yourself into the stone. I told him that some of his daddy and some of me were already rubbed into it.

"About a year ago, Paulie gave it to Wallace May. He and a buddy were on Wallace's land looking for arrowheads and shards. Wallace came down to see who was out there and to find out what they were doing. Paulie gave him the Clovis as an apology for not asking his permission and a thank-you for letting him stay to hunt for points. Wallace tried to give it to me a couple of weeks ago while we were talking at the Dairy Queen. I guess today he did. The truth is, it's a gift to me and you from our son with a message delivered by Wallace."

"What do you mean?"

Will closed his fingers around the point and leaned back against the pillows. He pulled the quilt up to his chest and repeated, exactly as he remembered it, his conversation with Wallace at the Dairy Queen. When he finished, Lana reached over, opened his fingers and took the Clovis point. She turned it over in her hand and studied it as carefully as if it were a precious stone.

"When I was at the wreck last night, I found it on the floor of Wallace's truck." Will said.

Lana looked at Will then back at the small piece of flint. She lay back on the pillow and turned it in her fingers. "You know, Will, we—you and me and Paul—had us a really great little boy. We . . ." She stopped, unable to speak.

Will put his arm around her and gently pulled her to him. She stretched her arm across his chest and quietly cried into the pillow. He took the arrowhead and put it on the bedside table.

"I guess I always wished that Paulie was my son, so when Wallace told me what Paulie said to him, that I was 'more like another daddy than an uncle,' well, I guess that's just about as good as I could hope for."

Lana nodded. "Will, you were a good daddy, and like Wallace said, 'Being a daddy is hard.' You've always said that your daddy was a hard man. That he was never proud of you. Maybe he didn't know how to tell you he was proud and that he loved you. Maybe he was afraid, but maybe you never gave him the chance he needed. Some men find it hard to be loved, so, I guess, they find it hard to love. So Wallace was right, being a daddy is hard."

Will stared at the ceiling. "Harder than I ever imagined."

Lana cleared her throat. "Will, I feel better. I feel . . . free. I've wanted to talk to you, to see if you knew, but for years I was afraid. Now we know out loud, so let's deal with it and not let it keep us from getting on with things."

"What things?"

"I don't know . . . life, being a cop, fishing, hunting, relationships, politics . . . whatever we need to get on with."

He closed his eyes. "What do you need to get on with?"

Lana rolled onto her side. "Learning to live a new life, whatever that will be. I have to find my way out of the alien."

"What alien? What are you talking about?"

"Nothing. It doesn't matter. I need to learn to live a new life. I need a do-over. As a matter of fact, I was talking to Vicky the other day about maybe finishing my education. I told her I thought I could be a good vet. I figured she would pooh-pooh the idea, but she didn't."

She turned her head and looked at Will. He smiled, then leaned over and gave her a kiss, "And why the hell not?" he said. "You're a strong woman and a start-over is always an option in life."

—✦ ✦ ✦—

They lay quietly, each with their own thoughts. After another half hour, Will got out of bed and looked around the room. "I've got to find my clothes."

"Oh damn, they're still in the dryer from before you seduced me," Lana said.

"Seduced you? You practically knocked me off my feet," Will said, patting her on the bottom. "I hope the downstairs maid hasn't come in yet."

"The downstairs maid is upstairs, buck-naked. Anyway, she'll be in the kitchen in a few minutes to fix more coffee and some eggs."

"Okay, but I've got to go pretty soon. I need to get home, get on a fresh uniform, get hold of Bob Joyce and the sheriff, then get back out to Lolly's."

Lana held the quilt across her chest while Will picked up a towel from the floor and wrapped it around himself.

"If Wallace was at Lolly's and drunk, then all you've got is a case of drunk driving," she said.

"I don't think it's that simple." Will replied. "Wallace was at Lolly's with a bunch of other men, all invited and paid for by Eugene Winslow. So why last night? Why would Eugene invite, for the first time, remember, Wallace to Lolly's, and buy him a bunch of beers? There was a reason, a plan, 'cause Popper ain't Santa Claus. He ain't known for kind gestures.

"And another thing," Will added, "According to two different people, when Wallace left the parking lot headed for home, he was going well below the speed limit. Something happened between Lolly's and the scene of the accident that made Wallace speed up considerably. You don't leave the road and fly fifty yards though the air going twenty miles an hour."

"Maybe he became bolder and sped up." Will shook his head.

"Or maybe somebody forced him to speed up."

—◆ ◆ ◆—

Lana carried the pot of coffee over to the kitchen table and poured two cups. Then set down his plate of eggs and a warmed-over biscuit from the day before.

"What do you think Ernie will do?"

"I don't know. If I get strong, compelling evidence, he'll back me up, but I need to talk to Sergeant Joyce for an update on what he's found so far. Then talk to Rufus and Eugene and everybody else who was at Lolly's."

Lana sat down at the table and poured some half-and-half into her coffee. "What if you don't find anything at the crash site? What if they stonewall you? Where do you go then?"

"I don't know, I'll figure that out later. But regardless of what happens with Wallace's accident, I'm moving forward on Paul's death based on the new information we have."

Lana looked at him without saying anything but with an expression that spoke volumes. Will sat back, let out a long breath and proceeded to tell her about his morning with Hank and everything the young boy had told him. After he finished, he smiled and said, "So what do you think?"

Lana just stared at him for what seemed to be a very long time, then smiled and said, "I think I was right to doubt the accident story. I think that Hank is telling the truth, and that you should use it to get that son-of-a-bitch Eugene Winslow. I think I have a shot at justice after all."

Will sat back, thought for a minute then said, "I'm thinking about asking Ernie to let me get an exhumation order for Paul's body. Would that bother you?"

"Not if it could help prove that he didn't die from an accident." Lana paused a beat, "What's the chance of tying Oris Martin into the deal? You and I both know he's bound to be in this up to his neck."

Will pursed his lips, "You're probably right, but I'll also bet he's content to be the puppeteer. Our problem is going to be finding the strings between him and Popper. I know they're there, just like the ones between Popper and Weldon, but the problem is how to expose them." He pushed himself up from the table, then bent down and gently kissed Lana.

She stood and put her arms around him. "Thank you, Will. Thanks for everything. Be careful now," she said, releasing him.

19.

Robert Joyce was leaning against his car smoking a cigarette when Will drove up.

"Hey, Will. You look like you got about as much sleep as I did." Will smiled, "Maybe less."

He took his dark glasses off and glanced at the accident scene over the hood of Sergeant Joyce's car. "Jesus, but he must have really been flying." Will stepped on the front bumper of Robert's patrol car and turned slightly as he pushed up to sit on the hood. His hip was hurting this morning and with even the slightest jolt or twist, a grimace shot across his face. "So, Robert, what do we know about last night?"

Robert flipped his cigarette across the road and exhaled. "We know that Wallace May was probably traveling in excess of seventy miles per hour. We know, based on your visit to Lolly's, that he was observed to be quite intoxicated when he left. We know that he was seen driving at a slow speed upon leaving Lolly's parking lot. We know that he left the road at the point marked by the red flag over there. We know from the tracks over the shoulder of the road that he applied no brakes; therefore, we assume, he was unaware that he had left the road.

"We believe that the rear-wheel skid marks on the shoulder of the road," Sergeant Joyce turned and pointed, "down there by the yellow flag, and the scrape marks and dents on the guard rail, may have been caused by another truck traveling at a high rate of speed behind Mr. May's truck."

Will turned from looking at the yellow flag and said, "Why? Why do we believe that there was a truck following Wallace?"

"Because the skid marks were made last night, just like the marks from Wallace's truck were made last night. The mud, gravel, and torn grass in both marks were disturbed within the past ten hours. If it had been from a few days ago, the rain would have smoothed out the damage. We, of course, can't be sure that the two events took place simultaneously, but it seems logical, looking at the condition of both areas."

"Have you got pictures of the skid marks as well as the marks left by Wallace's truck?"

"Yes, sir. We got 'em from last night and this morning. I was here until after three, as you know, and Sergeant Canipe was here from then until about thirty minutes ago, so nothing's been disturbed here. There's another thing, Will. We found some black paint on the guardrail. I planned on sending it to the SBI lab in Raleigh."

Will nodded his head. "Do it today, Robert. I want as much information as quickly as possible. In the meantime, I'm going to pay a little visit on Rufus Austin, Eugene Winslow, and Weldon Goins."

Will slid off the hood of the patrol car and strode back down the road to the spot marked with the yellow flag. He bent down and scrutinized the scrape marks on the guardrail. It looked like a rear bumper and a part of the undercarriage of a vehicle had hit the rail pretty hard.

So, mystery man, did you leave us a little calling card? Will smiled as he stood and headed back to his car.

—✦ ✦ ✦—

Lana came into the veterinary clinic through the back door. Carter Jeffers was sitting in his office reading the paper. Vicky was in the working lab with Sylvia. A McDonald's bag sat in the middle of Carter's desk with a cup of french fries and a half-eaten cheeseburger. He held a can of Coke in his left hand. "Hey, Lana. Everything all right? You sounded concerned when you called this morning." Carter asked.

Lana nodded. "Yeah, everything's okay. I don't know if you've heard, but Wallace May was killed last night. Will came by the house early this morning. He's been up all night. He really liked Wallace, so he was pretty upset."

Growing pale, Carter wrinkled his brow, got up, and walked to the door putting his hand on Lana's shoulder. "You sure you're all right? You look exhausted."

Lana nodded, a quick smile crossing her face, as she put her purse on the front of the desk. "I'm okay, just didn't get a lot of sleep." She looked over her shoulder toward the back door and then back at Carter. "When I drove in just now, I thought I saw Eugene Winslow driving out. It wasn't his truck but it sure looked like him."

"It was. I didn't see what he was driving today, but that was him. He came looking for some medicines that Don had ordered for Pine Bluff. Why?"

Lana shook her head. "No reason. It's just that he looked angry. He gave me, you know, a kind of dirty look. Anything happen in here?"

Carter shrugged his shoulders. "No. I got his stuff and he mumbled something close to thanks and left. I wouldn't worry about it. He gives everybody a nasty look. You know Eugene."

She nodded, her hands suddenly clammy. "Un-huh."

Vicky had moved to one of the examining rooms with a big collie, there was no one in the waiting room and Sylvia was still in the lab. Lana opened a blue folder sitting in her in-box and started sorting through it. When she had what she needed, she got up and walked into the lab. Sylvia was wearing a white lab coat and working at a table on the far side of the room.

"Hey, Sylvia," Lana said.

"Hey," Sylvia turned.

"What'cha doin'?"

"I'm doing some blood work for Dr. Newell, plus a few fecal checks for worms. What do you need?"

Lana dropped the blue folder on the table. "I need to know what a few of these items are that you're wanting me to order. I'm not sure I know where to get them or what to call them."

Sylvia picked up the sheet of paper.

"Numbers five, six, and seven," Lana pointed.

"Five is an extender," Sylvia explained. "Semen extender. When you gather semen for artificial insemination you mix it into a solution of extender in order to make it go as far as possible. There's a package of powder, usually composed of some type of milk, antibiotics, glucose, and a bunch of other stuff, and a jar of diluent. That's a sterile saline solution that dilutes the extender. In fact, that's, uhm, number six. Anyway, you mix the saline with the package of extender and bingo, semen extender. It's a kind of milk shake for a sow's rear end, if you get my drift."

Lana nodded and smiled. "Very graphic, Sylvia. I bet you were a hit at show and tell."

"Actually," Sylvia said. "I was a lot better at show than tell. You should be able to get all that stuff from Saxby's. Uhm, number seven is Agar. Also Saxby's."

"What's Agar?" Lana asked.

"Growth medium. That jello-like stuff we put in the petri dishes."

"You mean to grow bacteria or whatever?" Lana replied.

"Yeah. We use it in order to make more of the bacteria or viruses we're studying. Kind of like using eggs to make vaccines. In the really big companies they use fertilized eggs. They inject the eggs with the bacteria or viruses or whatever it is they're trying to grow, seal the holes with a drop of hot wax and then keep them in an incubator while the bugs grow and expand. We don't need that much stuff, so we use these small dishes and enrich the Agar with proteins. Eggs have their own protein. Now you know what I know."

—✦ ✦ ✦—

Dr. Newell came into the room as they were talking. "Sylvia, that's very good, and, Lana, if you're interested, I have a book on biological cultures and growth mediums. You might find it interesting."

Lana smiled at her. "Let's keep it simple, doc. It's been a while since biology class."

"No sweat."

Vicky walked into the cooler and removed the locked insulated container that held the cholera tissue samples. It looked like one of those metal boxes that hold radioactive materials, except the sign on the side said "Danger. Infectious material." As she walked out of the cooler, Vicky said to Sylvia, "Sylvia, would you please open the door to the sterile work room?"

"Sure." She opened the outer door and after Dr. Newell went in, closed the door behind her. Vicky set the container on the metal desk in the outer room and opened the door into the sterile lab. After retrieving the container, she walked into the lab and deposited the samples on the counter that ran along the far wall. She arranged some instruments and equipment along the counter, then left the room and walked back into the main lab. "Sylvia, what did you do with the sterile mixtures that we made up yesterday?"

"They're in the cooler." Sylvia replied.

Lana watched all of this and as Vicky was coming out of the cooler said, "Vicky, what are you doing, if I may ask?"

"Sure. I'm going to expand the samples of the cholera virus so we can study them in several environments and under different conditions. Looking for variations in response. That kind of thing. But we gotta be careful to keep the cultures alive and well segregated so we know which is which."

"Will that tell you how this thing started, or how it spread?" Lana asked.

"Not likely. It will possibly tell us where it came from. You know, what strain of the disease this is."

"So how do you find out how it got here?" Lana asked.

"That we probably can't ever be sure of."

"Why not?"

"Because there are just too many possibilities. Viruses, whether flu or cholera, can be spread lots of ways. Usually it's because somebody who has been at an infected facility walks into an uninfected facility without first changing their shoes or sterilizing their clothing. You remember when you drove the samples from Carl's to Raleigh?" Lana nodded. "The van you drove was sprayed with Clorox. Your clothes were burned. Everything was cleaned and disinfected. The same thing is supposed to take place at a hog facility before anyone or anything new enters the grounds. That's why every facility has a shower and covers for shoes and one's head."

"If everyone is so careful, and you said that Carl is really careful, how could this have happened?"

"Well, humans are only one of the ways it can spread. Other pigs are also a big cause. If a pig with the virus is introduced into the feed operation, simply by coughing or sneezing, it can spread the virus. A hog shed is worse than a kindergarten for spreading disease." Vicky started to move toward the sterile lab but then turned toward Lana. "I don't think we'll ever know for sure how this thing started. Like I say, there are lots of ways the thing can be spread.

"I was reading the other night about an operation in Holland that they think got infected by birds. Somebody found a bird with a broken wing in one of the hog sheds. They were taking it out of the facility when one of the medical examiners saw them and asked if he could have the bird. Apparently, when they tested it they found it covered with the cholera virus. That didn't necessarily mean that that was the way the virus came in, but it's a distinct possibility.

"One of the hypotheses was that the bird fed at an infected facility and then flew to an uninfected facility, walked around in the feed or drank the water and bingo, spread the virus. It's just a guess, though. They never could prove that that was the way the virus got there; however, it does show the myriad stealthy ways the damn thing can be transported."

Lana picked up her folder and pen. "Fascinating. Who would think that one bird could wreak so much damage? Well, I guess we'll never know what really happened to Carl, but thanks for the lesson in viral transmission."

Vicky smiled and headed back into the sterile room.

Lana paused at the door to the lab. "You know, Sylvia. I'm just curious. How much of that extender do you use for each sow?"

"Well, first off, I don't use it. I think sticking your arm up a pig's vagina is about as gross as you can get. I couldn't eat with that hand ever again. But Dr. Newell, who will be performing that little feat on Oris Martin's herd, uses about five or six milliliters per shot. That means per sow."

"So how much do you mix up?" Lana asked.

"Enough for the sows she'll do in the first round. I understand that will be about five percent of each farrowing operation. They'll check the results, and if everything goes the way it should, then she'll expand the program. There's a lot of controversy about some of this stuff. You know, having to kill the mother and all."

"What do you mean killing the mother?" Lana said.

"To get clean pigs, they open the sow just before the little ones are born and take them out. This means killing the sow; or to be more diplomatic, 'marginalizing the breeder.' They move the piglets to a sterile environment and raise them as the new breeders."

Lana's face must have shown her distaste for such methods

of animal husbandry because Sylvia smiled and said, "Not what you thought, huh?"

Lana shook her head as she picked up the requisition and headed back to her desk, "No, not exactly my cup of tea, but I'm sure it doesn't bother Oris."

—✦ ✦ ✦—

The late afternoon sun transformed the field of brown soybean pods into a lake of russet gold. Will leaned against the trunk of his car and watched as the greens and oranges of the late sky traded places. He marveled at the subtle range of colors in eastern North Carolina sunsets, but couldn't remember ever seeing a painting or photograph that showed the greens in the spectrum. Pink and reds were always there. Variations on yellow and orange were always there, but he never remembered any yellow-blue mixes.

Ernie drove up just as the sun vanished below the far trees. "Hey, Will. Sorry for the delay, but I got held up in court."

Will nodded and turned to rest his right forearm on the top of the trunk. "No problem, Sheriff. I love watching the sunset this time of year. You ever notice how much green is in the sunset sky?"

Ernie shook his head. "Don't think so."

"Well, next time look between the blue sky and the top of the sunset; it's real green." Will shifted his eyes from the sky to the sheriff's insignia on the side of the car and for a moment didn't say anything. "Okay, here's what I think. And by the way, Ernie, I appreciate your meeting me out here. I feel more comfortable talking where I know we're alone. No ears except yours and mine." He pushed up onto the trunk and put his hands on his knees.

"I didn't tell you my source on the Pine Bluff situation because I wanted to protect him for as long as possible. I'm telling you now because tough decisions have to be made. Henry

Grier, Odell's boy, is the one who saw and heard the argument that morning. He was on his way to his uncle's house when he heard the bulldozer running. He stopped on the other side of the bean field from Popper's farrowing facility and I'm sure saw just what I told you.

"What I don't know is what he's *not* telling us. He's scared of getting mixed up in business between white men, and I can't say I blame him. His uncle Rafe basically told him to keep his mouth shut. Rafe has some issues with Popper and Oris, according to what I'm told. In any case, he told the boy to forget all about it. But, Ernie, I know how good that boy can see, and I guarantee you he knows exactly who was at the shed that morning.

"I only found out about it because of something he said while we were fishing. He told me about a dream he had in the hospital. In the dream, he was at Paulie's funeral, and said he saw Paul Sr. standing beside Paulie's coffin. Beside Paul was the man he was arguing with on the morning he died. I was a little slow at first and what he had just said didn't register, but then it hit me. I asked him what he was talking about. Of course, he tried to change the subject but I didn't let him, promising him he wouldn't get in trouble. Then I asked him if he heard what they were arguing about. He was real uncomfortable, but after a while, and a lot of prodding, he told me the story. It was right after that that I told you."

Ernie never took his eyes off Will's face. "And what do you think this has to do with Wallace's death?"

Will nodded and continued. "If Hank's description of the events is right, then Wallace was the one driving the bulldozer that morning. That makes him, or rather made him, the only possible chink in the story about Paul's death. I remind you that as of now no one but you and me and possibly Rafe Grier know what Hank says he saw in the early dawn."

Will had decided not to tell Ernie about Lana's trip to Pine Bluff and his subsequent conversation with her about Hank's story. All Ernie knew about Lana's episode at the house was that someone broke in, rummaged around and vandalized her room. Anything more would only anger the sheriff and get Will a lecture about making the investigation too personal. Ernie might even discount the real meat of Will's story if he knew that Lana had been involved.

Ernie took a Winston out and lit it. He inhaled and looked out over the bean field, adding up what Will was telling him.

"I haven't talked directly to Popper about Paul's accident since last year," Will went on, "but I did talk around the subject with Weldon Goins the other morning. He got real defensive, as you would imagine. I've been thinking about how to bring it up to Eugene, but figured there was no point since I'm guessin' Weldon told him about our conversation anyway."

Ernie looked across the fields and asked, "You talk to Popper about Wallace's accident last night?"

"No, but Robert went out to his place a few hours ago. He told Popper that we're interviewing anybody who was with Wallace at Lolly's. Popper acknowledged that he was there but didn't mention that he was the one who invited Wallace. Robert asked him a lot of questions about what went on, and all he said was that Wallace drank a lot, as did everybody else. Thing is, Rachel said Popper wasn't drinking all that much. Robert asked him what time he left, when he got home, how he drove if he was so drunk, you know, general kinda stuff. Anyway, he says he drove straight home, down 212 to Church Rd. There's no way to check that out."

"What do you think?" asked Ernie.

"I think he's lying."

"So how come you didn't mention this in the office?"

Will looked over his shoulder. "The walls have ears. Plus I didn't want to bring Hank and Paul into the discussion unless we were alone. I remember what you said about looking like I'm on some kind of personal vendetta."

Ernie listened and calmly blew a smoke ring. "So, you think Popper, or somebody connected to Popper, waited for Wallace to come out of the parking lot at Lolly's, chased him down the road, possibly bumped the back of his truck, and finally ran him off the shoulder and into the cypress tree." Ernie scratched his cheek with his index finger. "He did this in order to keep Wallace from telling you or me, mainly you, anything more about the morning of Paul's death, which I assume was really murder or manslaughter, depending on intent."

Will nodded. "Well . . ."

"Hold on, I want to finish." Ernie said holding up his hand. "We got as our only witness, a ten-year-old colored boy. Who, should he ever get into a courtroom, the defense will rattle so bad he won't remember his own name. Our other potential witness is now dead and we got no way of knowing at this point if he was murdered or victim of another accident. So how do we use the information this young man has?" Ernie slid onto the trunk of Will's car.

"We go to Judge Spivey and get a court order letting us exhume Paul Reavis's body and possibly dig a big hole in Eugene Winslow's parking lot out at Pine Bluff."

Ernie bit his lower lip then took a long drag on his cigarette. "Why?"

"Why what? Why exhume Paul or why dig a hole at Pine Bluff?"

"Why any of it?"

"Because I think my friend Paul Reavis was murdered. I think he was murdered by Eugene Winslow because Paul found him burying diseased hogs under his parking lot. Because I think that we, or the medical examiner, just assumed that Paul was killed by the bulldozer and thus didn't look for any other signs of a fight. In fact, I wouldn't be surprised if Popper didn't tell Oris about the diseased pigs. Popper had to protect his bread and butter. Now if you ask me whether Oris suspected or maybe even knew that Popper killed Paul, I would be hard pressed to think he didn't. Popper may have told him some story about fixing up the parking lot and that Paul's death was an accident, but knowing Popper as well as he does, I doubt Oris believed it. And even if he did, he wouldn't want to jeopardize their operation. Maybe his were the hogs that introduced the cholera virus that recently wiped out Carl Ross. In fact, Ernie, I wouldn't be surprised if Popper was responsible for burning down the Ross farm. I'll bet you anything that there was some connection between the two that Eugene doesn't want discovered. Fact is, I think Wallace is dead because he knew too much and Paul is dead because he found out too much."

Ernie stroked his chin and flipped his cigarette into the dirt on the shoulder of the road. "No matter what, we're not going to find out anything about Wallace's possible role in all of this."

"True, but if we find out that diseased hogs are buried under the parking lot, then Popper has a bunch of questions to answer."

"You first got to get him to admit he was there."

"No, we have Henry to say he was there." A long pause followed.

"Okay, that's enough," the sheriff said, turning to Will. "But, Deputy, what happens if we exhume Paul Reavis and all we find is that he was backed over by a bulldozer, like we already know? And what happens if we dig up Popper's parking lot and find some pig bones that show no sign of disease? What then?"

Will glanced over at the sheriff. "I'll drive off that bridge when I come to it. We're investigating a possible homicide, or homicides, and if we can show a judge evidence that warrants a court order, then as far as I can see, that's our job. We've got new, and in my opinion, sufficient evidence to justify asking for authorization to exhume.

"Sheriff, you very pointedly reminded me that you've never whitewashed an investigation in your life, and I believe you. Well, if I'm going to be sheriff of Hogg County, then that's a precedent I'd like to follow." Will paused for a moment. "I know I'm right, Ernie. I know I need to follow the rules, be politic, and remember who my real boss is, but this whole thing stinks.

"Wallace didn't go nuts and drive seventy miles an hour down that road. He was drunk. He would've been creeping through the rain just trying to get home, unless somebody scared him. It's the same with Paul. What happened to him was out of character. It's just that until now we haven't had any hard evidence to support our suspicions. By the way, I think Hank would be a good witness. He's too young to have any ulterior motives, and he's too scared to lie. I think he saw what he told me. In fact, I think he saw more than he told me. When was the last time you left before a fight was over?"

Ernie didn't answer.

Will looked at him. "I hope you know that my personal ambitions have got nothing to do with this; neither does my relationship with the Reavis family. I'm just trying to do what the citizens of Hogg County would expect the sheriff's department to do—administer the law."

Ernie smiled. "I got no problem with that, William. I'll go see Judge Spivey as soon as we're ready. By the way, was Popper's truck banged up?"

Will looked down the road, the corners of his mouth slowly turning up. "Funny thing about that; Popper said he hit a fence post coming into his farm last night. This morning he took his truck to Dodson's to be fixed."

Ernie nodded and slid off the trunk. "I don't suppose you happened by Dodson's for paint samples sometime this afternoon?"

"By strange coincidence I had Sergeant Joyce go by. I also stopped by the place where Eugene said he hit the fence post. It had been hit all right, but I'll bet anything it wasn't last night. I'm having Luther take pictures of the post and see if there is any black paint on it."

"Will, you get together the paperwork we'll need."

20.

Lana paused beside the barn door and looked across the yard. The wind had picked up and was blowing leaves into small tornado-like eddies. The temperature was dropping by the minute. She'd told Arlo Byerly to be here by three, but it was almost three-thirty.

She pulled the old chestnut door open and went inside, shutting it behind her. Reaching around in the darkening room, she found the light cord. The musty space was surprisingly warm considering that the only source of heat was the old egg incubator standing against the far wall.

Originally, the room had been a workshop, the place where Paul used to cut, shape, and sand furniture out of the rare pieces of wood he culled from the piles of lumber at Moser Hardwood. A scarred, stained oak workbench stretched beneath the window with electrical outlets spaced at two-foot intervals along its length.

Over the years, Paul had acquired, from one place or the other, a sizeable assortment of tools, equipment, and furniture. He'd made the stretcher table Lana still used in the kitchen, the chairs surrounding it, and the wardrobe in his and Lana's bedroom. He was good at woodworking, and enjoyed it as an escape from his resentment of working for his uncles at Riverside. He made furniture until his construction business began to rob him of any spare time, or at least until he decided that it had robbed him of his spare time. Eventually he sold his tools, feeling he didn't have the luxury of a hobby anymore. Lana thought it was a mistake. Working on a piece of furniture seemed to calm Paul, to give him a rest from his frustrations.

After Paul gave up woodworking, the workshop was turned into a clubhouse for Paulie. It made an exceptional clubhouse, the fountainhead of many deep, mysterious secrets. But like its members, it matured and changed, most importantly into a venue for Scout projects.

When Paulie decided to raise pigeons as one of his merit badge projects, he, his dad, and Will, along with Arlo Byerly, charged all over the county swiping pigeons from under roadway overpasses and out of railyard equipment sheds. Arlo was a committed quail hunter and used the pigeons to train his dogs. What had started out as a hobby and training exercise became a source of additional income for Arlo. In real life he was a master carpenter, running a successful business doing additions to existing homes as well as restoration projects for some of the historical buildings around Mussel Ford.

After Paulie's death, and with Will's and Arlo's encouragement and help, Lana continued to feed and water Paulie's pigeons. She knew Will's ulterior motive was using the poor birds to train his bird dogs. Eventually, she would have Arlo come and take the birds away, but, at present, Lana couldn't bear the thought of not hearing their cooing as they settled in for the night or awoke in the morning. Their plaintive calls were a pathway to her dead son and husband, a slender amorphous fiber vibrating in a song of rest and remembrance. As she sat on the evening porch or lay in her morning bed, she imagined she could hear the birds wishing

Godspeed, and Paulie thanking them for the thought.

She pulled open the top drawer of the incubator and checked the temperature. The old incubator seemed to be working, though she wasn't completely confident that all the instruments were functioning properly. She turned when she heard the growl of Arlo's truck in the yard. The engine cut off and the truck door opened and closed.

"Hey, Arlo, I'm in the barn."

The door opened slowly and he looked inside. "Hey there, Lana. Sorry I'm late but I was doing a little job for Mrs. Thatcher down the road and it took me a little longer than I thought. Hope I ain't held you up too much."

Lana smiled. "Not at all. I was just looking around at what we need to move out of here." She took a deep breath. "Lots of memories in this old barn, Arlo, lots of memories."

He nodded and patted the oak bench by the door. "There sure are. Matter of fact, I remember toting this bench in here with Paul after we got it out of the old foundry over in Sessions County. I remember it being a heavy sucker back then, so I reckon I'm gonna need some stout boys to help me move it now."

Lana pushed the drawer back in and turned around.

Arlo motioned toward the incubator, "You mean for that thing to be on? There's better ways to keep this place warm. I got . . ."

"No thanks. This is fine. I don't need a heater. I'm not out here that often."

He nodded, walking toward the back of the room.

"You want all this stuff out of here?" he said, waving his arm across the back of the workshop.

"I think so. It's mostly stuff that Paul used. I won't have any use for it. I'm keeping the incubator and the ladderback chairs over there." She slowly looked across the work space. "And maybe the pie safe in the corner."

Arlo nodded again, figuring that getting the stuff out of the shop would require at least a day. He looked at Lana and smiled.

"Reckon that's all we can do today. I'll come back over the weekend and haul this stuff away."

"Okay, and thanks very much." She backed up a few steps, then turned and walked out into the yard. His words had drawn her into the past and she didn't want him to see her cry.

The breeze, by now cold and harsh, blew leaves across the yard with increasing force. Paulie's pigeons dipped and soared over the roofs as they dropped one at a time into the yard and through the pigeon coop's openings. Lana started toward the house.

A frantic beating sound stopped her. It was coming from the pigeon cages. She looked through the wire mesh and spotted a blue and gray pigeon pressed into the far corner of the first cage. Lana walked over to the side of the coop and looked at the frightened bird fluttering against the wire and barn siding. It appeared thinner and more streamlined than the rest of the flock.

She opened the frame door on the side of the pen and walked in. As she bent down to pick up the bird, it hopped a few inches away, but she gently grasped it, picking it up. As she turned the bird over to examine it, she noticed a red band on its right leg. On the bottom half of the band, stamped into the plastic, was what looked like a phone number.

The pigeon seemed to be healthy, with the possible exception of an abrasion on its back. She turned the bird back over just as Arlo came out of the barn.

"Hey, Arlo. What do you make of this?"

Arlo came into the wire cage and looked at the bird in Lana's hands. He put his hand out to take the bird, then carefully turned the frightened creature over and looked at the band.

"Huh. This here's a racer." From the quizzical look on Lana's face he knew to explain. "Pigeon racing is a big sport in some parts of the world. Owners release their birds at a designated point and then see how long it takes them to get back home. Fact is, I bet I know whose bird this is."

"Whose?"

"I figure this here's Burton Fidler's. I'm pretty sure this is his telephone number and I know he had a race this week." He looked at the small injury on the bird's back.

"Reckon this feller had an accident or a run-in with a hungry hawk, so decided to stop off here for a rest. Probably saw the other pigeons flying around this here coop. Smart little rats."

Lana cocked her head. "Why would you call such a fancy pigeon a little rat?"

Arlo smiled. "Oh that's just what I heard some fella on television call 'em . . . rats with wings. I guess in the big cities these li'l guys aren't much appreciated. Folks think they're kind of dirty. You know, like they spread disease and stuff, like rats."

"They never seemed that way to me," Lana said.

"Me, either," Arlo replied. "But some folks don't like 'em."

"That band looks kind of tight," Lana said. "You don't think it hurts him, do you?"

Arlo smiled, "I don't reckon so. Everybody uses 'em. Sometimes I hear the racers get a kind of foam band that's softer and lighter, but I don't reckon it makes that much difference, 'cept I'd think it'd git kinda wet."

"Should we call the number on the band?"

"Yeah, I reckon so. Burton will be wantin' his bird back."

"What would happen if you just threw him up in the air right here, what would he do?"

"I don't know. He's kinda tired right now and maybe his wound is worse than it looks. If he was in good shape, he'd make a beeline back to Burton Fidler's house."

"All pigeons do that? Fly home, I mean?"

"Naw. Most of them, the ones like you got around your house, will fly to the closest flock of birds. They're flock animals, and they want to be with their own kind. If they got food and water, they're happy. 'Course, when they find a good home, plenty of food and shelter, they ain't in any hurry to leave it." He looked at the birds circling above Lana's house. "Like these-here birds. They got it good at your house and they know it."

"If I wanted to get rid of them someday, where would I take them?"

"Well, if you decide to get rid of them, don't take 'em anywhere. Call me."

Lana smiled. "I'm not calling you. You'd sell 'em to some bird hunter. I want them free. I want them to have a good home."

"I wouldn't sell 'em if you didn't want me to, Lana. You know that."

"I know, Arlo. So, where would you take them?"

"About anywhere. There's a big bunch out at the cement yard, a mess of 'em over at the rail yard, but I'd probably take 'em to Martin Feed Mills. They got the biggest flock of all."

Lana smiled. "I bet that'd piss ole Oris off. Adding to his flock of grain moochers."

Arlo nodded. "Yeah, it might. He don't like 'em anywhere he owns."

"I knew he hated most people but hate birds?"

With that, Arlo shrugged his shoulders, smiled and turned toward his truck waving once. He put the racing pigeon in a small wire-mesh cage behind his seat. When he turned around, he saw Lana rubbing her arms with her hands and shifting her weight from foot to foot.

"It's getting mighty cold, Lana. You'd best be getting inside the house and out of the air. I'll be over sometime Saturday to start moving all that stuff out of the barn." He smiled and got into his truck. "Good to see you! I know Burton will be glad to get his bird back." The truck started up with a roar and Arlo backed out of the drive, heading north into the wind.

Lana waved, slowly turned, and headed back toward the house still hugging her arms.

21.

Oris drained his half-empty bottle of Coke in one gulp. It was late, sometime after seven and the office was closed. By five o'clock this time of year it was dark, and even though soybeans were still being harvested, seven o'clock was dinnertime.

Eugene had been none too pleased when Oris called and told him to meet him at Martin Feed Mills.

"Goddammit, Oris. I've got my boots off and am just before having my dinner. How 'bout in the morning."

"Got to be now, Eugene. Sorry."

"It's always got to be now, don't it?" Popper groused.

"Not always," Oris said, "but this time, yes."

—◆ ◆ ◆—

Oris had been at the mill for over thirty minutes, arriving just as the last worker was driving out of the parking lot. He punched his code into the burglar-alarm pad outside the main door and when signaled that everything was off, unlocked the front door and went into the big conference room, leaving the outside door slightly ajar.

He looked around. The room was too big for intimate intimidation. What Oris needed tonight was for Eugene to feel fear, to smell the anger and danger that Oris intended to exude from every pore. He walked down the narrow hallway to the back of the building, his steps echoing off the empty walls. Ronnie's office was perfect. It was Spartan and small . . . steel furniture and nothing but charts on the walls. He grabbed a coke out of the break room and returned to the office, walking around the desk and sitting in the gray swivel chair behind it. He looked at his watch then leaned back to wait. Five or ten minutes later he heard Popper come into the building.

"Hey, Oris! Where the hell are you?"

Oris looked at his watch and smiled, then stood up and poked his head out of the doorway, "Down here, Popper. In Ronnie's office."

Popper sauntered down the hall and brushed past Oris, half-heartedly shaking his hand as he did. He slumped onto the steel chair in front of the desk. "So, what the hell we doing in this shit-hole? What's wrong with the conference room?"

"Too many windows," Oris replied. "I want to keep this very private."

Eugene twisted his neck and looked around the room . . . sure enough, no windows. "Okay, we're private. What's the big mystery?"

"Actually, the big mystery isn't really a mystery. It's a known fact, or rather a series of known facts." Oris's eyes locked on Popper's with an intensity he rarely used with his friend. "Let me recite them for you, Eugene. I think you'll find 'em interesting. Fact one: Sheriff Tasker and Chief Deputy Moser had a meeting with Judge Spivey yesterday. Fact two: they presented him with a request, or requests, for a court order to dig up Paul Reavis's body, plus the whole fucking parking lot in front of the Pine Bluff farrowing operation. Fact three: they say they have firsthand eyewitness information about Paul Reavis's death, and it isn't, or wasn't, from Wallace May. Fact four: they're postulating a broad conspiracy to cover up Paul's death. Fucking fact number five: they implied that I had knowledge of the events at Pine Bluff last year! And six: they intend to bring charges if the information they get from their little digging party turns up something." Oris was, by this time, not only yelling but leaning across the desk, his face not more than two feet from Eugene's.

The blood vanished from Popper's face. He emitted a cold clammy sweat and his heart was racing. Thus reduced to a cowering heap, Popper moved back in his seat and stammered, "They're bluffing. They couldn't have ah . . . ah . . . an eyewitness. Wallace was the only one there. It's been over a year; if anybody saw anything, they would have said something. I know that they . . . uhm . . . they are trying . . ." Fear locked him frozen into his chair.

Oris let him blather and babble on. Let the terror congeal his organs into one quivering mass. Let him focus on his fate.

Finally Oris pulled back, and wiped his hand across his forehead. "Eugene, perhaps they are bluffing. Perhaps they are trying to scare us. Perhaps they're only guessing. But, my friend, they don't know that we know any of this. If they were trying to spook us into some irresponsible act, then why not publicize it? Why not spread a few rumors? Why go to a sitting judge and put your fucking reputation on the line?"

Eugene stammered, "Maybe they wanted us to know that they went to the judge. Maybe they fed us the information. How do we know what really happened?"

Oris sneered. "Because, you imbecile, I don't use sources that can't be relied upon. My source on this is a court insider, so I know I'm right. When people owe you their jobs, they're loyal and accurate."

Eugene ran his hand over his mouth. *Who could have been there that morning that he didn't know about, and why were they coming forward now? Why not a year ago?*

Oris let him stew for a few minutes, then asked, "Aren't you going to ask me who the eyewitness is?"

Eugene looked up, clearly startled. "You know?"

"Of course I know. You don't think the judge is going to grant permission to dig up a corpse without some evidence, do you?"

Popper shook his head.

Oris leaned back in the chair. "It's the nigger boy. The kid who almost drowned with young Paulie Reavis . . . Odell Grier's kid, saved by those Yankee bastards at Duke Hospital. Apparently he was on the road that morning and saw the whole thing. I don't know why he's coming forward now, but him being a kid, the sheriff wants some corroborating evidence."

A smirk spread across his face. "But you know something, Eugene? There ain't even the slightest hint that he saw *me* there. 'Knowledge of' ain't the same as 'guilty of.'" Oris leaned back and let this last revelation sink in. Never mind that neither Ernie nor Will had implied that Oris had knowledge of the incident, though both believed that to be the case. Oris threw that tidbit into the pot so Popper could understand his level of anger and indignation. He needed action, and he needed Eugene to understand the immediacy of the problem.

"Let's say he did see something," Popper replied. "His word against ours. They can't dig up nothing to hang us with. Paul was run over by a bulldozer. His bones ain't going to tell no different."

Oris lowered his eyelids and looked at Eugene. "Didn't run over his head, though, Popper. Maybe they see where you planted that pipe wrench in his forehead and things don't add up. As for them pigs, my understanding is they died of influenza. 'Course somebody could've lied to me about that. Whatever the case, if I was you I wouldn't enjoy the wait.

"But, you know, my memory about all that trouble is mighty vague. I was in Raleigh at the time, and you told me the same thing you told the sheriff. A real honest-to-God tragedy. And they just keep on coming, too. That thing the other day about Wallace May. Not good, not good at all. Lots of press, lots of attention—all the wrong things."

Popper tried to work up some indignation of his own, but he had no heart for it; besides, he knew it would be wasted. Oris had no soul. He had no friends except those he could own and they were no more to him than a herd of Yorkshire boars at one of his farrowing lots. Eugene had to save himself.

"Young Henry Grier lives out near Mitchell Creek," Popper mused, "I hope he's learned his lesson and come to respect how dangerous that water can be. I hear we're in for a big blow out of the northeast sometime tomorrow or the next day. A bad place for a young boy to be, wouldn't you think, Oris?"

"Very dangerous, Eugene. Let's pray he goes nowhere near the creek during such violent weather."

Popper pushed back his chair and slowly got to his feet. He raised his eyes to meet Oris's, slowly inhaled then nodded, a look of resignation crossing his face as he exhaled. "I'll be seein' ya." He turned and walked out of the room, down the hall, and out into the cold empty mill yard. It was black night now so Popper raised his collar against the biting wind.

22.

Will smiled across the table at his mother. Mamie Neal finished putting the serving dishes on the table and retreated to the warmth of the kitchen. Will picked up the bottle of Balletto Pinot Noir and poured his mother a half glass, then filled his own.

"Mother, this is a pleasant surprise and something we should do more often. Thank you for the invitation. My home cooking is not, as you might imagine, quite up to Mamie's standards." Sarah Moser smiled and raised her glass of wine toward Will.

"To a nice dinner with pleasant conversation," Sarah said. Will touched glasses. "Hear, hear."

Sarah served Will from the hot casserole as he helped himself to the vegetables in the small bowl to her right. It was an adequate amount of food, just the quantity that he should be eating but rarely did. Mamie was a good cook and when Sarah told her that Will was coming over she knew immediately what she would fix. It wasn't breakfast but she didn't hesitate to order some fresh shrimp from the market for her cheese grits and shrimp casserole. She added onions, some bacon, and just a touch of venison sausage. Mamie missed Will's visits.

"So, Mother, I hear you might be going to Florida with the Chamberses next week."

"They were nice enough to invite me, yes. I enjoy Palm Beach when it's cold in Carolina. The dampness this time of year seems to seep into one's bones. Anyway, I'll be there for two weeks. I've thought about getting a small place down there. Maybe something at The Everglades? What do you think?" Will thought for a moment, then said, "Well, it ain't my cup of tea, but if it's a place you like, why not? Anywhere else appeal to you?"

"Well, I've also thought about Boca Grande. The Holdernesses have a house there and they have invited me several times, but I like the vitality of Palm Beach. There always seems to be a lot going on; plus there's a quite wonderful group of ladies in Betty Ann Chambers' bridge club that I've gotten to know." Will drank some of his wine and waited for Sarah to finish.

"I don't know," Sarah said. "Maybe I'll look around when I'm down there this time and see what's available. If I see something that appeals to me, perhaps you could come down and help me. I always did depend on your father for making that kind of decision."

Will smiled and said, "I'd be delighted to, Mother. I've only been to Palm Beach once before and I'm sure that it's quite different than what I remember. A classmate of mine at Vanderbilt, Kennan Thomason, has a house there. He's asked me to come down a few times but I haven't been but once. And it's been a while. Anyway, I'm sure he knows what's what in the real estate market."

Sarah smiled at the thought of Will helping her. She had never asked him to do anything more than a few small favors around town, feeling with some justification that their relationship never warranted more trust. But relationships between a mother and her child, no matter how strained, can never be completely severed, never washed totally from the soul of either the child or parent. Sarah Moser, though distant, unreflective, and controlled, still saw in her child something of herself. They enjoyed their dinner and conversation, making sure that it never fell into past differences. Talking mainly about local news and personalities, they occasionally ventured into state politics.

"I've gotten some very good reports on your recent speeches. It seems that you have won the votes of my entire bridge club," Sarah said.

Will smiled, "Thank goodness. Some of the ladies in your club are pretty tough inquisitors, especially Ruth Kaster. Now that is one well-versed lady, fair but tough."

Sarah nodded, smiling. "Ruth has, of course, been more involved than most of us, but then she is the most naturally attuned to politics." Sarah started to say something more but suddenly paused and looked, Will thought, perplexed. When she didn't continue, Will said, "What?" She looked at him but didn't answer. He said again, "You were going to say something else but seemed to reconsider. What were you going to say?"

She sat for a moment longer. "You remember the other day when you cautioned me about spreading rumors, and to try and stop them if I heard them?"

"Yes. I remember."

"Well, yesterday I heard something that I don't know how to handle."

"Maybe I can help. What was it?"

Sarah paused, hunting for the right words. "At our weekly bridge club, during a refreshment break, I overheard a conversation between Ruth Kaster and Emma Martin, Oris's wife. It was none of my business, but with your position in mind, I did focus on it more than I probably should have. Ruth said to Emma something about a request that you and Sheriff Tasker made to Judge Spivey. Something about exhuming a body or digging up a body. I couldn't really understand what they were getting at, but I clearly remember this.

"Ruth said something about the Grier boy, and Emma, and I am certainly not surprised by this, said louder than she should have, 'You mean he's gonna take the word of some little colored boy on a matter that important?' "

Will's face showed concern.

Sarah waited for him to say something, but when he didn't she continued. "Will, I didn't say anything. I really shouldn't have been listening in on someone else's conversation, so it didn't seem . . ."

He cut her off. "Mother, you were absolutely right. That was no place to say anything, but thank you so much for telling me. This is a very important fact for Ernie and me to have. You did exactly right. Thank you." He arose from the table and hastened to Sarah's side, bending down and giving her a kiss on the cheek. "I need to go. Thank you for a wonderful meal, and for . . ." He didn't know the words, so threw up his arms and grinned.

Sarah smiled and said, "For wanting to help my son."

"Yes, for that and for everything else." She held his arm so he couldn't bolt without something more.

"I would like to know what this means, William."

"I'm not sure I know entirely, but one thing it means is that she knows something that she shouldn't. Therefore, I need to know how."

"I know how." Sarah said, releasing his arm.

Will, shocked, stood with his mouth open.

"You're not the only detective in this family," she said with not a small amount of pride.

"Okay, shoot, Ms. Marple."

"Ruth Kaster's son, young Dunbar, is Judge Spivey's law clerk. I have to presume that whatever the judge sees, he sees. I also presume that when she mentioned Dunbar to Emma she was talking about her son, not her husband."

Will slowly nodded his head. "You're exactly right! Furthermore, if Ruth knows and Emma Martin knows, then Oris does as well."

"What does that mean?" Sarah asked. Will took a step backward and started to turn around.

"It may mean that Hank Grier is in trouble. But it definitely means that the sheriff's department of Hogg County, and William Moser Jr., owe a debt of gratitude to Sarah Moser, chief detective. Thank you, Mother. I'll let you know more when I can, but in the meantime, know that you have done a great service to everyone around here."

Bowing his head to her, he turned and left Cromwell House with a feeling of belonging that he hadn't felt for many years.

23.

Will walked down the hall and into his office. He dropped his coat on the leather couch and dialed Ernie's number at home.

"Tasker."

"Sheriff, it's Will. I just heard something that concerns me. In fact, it may constitute a crime at the highest level of the judicial system."

"And that would be?" Ernie said.

"That would be a leak in the office of Judge Spivey. A leak that has probably warned Oris Martin and by extension his buddy Eugene Winslow about our request for an order of exhumation of Paul Reavis." The sheriff remained silent. "Ernie, if my information is correct, and I am one hundred percent sure that it is, Oris knows what we have asked the judge to do. But even more worrisome is the fact that he also knows that Hank Grier is the basis for our request."

"And how do you know that, Will?"

"Because my source overheard a conversation between two

people who know what they're talking about. One of them commented, 'How could the judge trust the word of some little colored boy?' or something to that effect."

Ernie waited a minute. "If true, what do you think this means to us?"

"I think," Will replied, "that it means nothing as regards our request for exhumation, but a lot as regards Hank's safety. If Wallace's death was murder and not an accident, then there's a good chance he was killed because of what he knew about Paul's accident, or murder. The same may now be the case for Hank Grier. Oris and Eugene know that Hank is the basis for our request to the judge; therefore, they know Hank knows something that we believe justifies exhumation. In my opinion, this puts him at risk."

"How the hell did this information get out?"

"I don't know for sure but my source reminded me that Dunbar Kaster Junior is Judge Spivey's clerk and the conversation overheard was between Ruth Kaster and Emma Martin."

"And you think that everything Sarah heard was accurate?"

"I didn't say it was Sarah."

"Listen, Will, I'm not completely stupid. Who else would overhear a conversation between Ruth and Emma, both of whom are in Sarah's bridge club?" Will smiled and made a low grunt.

"Anyway, assuming that it was accurate, I agree that Oris, and by extension Eugene, now know that Hank Grier has some knowledge of Paul's accident. Whether it was Dunbar Junior we don't know, but I agree that he is the likely leak. I'm sure it wasn't the judge and I'm equally sure it wasn't you or me. So what now?"

"I've called Bob Joyce," Will said, "and had him check by the Griers. I don't think Popper is stupid enough to do anything tonight, but I'm sending a car by every hour just in case. I'll go by in the morning."

"Don't get Odell and Nancy too uptight until we can figure out exactly what we got here," Ernie said.

Will nodded, "I won't get Nancy involved any more than I have to, but Odell has to know that he should be on the lookout for anything suspicious. I don't want to make him more nervous than he is now but I need him to make sure he knows where Hank is at all times. I might have to tell him more than we want, but I think it's worth it. We may be borrowing trouble here, but after Wallace's accident I don't think we can take anything for granted."

"Okay, but make sure he understands what is fact and what is guesswork. All we really know is that somebody knows about Hank that isn't supposed to."

Will nodded. "I need to talk to Robert and see if he found out anything from the paint sample. I also need to put some quiet eyes on Popper and maybe Weldon. I can't think they would be so stupid as to do something rash, it being so soon after Wallace's death, but you never know what fear can do. Popper is bound to know we're closing in on him, or else why exhume Paul and dig up the parking lot? This is just the kind of thing that could make him do something crazy, especially if it hinges on a young, defenseless black boy. I guarantee he wouldn't lose a minute's sleep over creating an accident for a black kid." Will was tapping on the top of his desk with a pencil. "You know, Sheriff, you probably need to go to the courthouse in the morning to tell Judge Spivey there's a leak in his office. He needs to find out how this information got out. If it is Dunbar Junior, he needs to know."

Ernie breathed out through his mouth. "The courthouse is closed on Saturday, so I'll need to go by the judge's house. That'll be better than going to the courthouse anyway . . . fewer eyes and ears around. I'll only tell him what is absolutely necessary, but I am going to tell him that we suspect the leak. I won't mention our theory about Oris and Popper having something to do with Paul's death, but I need to tell him about Ruth and Emma's conversation and what was said. I'll beg off saying who heard them for now.

"He needs to understand how serious this is, so I want him to be really pissed that somebody in his operation may be betraying their sworn duties."

"Okay, I'll go out to Odell's around nine or ten. I'll call early to make sure he'll be around. I forgot it was Saturday. It's supposed to be really shitty weather tomorrow. Something big coming in. How about we meet at the office sometime in the afternoon?"

"How about three o'clock?" Ernie said.

"Fine. See you then."

24.

The pecan tree in Odell Grier's backyard bent and groaned under the constant assault of forty-mile-an-hour winds. The storm had started at five in the morning and intensified ever since. The rain began in earnest at seven, and by nine, when Will drove into Odell's yard, it had already flooded the driveway and most of the backyard.

Will drove as close to the back door as possible, then jumped out and ran the last ten muddy yards. "Damn," he yelled as he slid through the door and into the Griers' kitchen. "It's getting serious out there."

Odell smiled and said, "You thought this was supposed to be some wimpy little shower?"

"No, but I didn't think we were still in hurricane season."

"You know northeasters can be worse than hurricanes, unless you're on the coast, and lots colder, too."

Will took the dishtowel offered by Odell and sat down at the kitchen table. He dried his hair with a few rapid strokes and then wiped his hands and face.

The room was bright and cheerful, even on such a dreary day. Yellow-and-blue curtains covered with what looked like hand-painted images of wildflowers hung on either side of the big window above the kitchen sink. Similar ones hung around the large bay window that looked over the side yard and barns.

Will smiled and tried to think of a good way to start, but before he could, Odell took the towel from him, flipped it into the sink and sat down at the table.

"Okay, Will, what's going on? A seven A.M. call on Saturday morning means you've got something on your mind other than a neighborly visit—especially on a day like today." He reached behind him and took the coffeepot off the burner. "Coffee?"

Will nodded, and Odell filled the mug sitting in front of him. "Cream?"

"No, thanks." Will leaned back in the chair and looked around the room.

"Nancy's upstairs doing some sewing for a church project, and Henry's out in the barn," Odell said as he watched Will's eyes move around the kitchen. "Just in case that's what you're trying to see."

Will smiled, "You don't miss much, Mr. Grier. You want to tell me what I'm here for, or haven't you figured that out yet?"

"I haven't figured that out yet, but I'm guessing it's either about Henry or me getting almost killed in a suspicious accident recently."

Will leaned forward in his chair and stared for a few seconds into his coffee. He wanted not to look or act too concerned.

"Well, you're right. It is about Henry, or it might be about Henry. I'm going to tell you something I promised him I wouldn't. We'll talk about how to handle it and what to tell Henry and Nancy when I'm finished."

Odell leaned back in his chair. His eyes were calm and steady. He didn't move a muscle or make a sound until Will had finished telling him everything that Hank had said about that morning at Pine Bluff.

When he'd finished, Will crossed his arms on the kitchen table and waited for what he assumed would be a barrage of questions, but the only thing Odell said was, "But that ain't what you're here about, is it? You're here to tell me about something that's happened since. The thing that makes it impossible to not tell me about Henry seeing that brush-up at Pine Bluff."

Will nodded and continued. He told Odell about his suspicions concerning Wallace's accident, the fact that it might be related to Paul's death, and that they'd gone to Judge Spivey for permission to exhume Paul's body.

"Odell, someone close to our office overheard a conversation that gives us reason to believe that Eugene may know that we're seeking an exhumation order from Judge Spivey, and that the basis for our request is Hank's observation of events surrounding Paul's death." Will put his hand on Odell's arm. "Listen to me, Odell. A lot of this is just guessing right now. You need to keep this between us for the moment. I wouldn't say anything to Nancy yet, and for sure don't tell Hank that you know about what he told me. He'd be so embarrassed that he didn't tell you himself that he'll likely clam up on both of us. And he'd be disappointed in you for finding out, and me for telling on him."

Odell stood up and slowly turned around. He poured a cup of coffee for himself and motioned to Will.

"No thanks, I've had enough."

After a minute Odell said, "I agree that we don't need to tell either Hank or Nancy right now, but I can't keep this from Nancy very long. You think Popper means to do something to Hank, don't you?"

Will shrugged.

"Then you'll understand that I can't just sit here and wait for that bastard to hurt my boy. You wouldn't do that, and neither will I."

Will motioned for Odell to sit down. "You know how I feel about that boy, and you know I'd never let anything happen to him. Sheriff Tasker is over at Judge Spivey's right now telling him about the leak in his office. We're going to try and get a warrant for Eugene so we can at least question him. I don't imagine he'll confess to anything, but he'll certainly be put on notice that we're after him. If he knows we're looking, he isn't likely to do anything rash."

Odell shook his head. "Likely ain't good enough. I got no intention of living with likely. Henry means more to me than . . ."

Will's radio crackled and came to life. He looked at Odell and held up his hand.

"Four to two. Unit four to unit two. Come in, Will."

Will keyed his radio. "That you, Robert?"

"Roger that," the deputy replied.

"Switch to ST channel," Will ordered as he changed from the general com channel to the special tactics frequency.

"You on, Robert?"

"Roger that."

"What's up?"

"Will, I'm out at the subject's house and his wife says he ain't been here all night. He went out right after getting a call around seven last night, and he didn't come back. She says he didn't even have his dinner."

"Who was it that called, Robert, and where'd he go?"

"She doesn't know, or won't say."

Will looked at Odell, who was leaning against the kitchen counter. "What was he driving, Robert? I think his other vehicle is still being repaired."

"I don't know, Will. I'll go back in and ask her if you want."

"Please. And Robert, make it look like we want to know so we can be sure he's okay. I don't want to do anything to make her suspicious."

"I think she's a little suspicious already," Robert said. "When I asked to see him, she wanted to know what for, and so I told her I was following up on questions from the night of Wallace May's death. I told her I was questioning everybody who had any knowledge of that evening. She kept saying that he didn't know anything about what happened after he left."

"Okay," Will responded. "See if you can find out what he's driving. Call me right back." Will leaned back in the chair and looked at Odell. "You heard it. We'll just wait and see." Odell nodded then looked out the window toward the barn.

"I wonder where Henry is? He was finishing tying down the stall shutters and then was supposed to come on back in." Odell walked over to the coat hooks by the back door and took down his slicker. His limp was markedly better but he still had his cane for safety's sake. "I'm just going out to check on him, Will. I'll be right back."

Will nodded and walked over to the window. He watched Odell run toward the barn, stiff-legged like he was in a three-legged race, splashing through the huge puddles of water with his cane flailing about.

"Four to two," Will's radio sputtered.

"Go ahead, Robert."

"He's in a ten-year-old blue Ford pickup. I seen it before. It's kind of a dark Carolina blue, with rust. He mainly uses it around the farm to carry really grody stuff. His wife said his new truck is still being painted from the accident. Where you want me to go now?"

Will watched as Odell came out of the barn and started walking toward the small shed on the far side. The wind appeared to be getting stronger. A gust knocked Odell against the barn. He pushed away from the structure and turned, walking with his back to the wind.

"Where are you?" Will asked.

"Headed down 216, a few miles from Lolly's."

"Okay, keep on coming down 216 and then head over to Pine Bluff. Maybe you can spot something."

"Spot what?"

"I don't know what. Maybe the truck, or . . . hell, I don't know, Robert—something."

"You think," Robert replied, "that he could be snooping around out in your area?"

"Could be. We know he didn't go home last night. Listen, since you're near Lolly's anyway, check and see if he showed up there. Then come toward Pine Bluff and Cane Creek Road."

"Roger that. I'm almost there right now. I'll check in with you if I turn up anything."

Will clicked off his mike and stood staring out the window. Odell came back around the corner of the barn and yelled Hank's name. Will could see him looking toward the house but then turn toward the woods that bordered Mitchell Creek. Odell yelled again, and then again. He spun around and headed back toward the house, pushing off on his cane and leaning into the cold northeast gale. Will walked over and opened the kitchen door, then leaned out over the stairs in order to hold open the screen door.

"Raining like a son-of-a-bitch, ain't it?" Odell muttered, as he grabbed the door jam and pulled himself through.

"Getting harder by the minute. Where's Hank?" Will asked, his hand pulling the screen door shut.

"Don't know. Maybe he came into the house through the front." Odell threw off the raincoat, walked across the kitchen, and out into the downstairs hall. "Hey, Nancy! Hank up there with you?"

"No. I thought he was with you in the barn," she yelled from her workroom.

"He was, but when I went to help him, he said he could do it by himself and for me to go ahead back to the house. You know how touchy he gets when I try and help him. I figured he'd be right behind me."

He looked worried. "I thought," Odell continued, looking up the stairs, "that he might've come in through the front door."

Nancy Grier stepped out into the upstairs hall and looked down at her husband. "He's not up here. Maybe you better go out and call him again. It's too nasty for that boy to be outside now. And make sure he didn't go down to that rickety old clubhouse. He might try and do something stupid like board it up." Odell nodded and turned back to the kitchen. He closed the door and motioned Will to walk to the other side.

"He ain't at the barn, and if he ain't there, then he's done what she said, and gone down to that damn clubhouse of his."

Will reached for his coat. "Where's the clubhouse?"

Odell looked out the kitchen window past the barn. "It's about two hundred and fifty yards across that field and into the woods on the edge of the creek. Hank and Paulie built it about two years ago. It's mainly a bunch of outside slabs from Carter's mill and half a dozen pallets from the feed mill." He grabbed his raincoat and looked over at Will, clearly showing how scared he was. "You think Eugene's already here, don't you, Will?"

Will zipped up his raincoat and opened the kitchen door, stepping out into the backyard, "I think we need to find Henry and then talk about who's looking for who."

Will and Odell went as fast as Odell could across the twenty yards between the house and barn and then out into the bean field on the far side. By the time they got to the edge of the woods next to Mitchell Creek, both men were breathing hard. Odell's cane had mired half-way up the handle on several occasions. Will could tell he was hurting. The wind was blowing gusts of around fifty miles an hour and the rain stung their faces.

"Which way?" Will shouted.

"This way," Odell responded as he headed into a chaotic wood line.

They kept their heads down and struggled through the tangle of dead wood and recently downed leaves and limbs. Odell hollered. "Henry! Henry Grier!" They stood still, listening through the howling storm for a response.

"Let's keep on going. The clubhouse is still a ways off," Odell said.

Will followed the bigger but now less agile man up the wet slope and over the top of a small rise. Below them the creek was starting to move up its banks. The water was in the beginning stages of a boil—and rising fast.

"Four to two. Four to two. Come in, Will." Will stopped and keyed his shoulder mic.

"This is two. Go ahead, Robert." Will stood at the top of the hill while Odell slogged down the bank and stumbled through the woods toward the rough-hewn cabin.

"Will, I found what I think is his truck. It's parked off the road next to one of the field tracks on John Keaton's farm. And for what it's worth, he didn't go by Lolly's last night."

"Which farm, Robert."

"The one about a mile or two from the Grier place . . . near the land John sold to Wallace."

"You mean off Pine Bluff Road?"

"No, off Olivet."

"Christ!" Will yelled into the mike as he tripped over a piece of wood hidden under the leaves. "It's the same damn road, Robert! Olivet runs into Pine Bluff. Where are you on Olivet?"

"Maybe a half-mile from the creek."

"You near John Keaton's feedlot?"

"Yeah, not far. The truck is on the road that runs into the feedlot."

Will wiped his hand over his face and swore into the wind. "Shit. The son-of-a-bitch is huntin' the boy. Goddamn his sorry ass."

"Say again, Will?"

Will turned his head back to the mic and said, "Nothing, Robert. Listen, I want you to park next to Mitchell Creek about where Wallace went off the road. Then start down the creek toward Wallace's feed operations, but on the opposite side of the creek. I think our man might be looking for Henry." Will thought for a few seconds then said, "And Robert, he could be armed."

"Roger that."

Will switched his radio back to the general com channel. "Base, this is two. Come in please," Will said.

"Two, this is base."

"That you, McKee?"

"Roger that, Major."

"Okay listen, John! I think the sheriff is at Judge Spivey's house; get hold of him and tell him to come to Odell Grier's place. Tell him I'm looking for the young boy we've been worried about. Tell him there may be a problem. You copy?"

"Roger. I copy."

"And John, tell the sheriff he needs to bring some cavalry."

"Okay, Will. Cavalry on the way."

Will wiped his face again and started down the bank toward the clubhouse. Odell came out of the cabin and slipped on the mass of wet leaves and moss that covered the ground behind the cabin. His face contorted in pain as he pushed up with his cane. Will, whose own hip was starting to ache, limped up to the cabin as Odell got to his feet.

"He ain't here, Will. But he was. The door was tied and the window shutter's locked down." Will examined the ground for any sign of a struggle.

"Odell, walk up the creek bank and see if you can find any sign of him." He paused for a second and then took a small thirty-eight snub-nose out of an ankle holster and handed it to Odell. "I ain't sayin' you'll need it, but take it just in case."

Odell stared at him. "He hurts just one hair on that boy's head and he's a dead man, Will. You better understand that."

Will nodded. No reason to start with the platitudes about the rule of law. "Keep your head, Odell, but don't stop to ask questions if Hank's in danger. I'll handle any problems that come up." Odell nodded and limped rapidly along the creek bank toward the road.

Will turned downstream, rubbing his hip with the heel of his hand. "You don't even have to harm a hair, Popper. You even look at Hank with that piece-of-shit face of yours and I'll blow your fucking head off!" he mumbled.

He pulled his nine millimeter out of its holster and yelled. "Hank! Hank Grier! Answer me, Hank!" Nothing came back except the same desperate calls made by Odell.

The wind whipped a branch across Will's face cutting a small slash in his lip. Blood flowed into his mouth as he rubbed his fingers over the cut. *Okay with me. Blood's what I'm after*, he thought. He moved downstream at a pace he knew would put severe strain on his hip, but he didn't care. Speed was called for, not self-indulgence.

He stopped a hundred yards down the bank to catch his breath. After a minute or two, he cupped his hands over his mouth and yelled, "Paulie . . . Paulie Rea . . ." Realizing what he had just yelled, he shook his head, called "Hank Grier," then strained to listen through the wind. Nothing returned to him but the sound of slapping branches and moaning pines. *I know I heard something. It was too . . .*" The sound came again, from down the creek. It was high and shrill, like an animal caught in a trap. Will raced through the woods along the creek, his arm in front of his face to keep the limbs away. Water ran into his eyes.

There, out in front, he saw a movement—ahead and slightly to his left. It was Popper. Will stopped and wiped his face. Popper had Hank by one of his legs and was dragging him along the ground. Hank's arms flailed against the wet ground, so the boy was still alive.

When Popper saw Will, he pulled the boy behind a huge red oak, then leaned around the trunk, pointing a gun in Will's direction. Will crouched, in order to conceal himself. Popper stuck his head further out from behind the tree to locate the deputy. So Will rolled behind a poplar, flattening himself against its trunk. He pushed up to a standing position, holding his pistol vertically against his chest. Slowly he turned to his left and looked around the tree. The big oak behind which Popper and Hank were hidden was about fifty yards away, but on the other side of a steep ravine.

Will leaned back against the smooth gray bark of the poplar and thought, *Okay, when I move, that son-of-a-bitch is going to shoot my ass. Why couldn't it be somebody else? Why Eugene Winslow? Shit.* He looked back around the tree, but the other side. He could see Popper holding a pistol, looking down at Hank, and trying to adjust his grip on the boy with his other hand.

Will looked at the edge of the ravine . . . fifteen yards, maybe twenty. If he could make it, he'd have some cover, and if Popper came after him, he'd have to let go of Hank. No way he could drag the boy with him. Will turned back around and took a deep breath. One more look: okay, Popper was still occupied with the boy. Will turned and ran toward the edge of the gully. His hip burned. The rain blinded him, making him bounce off a small dogwood tree near the bank.

The explosion seemed to come from far away. Across and further down the creek, or from Wallace's fields next to the hog lots, or the clubhouse; somewhere farther away than the red oak forty yards in front of him. But he knew, deep in his brain, that Popper had fired, and he knew it was at him. Will had been so focused on the edge of the gully that the shot seemed distant, meant for someone else.

Will's left shoulder flew backward with such force that he saw his feet over his head. The impact of the bullet into his shoulder and upper left chest spun him around so hard that the pin or pins in his right hip seemed to tear loose from their bone anchors. He lay on the ground knowing that at any minute another shot would come and end it.

But nothing happened. He turned his head and raised it slightly off the wet ground. Will still held his nine millimeter in his right hand and moved it toward his face so he could wipe his eyes with the heel of his hand.

Popper was on his feet, trying to drag Hank toward the edge of the creek. The boy was fighting back. Will tried to stand but the pain in his right leg was overpowering. He slid his arm under himself and pushed up to a kneeling position. No good. He'd have to crawl. He fell forward and began to pull himself toward the gully with his right arm, his left being practically useless, while pushing with his only good leg, his left. It was like being back in basic training, low-crawling along the PE course. Only this time he had only one good leg and one good arm, and they were opposite at that.

As he got to the edge of the gully, he noticed a bare pine log stretched across the bottom of the ravine. One end was pushed behind a tree root and the other behind a rock. If he could get to it, he would cross the water-soaked gully and crawl up the other side, not quite as steep as this.

Will pulled himself over the edge of the gully and slid down the bank through the mud and leaves to the water's edge. He grabbed the middle of a convenient root, and pulled himself onto the log. His right leg hung off the lower side of the log while his left pushed through the muck that had accumulated on the upper side.

The wind blew leaves across the top of the gully and over the lip of the bank as he looked up to see where he was going. Carefully he pulled himself across the crude bridge and up the far bank. He got what traction he could with the heel of his left boot and the butt of the pistol in his right hand. Slowly, slowly he looked over the top of the ravine toward the bank of Mitchell Creek. He wiped his eyes one more time, and looked toward the oak only to see Popper looking back toward the trees on the far side of the ravine. Popper hadn't seen Will pull himself over to the gully and slide down. Finally a break. Will put the gun down and wiped his face again.

—✦ ✦ ✦—

He heard explosions. He saw men running from behind and out of the wooden building in the middle of the rubber plantation, firing at Lieutenant Pratt and his men as they did. He saw it all again, and again the only fucking thing he had was an automatic pistol.

The Vietnamese officer heard him yell through the storm. He grinned and slowly turned his head, raising his gun at the same time, but this time Will was calm and steady. His eyes were clear and his hand and arm were braced against a tree. Not today, motherfucker, not today. Lieutenant Pratt, you owe me one.

—✦ ✦ ✦—

Will fired the nine millimeter. The bullet covered the thirty yards in the smallest part of a second, but he felt he was seeing it all the way. It tore through the top of Popper's throat and exited his head at the base of the skull. His esophagus, spine, and all surrounding muscles and tissues parted before the devastating slug, and his head popped backward like a child's Pez dispenser. Popped right off.

Will closed his eyes and dropped his head forward onto the wet leaves and mud. It was quiet and he was warm.

25.

Hogg County was starting to dry out. The sun shone between layers of white and gray clouds and warmed the asphalt parking lot outside the emergency room. The storm had dropped over four inches of water and torn roofs off numerous sheds and trailers. It hadn't been as bad as some of the late-season hurricanes, but there was a collective sigh of relief when the front moved back out to sea. Maybe the county could pry a little money out of the state for cleanup.

Lana smiled at Bob Velez as she passed through the emergency room doors behind the hospital.

"He's a tough son-of-a-gun, I'll say that for him," Bob said with a smile.

Lana laughed. "Yeah, 'tough' is a good description. I personally think 'hardheaded' is more accurate, but I'll take 'tough.' "

Together they walked over to the visitor's parking area, and as they neared her car, Lana stopped and turned. She leaned forward and gave Bob a hug. "Thanks, Bob. I'm not sure he could have made it without you. We owe you a lot."

Dr. Velez smiled and returned her embrace. "He's a good man, Lana. You deserve each other, and more to the point, you need each other."

He loosened his grip and stepped back, holding her at arm's length. "Now listen to me. He's got some hard work ahead of him. We're sending him to Duke in a few days. They'll fix his shoulder first, then the hip. Actually, he should have had his hip repaired long before now. I told him years ago that that Army hip was a second-class product, but he never paid any mind. Like you said, hardheaded."

Lana smiled. "Better late than never, Doc. Anyway, thanks for everything." She patted his arm and slid behind the wheel of her Jeep Wagoneer. Bob shut the car door and waved as she pulled out of the lot.

—✦ ✦ ✦—

The surgical care corridor in the Hogg County hospital was quiet. Nurses moved soundlessly between the rooms and the nursing station. Will had been waking and sleeping for the past few hours. Tubes of various sizes and thicknesses put in and took away the fluids necessary for his recovery. His pain was moderate. Unlike the ward on the hospital ship off Vietnam, Will's room this time was spacious and, more importantly, private.

A bullet in the left shoulder was serious, but compared to the shrapnel and trauma of his first wound, it was almost minor. It made sense that his hip gave him more discomfort than his shoulder, and he was relieved to be going to Duke for a new one, probably about time.

—✦ ✦ ✦—

The large wooden door swung slowly open and a stocky older man stuck his head into the room. At first Will thought it was Ernie Tasker, but as he focused more clearly on the face before him, he realized it was Oris Martin.

"Hey, Will. It's Oris. You mind if I come in for a few minutes?"

Will cleared his throat, "No, Oris, I don't mind."

"I just came by with Oleen Winslow. The medical examiner needed her to identify the body and I didn't want her coming alone. She's talking to Reverend Winston down in the chapel." Will didn't say anything. Oris stretched his neck some, then continued.

"Sorry you got messed up, Deputy. And I'm real sorry my friend Eugene Winslow somehow went off the deep end and got himself involved in something so unsavory. I can't explain it, really. Eugene was a strange man sometimes. Hard to predict."

Will looked at and into Oris. He was searching for the lie he knew was there. The lie that by habit and use now had a body of its own.

"What you think made him grab that boy, Oris?" Will said.

"No idea, Will. Like I said, Eugene was a strange man sometimes. Always was a dark sort. Even when we was young 'uns."

"Yeah, but what made him grab that boy now? What do you think set him off like that? Y'all talk all the time. You notice anything funny?"

Oris shifted his weight. "Funny like what?"

"Funny like anything unusual."

"Naw. Nothin' funny."

Will pushed himself up against the headboard and his pillow raising his head and chest. He started to say something but Oris cut him off.

"Anyway, Will, I don't want to bother you. I just come by to see how you was doing and to tell you that we're all glad Popper's aim wasn't so good for once."

"It was good enough. He hit a moving target running like hell through the trees."

"Well, he missed anything important. That's all that counts. I'll . . ."

"Oris, since you're here, I'm curious about something else."

Oris looked at his watch. "Yeah, what would that be?"

"What did Popper tell you about the morning Paul got killed out at Pine Bluff?"

"Nothing he didn't tell you and Sheriff Tasker. I mean, what's to tell? Don come in and found Paul under his 'dozer—terrible, terrible thing."

Will kept looking at Oris's face. Tried to see the lie looking back. It was there. It surely was there no matter how hard Oris worked to keep it inside and hidden.

"You think Popper could'a been lying?"

"How the hell would I know. Lying about what? For what reason?"

"Maybe he was there before. Maybe he was doing something illegal that Paul found him doing."

"Illegal like what?"

"Burying diseased hogs, for example."

"What the hell you talking about, Deputy? We ain't got a touch of problem with sick hogs on any Martin Farms properties, never have. Anything like that come up, I'd be the first to know."

"What if you weren't? What if Popper didn't want you to know?"

"Well, I guess I wouldn't know. Leastways not until something happened. Anyway, what's all this got to do with Popper going nuts and grabbing that colored boy?"

"I don't know. That's what I'm going to try and find out."

"Great, but if you got questions for Martin Farms or anybody at Martin Farms, you call me first. I don't need any problems screwing up my new breeding programs." Oris turned to walk out of the room. "Good luck, Deputy. See ya."

"Oris, one more question."

The older man turned around with a particularly sour expression. "Yeah?"

"When was the last time you talked to Eugene?"

"I don't know. Few days ago."

"What did you talk about?"

"Who knows. Pig business, I guess."

"Where did you talk?"

Oris's eyes started to close. He looked at Will through slits. A wall was coming down.

"Deputy, isn't it about time for you to take a pill or something instead of worrying about my conversations with an unbalanced man? Why don't we continue this conversation later. Maybe when you get back from Duke."

"How did you know I was going to Duke?"

"I know a lot about a lot of things."

"Like what happened to Popper."

"What the fuck . . . ? I know you shot his ass in the woods by Mitchell Creek. I know the son-of-a-bitch was off his rocker, a danger to ever'body around him. What the hell else you want to know?"

"Nothing right now, but when I'm back in a few weeks, we'll talk some more about Popper and what y'all discussed last week. I'll also want to know about any conversations you might have had with Judge Spivey or anybody on his staff. That's some of what I want to talk to you about."

"You can talk all you want. I don't have to listen."

"Maybe. But maybe you do. I am the law—after all."

"Sheriff Tasker is the law. You're the pretend-law."

"Whatever. We'll talk, Oris."

"You're as fucking crazy as Popper. Must be the shit they're pumping into your veins."

"Could be, but I'll see you then. Don't leave the state."

"You call me when you get your sanity back, Deputy. Or better still, call my lawyer."

"Count on it."

Oris turned and walked to the door. As he put his hand on the handle, he turned back into the room.

"One more thing, Will. Don't think you can fuck with my mind like you did with that half-wit Wallace or poor ol' Eugene. I didn't get to be where I am playing the fool. And leave my friends alone."

Will smiled slightly. "Oh, I wouldn't worry, Oris. I doubt you got any friends. Admirers maybe, hangers-on certainly, sycophants most assuredly, but I doubt friends. 'Least, not friends who aren't expendable . . . like Popper."

Oris began to shake, his face scarlet as he came back to the foot of Will's bed.

"Don't you threaten me, Deputy! Bein' a Moser don't mean dick to me. You only think your shit don't stink. You ain't nothing but a lot of hot air and snot, just like your daddy. Think you're better than folks. Everybody round here knows about you. How you been playin' policeman cause you couldn't wear daddy's shoes. Fancy lace-ups didn't fit, so you got yourself some boots . . . shoes for flatfoots. Well, you won't find nothin' on me. You can look til you go blind, I don't give a shit. God-actin' Mosers ain't nothin' but a bunch of stuck-up losers, and you gone to the head of the line. Fuck you and fuck the Mosers. And good luck, by the way, on ever being high sheriff of Hogg County, shit-for-brains."

Will watched the angry face of the man in front of him, looking for clues. But no point looking for Oris's soul, he had none.

"This has nothing to do with Mosers or Martins, Oris. Nothing to do with elections. This has to do with the law. Nobody, including Mosers and Martins, is above the law. I'm going to find out what Popper was up to and why, no matter where it takes me. If that happens to be to your door, so be it."

"We'll see about that," Oris said, and left.

26.

For the first time in days, maybe even months, Lana drove without the preoccupation of crisis. Will would be okay, and the man who'd tried to kill him, and probably had killed her husband, was dead himself. She had a vague sense that the satisfaction she felt at the death of another human being wasn't particularly healthy, much less Christian, but she also knew that Popper's death had gone a long way toward ridding her of the guilt and hate that had been her companions for so long. She rolled her window down, letting the cool air and earthy smells of the clear December day fill her nostrils and rejuvenate her lungs.

Turning into her driveway off Roanoke Street, Lana pulled around the giant hydrangea bush at the corner of the house. She stopped near the back door, then backed toward the barn and the wire door at the side of the pigeon coop. She had things to do and needed to get on with it.

—✦ ✦ ✦—

"Hello? Anyone here? This is the slowest diner ever. Where's the coffee?" Will sat in a large wicker armchair, the *News and Observer* front page and editorials spread on his lap, the rest strewn on the floor. His left shoulder was still bandaged, his arm in a sling. His right leg and hip were braced with a removable device that looked like something from a harness shop.

"Hold your horses, Deputy, I'm moving as fast as I can," Lana called.

"Now that's pathetic. I'm the one with the bionic hip and humped-up shoulder, and I can move faster than that."

Lana pushed open the door and looked around the corner. "Okay, Superman, then why don't you get your crippled butt and cape outta that chair and come help."

He laughed. "I didn't say I could move faster than that *now*."

Will had gotten out of the hospital toward the end of January. The most serious of his operations had been his hip reconstruction. New pins had been added and a partial replacement achieved. In order to maximize his range of motion, his doctors got him up and into therapy almost immediately. The pins that had held his hip in place since Vietnam had finally proved to be worthless. The bone damage from his falls had been the final straw. Once he was released, Lana had made sure to be around him as much as possible so that he didn't try and overdo his activities. She enjoyed helping out and Will clearly enjoyed letting her.

Lana carried the tray of coffee, scrambled eggs, bacon, and sugar cakes out to the porch, and put it on the table next to Will's chair. She returned his smile, then ran her hand through his hair.

"I'm glad Popper wasn't as good a shot as you thought he was."

Will put his head back against the headrest and looked at her. "I'm glad he wasn't either, but he was good enough. I'd like to point out that he hit me on my left side about six inches above my heart while I was running through the woods. That ain't sloppy shooting."

Will reached over and picked up a fresh mug of coffee from the tray. He took a few sips, then put it down, almost tipping it over as he did. "Damn, that was almost a disaster." He looked down and saw something lying, partially hidden, on the table. He moved the paper aside and there lay a small piece of flintstone—his Clovis point. He'd kept it with him since showing it to Lana.

He picked it up and turned it over a few times. Searching the uneven surface until he found the particular groove he was looking for, Will closed his eyes and slowly rubbed his thumb along the smooth flint depressions. It was comforting. A lot of worries and prayers were rubbed into that flint, centuries of 'em.

He smiled thinking of himself and Paul, along with the rest of the scouts from Troop 20, scouring the fields of Hogg County. Other images, too: Paulie and Wallace walking the freshly plowed soybean field next to the creek looking for scrapers, potsherds, and flint points; quail hunting trips; and fishing outings, so many times past, so many ghosts.

Lana watched as Will rubbed his thumb against the side of the stone and after a few moments, reached down and put her hand on his. He looked up as she gently took the Clovis.

She held it between her thumb and forefinger, studying it carefully, as if looking for something lost in its grooves. When she came to the large depression on the side, the one Will had been rubbing, she too ran her thumb along the groove. It was warm from Will's touch yet still cool and smooth by its nature. She held it up to the light and the light told her that this thing, this stone point, had been made by and for, men. It was a man's artifact.

She put it back in Will's hand and said, "Make sure to keep this safe, Will. From time to time I might want to speak to some of the men and boys living in this stone." He looked at the Clovis and nodded.

Lana picked the front section of the paper off his lap, and

started to read as Will leaned back with his eyes closed and rubbed the Clovis.

"You see where the feds have closed down damn near ninety percent of Oris's feeding and farrowing operations?" Will said.

Lana kept on reading the paper, "Uhmm, so I hear."

Will looked at her, "What's Dr. Newell say about it?"

"About what?"

"About Martin Farms' problems."

Lana looked up. "Oh. She says it must be some of the disease from Carl Ross's operation. Spread somehow to Oris's place. She says the state and feds are going to be real strict about this outbreak. Looks like they're going to close and burn down every feed and nursery facility Martin Farms has."

"As in put him out of business?"

"Looks like it."

"How do you think it could have happened? Disease spreading that fast?"

Lana glanced at him and then back to her paper. "How would I know? Maybe when I become a vet I'll know such things. Right now I just know he's screwed for sure."

"How does Dr. Newell think it could happen?"

Lana put her paper down and looked at Will. "Vicky says that there are lots of ways for cholera to spread . . . people, animals, other hogs. Martin Farms ships pigs between facilities every week. One diseased pig can infect a whole house. Must be spread between pig shipments. Anyway, who cares?"

Will shrugged. "I'm not saying I care especially, but I am the law. I am curious about such things. Seems like a lot of places were infected in an awfully short time."

"Meaning what?"

"Meaning nothing. It just seems real sudden."

Lana shrugged. "Just one of those things. An act of God . . . force majeur, remember that? Been a lot of that going around."

Will leaned back in his chair and closed his eyes. The late morning breeze felt good. The temperature was in the low- to mid-seventies, unusual for the last weeks of February.

"I saw Arlo Byerly the other day." Will said. "Ernie and I stopped for breakfast at the K&W and Arlo was there." Will sat up in his chair and turned toward Lana. "I didn't know you were getting rid of all that stuff in the barn. Arlo said it took him and a couple of boys the best part of a day to get that junk out. He said that when you want, he'll come back and get that old incubator. He said that as soon as you finish with it to call him."

Lana glanced at Will over the top of her paper, then looked back to the article she was reading. "I'll call him sometime next week."

"What you using an incubator for?"

"Providing a little heat for the barn, why?"

Will sat back. "No reason, just bein' nosy. Arlo said you might want him to come and take the pigeons away."

Lana kept reading. "I might. Getting to be a bit of a pain to take care of them, plus I don't love the idea of the poor things being staked out for those hounds of yours. They deserve better. They need to be doing something more useful."

"Useful like what?"

"Like flying around and being pretty. Eating harmful insects. I don't know, whatever they do."

"They eat corn, gravel, and other grains."

"Okay."

Will looked up into the sky. "Come to think of it, I haven't seen but one or two around lately. Wonder where they are?"

"Who knows? Maybe they joined a better class of pigeon somewhere. Maybe they're under the highway bridge near the cement plant or out gorging themselves at Martin Feed. Who knows?"

Will looked down at the Clovis point in his hand. "Well, wherever they are, they're probably finding something to eat. Speaking of which, I appreciate the breakfast and coffee. You're a good cook, Lana, and good company. I appreciate all you've done for me since I got out of the hospital. In fact, I appreciate all you did for me while I was in the hospital. It's meant a lot. I . . ." Lana had gotten up while he was speaking and came over to his chair.

She leaned down, putting her finger over his mouth, "Shh-hhh. It's been my pleasure. I like looking after you, always have." With that she kissed him gently on the lips and smiled.

Will leaned back in the chair and closed his eyes. "I miss hearing the pigeons, though."

27.

Will parked his car next to the sheriff's. He'd only been allowed to drive himself for a few days and he was still getting used to the one arm, one leg technique. The sheriff had been especially adamant about Will's attempts at driving himself.

"Will, what the hell kind of example you gonna be, weaving all over the road with a stove-up shoulder and bionic hip?" When Ernie finally did give his approval, it was a great relief.

Things were about back to normal. Eugene Winslow's funeral had been two months ago, and while Will couldn't go because of his hospital stay, he did get a full report from the sheriff. Lana hadn't gone, even though she had considered going just to make sure the bastard was safely in the ground. Ernie had decided not to exhume Paul Reavis's body, the primary reason now being buried as well; however, he did dig up the parking lot next to the Pine Bluff farrowing facility. Many pig bones were uncovered, much to the faked surprise of Oris Martin, but the testing to be done for disease had been a waste of time, since before the results were in, the cholera epidemic hit Martin Farms with a vengeance.

No one could remember the like of the recent outbreak either in severity or distribution. Whole farms were skipped over, the infection being restricted almost exclusively to Martin Farms operations. Even some of the Martin Farms co-op operations were skipped. John Keaton's huge joint venture with Oris was wiped out but his independent feeding operations were spared. It was almost like the angel of cholera had passed over some homes while inflicting others. Everyone assumed that diseased pigs passed from one facility to another within Oris's operations was the cause, but Oris wasn't so sure.

What particularly galled him was the seeming lack of attention he was getting from the sheriff's department. Oris had concocted a vast theory of vendetta and jealous conspiracy. He was sure someone had sabotaged his company, and he was demanding a full investigation from state and local authorities. The state and federal agencies had done their job, namely burning down almost every hog farrowing and feeding operation managed by Martin Farms, Inc. They had not yet determined the cause and source of the outbreak but they were still working on that, even though most of the scientists involved held out little hope of finding either.

Will heard Oris's loud screams of protestation as he walked into the sheriff's department and headed back toward his office and the conference room.

"Goddamnit, Ernie, I'm telling you that somebody sabotaged me. Somebody spread that goddamn virus to all my places. How the hell do you explain the fact that nobody else's place was hit, huh?"

As Will opened the door, he saw Ernie leaning back in one of the conference-room armchairs, a bemused expression on his face. Oris was standing in front of him, his legs splayed and his arms akimbo, a fist curled up in each. He turned as the door opened, glowered at Will, then turned back to the sheriff. "Well?"

Ernie slowly stretched his neck. "Oris, I don't imagine that Carl Ross would think of his operation as 'nobody else'."

"Fuck Carl Ross. He's probably the cause of all this shit to begin with. I'm talking about these recent infections. Damage to big, well-protected operations, not some small-time hick's feed-lots." Ernie was clearly agitated, but Will could see that he wasn't about to let Oris know it.

Ernie looked over at Will, "Hey, Will, take a seat. Oris here is just telling me how the sheriff's department is shirking—you did say shirking, didn't you, Oris?—its duty by not finding the person or persons responsible for sabotaging his company's operations." Oris turned around as Will pulled up a straight-back chair that he could sit in while keeping his leg and hip straight.

"Don't let me stop you, Oris," Will said. "I'm sure you have some vital information that we can use in our investigation. Something that the state and federal boys missed. Something that leads you to believe malicious intent." Oris squinted his eyes as he glared at Will.

"You think this is funny, don't you, Deputy? You think I'm just overreacting, don't you?" Will kept his gaze steady, focused on Oris.

"As a matter of fact, nothing about this whole episode strikes me as funny. Wallace getting killed wasn't funny. Paul's murder, and I'm damn sure that it was murder, wasn't funny. Threats to Lana Reavis lacked humor. The attempted murder of Odell Grier wasn't at all funny. And finally the attempted murder of Henry Grier wasn't the least bit funny. No, Oris, I don't find any of this funny."

Oris stood somewhat nonplussed at this response. He hadn't expected to have the subject switched on him. He hadn't expect-ed to stand accused of something. He cleared his throat and, as was his nature, returned to the attack. "I don't know what the hell you're getting at with all that stuff, Will, but I'm talking about something entirely different. I'm talking about who murdered my company. I got nothing to do with all those other things. Seems like you done a pretty good job of killing the man who could answer for some of that stuff, although you ain't got proof about any of it as far as I can tell. You . . .

"You don't, huh? Popper, your close friend and partner for forty years, never talked to you about any of that stuff? You never asked him about Paul's accident? You weren't curious about Wallace's accident? He never told you about a knife that he lost that showed up stuck into a desk in Lana Reavis's bedroom?" Oris stood with his mouth open.

"You're right, Oris, that I can't yet prove anything beyond reasonable doubt, but we have time and I'm not through. Not by a long shot."

Ernie said nothing. Oris opened and closed his fists and shifted his weight from one foot to the other. After a long pause to regain his composure, Oris said, "I see. The two of you are focusing on things that happened years ago and ignoring something that happened just a few weeks ago. With the exception of Eugene's recent mental aberration, you've decided that all the other accidents were murders or intentional acts of malice, but that my company's murder was a natural occurrence. Have I got it straight?"

Ernie shifted in his chair. "Nobody said that, Oris. Will said that lots of things need investigating. Your recent outbreak certainly bears investigating, but most of that has to be done by people who know and work with such biological problems. We in the Hogg County sheriff's department don't have the expertise to find out where the virus came from or how it got into your operations.

"Now if you have any evidence of intentional infestation of your operations, we will be glad to investigate; however, without something concrete to go on we can't very well conduct a proper investigation."

"We're going to be doing a number of investigations," Will added, "talking to lots of people, Oris. If something comes up that points to foul play, we'll certainly let you know. In fact, if we have any questions about any of our investigations, we'll give you a call."

Oris's eyes bored into Will. "Tell you what, Deputy. You call my lawyers if you got any questions for me. I've already told you what I know about all your accidents. Maybe your girlfriend needs to be questioned some. Maybe she knows something about some of this. Maybe she knows how cholera can spread so fast. She seems to be real curious about such things, leastways has been in the past."

Will slowly got to his feet. "My girlfriend? Are you referring to Paul Reavis's widow? Paulie Reavis's mother? Is that who you're referring to?"

Oris backed up a foot or so. "You know perfectly well who we're talking about."

"Yeah, I know who you're talking about, and rest assured I have talked to Mrs. Reavis about those incidents as well as the most recent ones. In fact, I've talked to her more than I've talked to you about them. Maybe I need to spread my questions around a bit more."

Oris turned and started toward the door, pausing before walking through. "Like I said, call my lawyer."

"Oh, I will, but before you go, take this with you," Will said. "If I hear about you or any of your henchmen bothering Lana Reavis even a tiny bit, we'll have a discussion you won't like at all. You understand me?"

Oris looked at Ernie and then Will, but said nothing else. He didn't need to. The door slammed behind him.

Will twisted his shoulders against the built-up tension and sat back down in his chair. Neither man spoke. Finally Ernie said, "You think somebody sabotaged his operation?"

"Maybe, but unless somebody confesses, I don't know how the sheriff's department is gonna prove anything. Seems like that's up to the doctors and researchers at state and the fed."

"You're probably right. It'd be hard as hell to narrow down

the number of people who have a big enough beef with Oris to want to put him out of business. Lots of people in that club! Well, I've gotta get on to more mundane business. You take it easy for a while. Tell Lana hello. Hope she's getting better. Hope she's feeling better about the world."

Will smiled. "I hope so too, Ernie. I'll tell her you said hello. In fact, we are going to the movies tonight. I'm going by her house right after I go by Odell's. I want to see Henry and make sure he's okay. He and Nancy been visiting her folks for a few weeks and are back today. I told 'em I was coming by."

Ernie got up and patted Will on his good shoulder as he left the room, then headed toward his office.

—✦ ✦ ✦—

It was late afternoon when Will pulled into the Grier's yard. Odell and Hank were by the barn and waved as Will drove in. Hank ran to the squad car the minute it stopped, though Odell, still using a cane, came over a bit slower.

"Hey, Will!"

"Hello, young man." Will replied as he eased himself out of the car.

Odell smiled as he came up. "Hello, Will. Don't we look like a couple of stove-up old men?"

Will laughed, "That's because we are a couple of stove-up old men." The two men shook hands, then leaned against the car. Hank was looking at Will's leg brace and sling.

"You want to come in for a cup of coffee? You know we always got a pot brewing." Odell said.

"Thanks, Odell, but I'm on my way over to Lana's. We're gonna catch a flick in town tonight. I just came by to see how you guys are doing." He looked at Hank, "Plus I wanted to bring something by for Hank."

Odell nodded. "Okay, you guys talk. I'm gonna go inside and sit down for a while. The old leg needs some TLC."

Hank stood and looked up at Will, dying to know what he had for him. Will put his cane against the car and reached into his pocket. As he removed his fist he turned it over with his fingers closed. Slowly he opened his hand. Lying in the middle of his palm was the perfect gray-white Clovis point. Hank looked at it but didn't move to take it. Will moved his hand toward Hank. "Take it. It's for you." Hank slowly picked the stone arrowhead from Will's hand, handling it like it was a precious stone.

"It's a Clovis point, the oldest and rarest of all the arrowheads. I want you to have it. I want you to be the next in line. Mr. Reavis found this when we were about your age. We were on a camping trip in the Boy Scouts. He gave it to me as a friendship present. A year or so ago I gave it to Paulie and recently he gave it to Wallace May. When I found Wallace after his accident, I also found the Clovis in his truck. I've carried it since then.

"There's a particular spot on the side, a big groove really, that feels good to rub. Kind of like one of those worry stones the people in Greece use. I been rubbing it a lot lately. It helps me think. I reckon that everybody from Mr. Reavis to me to Paulie to Wallace and now to you have rubbed some of themselves into this stone. I reckon this arrowhead has some of a lot of people in it, maybe even the native who made it thousands of years ago.

"The Indians believed that the spirits of their ancestors were still with them, were all around them, in fact. I think they might be right. I think this arrowhead holds the spirits of Mr. Reavis, Paulie, Wallace, me, and even the ancient Indian warrior who made it. The more you rub, the more of you goes in it. It's yours now. And I want you to know that your buddy Paulie Reavis is always with you. I want you to know that I'm always with you, and if some day you have a son or buddy that means the world to you, you might want for them to have it. You can do with it what you want. You can call on all the spirits that live there whenever you need them. They're there for you." Hank turned the stone over and over in his hand. After a minute he looked at Will.

"Will, this is the most wonderful thing I own. Can I show

Daddy?"

"Of course you can."

"Can I get him to rub it and put some of him in it, too?"

"I reckon so."

Hank rubbed the large groove on the edge of the Clovis watching his thumb slide across and through the smooth indentation. "It feels good. It kinda fits my hand."

"What you're feeling is all the good thoughts in the flint. You're feeling Paulie and me and all the others who live inside." Will opened the door of his car and dropped his cane on the far seat. He turned as he backed into the open door and rubbed Hank on the head. "We'll go fishing, Son, when the weather turns better. Maybe your daddy can go next time, too."

"I'll make sure he can," Hank said, as he looked at the Clovis. "We'll take everybody."

ACKNOWLEDGMENTS

As always I am indebted to Linda Whitney Hobson for her editorial assistance and many valuable additions to my manuscript. I am also appreciative of the artistic skills and visual interpretations of Mr. Joel Shelton in designing the cover art work for this book. I also appreciate the patience of the many individuals at the N.C. State veterinary school, who answered my questions on the diseases and safety precautions necessary in raising hogs on an industrial scale.